I0558850

Title: The Tower of Taal
ISBN: 978-0-473-66675-0
Copyright © Jim Gould
Cover design by: Artography By James

For Deborah, without whom I would not have had the courage or perseverance to complete this novel.

THE TOWER OF TAAL

J G Gould

CHAPTER ONE

Stroika, an ancient city. Some even said it was the oldest of all in the country. It had stood against the harsh winds, the freezing winters, and the torrential rain for five centuries. It had stood against all invaders throughout turbulent times and been a peaceful home to its residents with its beautiful gardens and stoned walkways. The city was a major trading center for much of the surrounding country, with roads leading all the way to docklands in the Bay of Dreams. Merchants from all of the country's regions came to sell and buy everything from produce to weird and wonderful devices, and some even said magical potions and artifacts. Although the city was wealthy and had many grand buildings, towers, temples, and walkways leading to parks for the citizens to enjoy, many of the citizens led simple lives, content with what they had and the simple joys that family brings.

The roads in Stroika were well constructed and allowed for the use of carts and horse-drawn vehicles. Paths on either side of the streets allowed for the safe travel of pedestrians while shopping or browsing the local businesses. Certain areas were closed off for use by street traders and auctioneers, and these were always the busiest parts of the city. These marketplaces were not just for trading but also for street performers, artists, fortune tellers, and many other diverse forms of businesses and entertainment.

On this day, acrobats amazed the audience with leaps, jumps, and rolls, each more daring than the last. A juggler threw fiery brands into the air before catching them as they fell and propelling them skywards once more. Vendors sold food to passersby, and people haggled with fruiters and butchers. An old woman, clad in long swathes of silk, spread her cards on a table before her, occasionally flipping one over and speaking to her eager client.

Children ran and played, their mothers watching from a distance as they gossiped and talked about their home lives. Musicians kept the crowds in good cheer, some stopping to dance to the merry tunes while others clapped along. The auctioneer today was Josua, who had arrived from Londra a few months earlier. He called out to the bidders, encouraging them to make even higher offers as he demonstrated what his latest product, a carved box that could be held in one hand and that glowed green along its edges, could do. The citizens hardly noticed the sounds coming from outside the city walls, and they paid no attention to them. Perhaps they had become complacent over the years, secure in the knowledge that they were safe even in times of war. They never feared, as the city was well defended with its towers and its high, thick dual walls. No enemy had ever made it past the first wall, let alone the second. And so, their daily lives went on while the battle continued outside. They knew about the war from travelers and traders, but it had been, for a long time, hundreds of kilometers away. On hearing that the war was coming closer, the citizens blocked the entrances to the city and decided that once again they would wait until the war ended and things returned to normal. Stroika had not been involved in a war for four hundred years; it considered itself neutral, and to date no one had ever attacked it in earnest, and those that had dared such a feat had given up without ever breeching the cities walls.

Fredrick had been married to Karo for 30 years; they both worked for local shopkeepers, earning a meagre wage but enough to provide them with a home and food on the table. Their children had grown and moved out, which had, as is normal, brought both joy and sorrow. There was joy that they had their home to themselves and did not have to take care of them, but sorrow for exactly the same reason as most parents would agree. Fredrick's clothes, while old, were clean, and he presented himself at his best whether at home or out in the streets buying supplies. Karo wore a simple dress, plain in colour but suited her figure; she wore no makeup; she did not need to, and Fredrick could not help but smile as he felt himself extremely fortunate to have such a beautiful woman for his wife.

A simple meal, even for an ordinary man, was laid before them. Fredrick led his wife in prayer to the gods for the wonderful meal that had been provided to them. He took the bread in both hands and tore it in two, passing one piece to his wife. Then, cutting a thick wedge of cheese, he gave this to her as well. Meanwhile, she poured him a glass of hinga juice. This was the local wine, but it was very cheap due to the massive growth of the hinga berries in the region.

They talked about their day, work, and the goings on around them in the city as they always did, laughing at the funny parts while being more serious about work, and what a commotion there had been over a cart whose wheel had come away and it had listed to one side spilling its contents and enraging its furious driver. Karo mentioned that on her way home she had seen a man trying to sell a strange box and that she had been curious as to what it was but had not had time to stop and enquire further. Fredrick suggested it was just another useless trinket that would be sold to some unsuspecting fool for a high price and that it would have no use at all apart from as an ornament. Karo pursed her lips: "Yes, I suppose you are right, you usually are." This caused Fredrick to laugh, he knew he was being teased, and it was part of what made them such a happy couple.

Fredrick looked into Karo's eyes the way he always did and saw them smiling back at him. He raised his wine glass up towards Karo to toast their love, but as he did so, his hand was shaking, and wine spilled over the lip. "Are you okay, my love?" Karo asked. She was worried; Fredrick was not getting any younger, and he had recently had a nasty fall.

It was then that she noticed that it was not Fredrick shaking; it was the room itself. The table and chairs were vibrating, and the floor itself now shook. Fredrick ran to the window and looked outside. At first all he could hear was a low rumble as he watched the nearby buildings shake, the leaves of the trees rustle, and people running this way and that. Produce fell from market stalls, and the vendors scrambled to gather their wares.

Now came another sound, something different: a high-pitched screeching that stopped suddenly and was replaced by a whistling noise. The noise grew in intensity, and he realised it was very quickly getting closer. In seconds, it had become a great whooshing and thudding noise, and then he saw the ball of fire coming directly towards his window. That was the last he knew; the fiery hell took him where he stood, so hot that it immediately turned his body into ashes that were blown backwards into the room.

Fredricks house was now just rubble, and it had taken the two buildings either side with it. The terrace was aflame, and small explosions from various combustible materials had sent shards of brick, wood, and glass some distance away. Many other buildings in the city were attacked in the same way and now also lay in ruins. Properties blazed with fires that spread rapidly to their neighbors or set fire to trees and bushes along the streets. People were running, some covered in blood from various injuries while others lay in the street with broken bones caused by falling debris; and here and there the bodies of the dead, men, women, and children, lay motionless.

Through this mass of burning debris, a man dressed in a long black hooded robe emerged. The hood of the robe was pulled down as protection against the falling ashes, some of which still burned and now landed on the arm of his clothes, sending a small blue stream of smoke into the air, which he quickly slapped out with a curse. The sound of the woman's painful moans made him stop and turn. He could not see anyone but was sure the sounds were very near. He Listened closely, yes, there it was. Taking several steps into the crumpling ruins that had recently been a house he noticed an arm laying limply over some smoldering wood, the fingers wriggling slowly with effort. Pulling the debris away, he noticed the woman and was shocked at what he saw. The skin was peeling from her face and neck, which were burnt and blackened; blood caked her hair; and one eye was closed, bruised, and bleeding. Looking down the length of her body, he could see the metal spike that impaled her and knew her death was imminent. Taking one hand as he knelt beside her, he knew this was all he could do to offer her some comfort. Placing the other hand on her head seemed to make her feel less pain, and she looked up at him with her one open eye.

"Fredrick , my love, is that you? I thought you had surely died." She gave a slight smile. "My love, to see you at the end is all I could have hoped for".

A lonely tear, streaking the soot as it flowed down her cheek. Karo breathed a long, slow breath outward, and was gone, her hand going limp in the stranger's grip.

The man stood up and turned to look at the destruction around him. Fires burned everywhere, and now a different rumbling was heard, that of a thousand horse soldiers riding to slaughter any surviving Stroika's citizens. There would be no mercy here, for this city had denied giving power to the invading force, and it would now seek its revenge. This invading army had woven fear and destruction across the land for two years now, and its conquest was almost complete.

"M'lord!" a voice shouted. A tall soldier dressed in leather armor and carrying a large two-handed sword came running towards the hooded stranger. The man lowered the hood of his robe, revealing long black hair that was held back by a silver band.

"We cannot hold them here Lord; we have fallen back to the inner city." after taking a few breaths, adding, "We cannot win; they are too strong. The whole city is almost theirs".

General Corvious looked straight into the other man's eyes and said, "I am the last commanding officer. All the rest are dead, and the men are scattering. There is nowhere for them to hide or run to."

Corvious waved a hand in an arc around him, pointing out the devastation caused by the fireballs as the town's timber and stone houses had been set ablaze. It was plain that the invaders did not need the buildings, but merely wanted to enslave or kill the population. This city, the strongest in the land, was being made an example of so that others would surrender without a fight.

"It's over; no one can stop them now." Corvious raged through gritted teeth.

"The Bastion army is heading to Dresslon. Only Varsile stands in its way now, and then what?" The stranger's almond-shaped eyes opened wider as he considered his own question: "Of course, Taal!".

"Taal? What could she want with Taal?" Covious asked. "There's nothing there but the ruins of a long-forgotten castle and an old tower."

"I have to go to Corvious; I will bring reinforcements. You need to slow the Bastion down as much as you can until it arrives. Fall back to Varsile if you can. Do not allow them to reach Taal".

Corvious did not respond. An arrow now protruded through his neck from back to front, blood trickled down onto his chest, and the wheezing sound of a dying man's last breath issued forth. The archer notched another arrow and went to take aim, but his second target was no longer there.

The hawk circled, its eyes peering into the mist below. Without hesitation, it swooped down through the white swirling veil that masked the field, catching its prey in razor-sharp talons before rising skywards again with a shrill. Its eyes blazed with the fire of the perfect hunter, while the dull, dead eyes of the rabbit dangling below stared outward and saw nothing more.

After a while, the noise had ceased, as had the cries and the screams. The sound of metal clanging against metal, the dull thud of wood on wood, and the hollow-sounding thump of hooves were now all gone. A few voices cried out for companions to come to their aid, or with a mournful sadness at what had passed. The green grass was now glazed with a hint of red, and the clear water had been muddied from the many feet that had ran through it.

The two men, one sitting and one kneeling, neither saw nor heard the end of the rabbits innocent life from a short distance away.

"Take the sword; take it to Arielle." Shaan ordered.

"I cannot," replied Philippe, "for without the sword there can be no king, and without a king the land will die."

"It is not a sword that makes a king, but his actions and deeds, the power of his heart, and the love for his people." Shaan looked deep into Philippe's eyes. "It is time for a new king.".

"Now that evil has been driven from the land, there is no need for the sword. Now do as I say, then go forth and find such a man; be his right hand, his friend, his confidant, as you have been mine."

"But sire, you are that man. I will fetch help and have your wounds tended, then we will..."

"No!" Shaan spoke firmly. "My time is over. I was not born to live my years peacefully, but to bring peace and then move on. My work here is done."

Blood was now seeping down the side of Shaan's armor where his breastplate had been pierced. Six inches of the spear's shaft still lay embedded in his chest, fixed by the barbs on the spear's blade.

"Go now, while there is still time."

Philippe took the sword and mounted his horse, and with one last look back, he spurred it on. The grey mare galloped gracefully despite the lengthy battle she had endured; several times she had to leap over the prone bodies of comrades and enemies alike. Here and there, the results of battle could be seen; broken weapons and dead or dying soldiers appeared as monuments to the cruelty of war. No longer did the men scream out their brave war cries; now their screams were of the damned, the utterances of last words and curses at victorious enemies. As Philippe drove his horse onward, his eyes were clouded with tears; how had it come to this? This perfect land of justice and peace had turned in on itself and now seemed more like a nightmare world of pain and suffering.

The sun was setting when he arrived at a lake, and it cast a warm glow over the still waters and through the mists, giving the effect of a hazy dream. Philippe took the sword and looked at it; he had never been up close enough to examine it before. The blade was a curious colour, not silver as Philippe had expected, more a pale gold. Rune symbols had been carved down its length, and at the tip, was carved a dragon's head, its tongue snaking out to form the sharp, deadly point. Philippe's mind turned back to Shaan; how could he have left his friend to die alone? He turned his horse and headed back to the battlefield;

He could not allow Shaan to die, not now, after all they had been through and knowing that evil had been forever driven from the land. Now it was time for Shaan to rule the kingdom once more, and for the country to return to its former glory.

Shaan rolled to one side, tried to get comfortable, but could not. He knew he would not live long enough for Philippe to get help; he knew his time had come. Theodore's spear had pierced his armor and body so deeply that it had been driven all the way through and out of the other side.

His mind played over again the last time he had seen the Queen. How he had forgiven her weakness and set her free; how he had hoped to see her again just once more before he died. His eyes misted over with droplets of water, or perhaps sweat from his brow, or maybe they were tears; he could no longer tell. His mind no longer worked on a physical level, and slowly he sank deeper into his dream, down to the darkest levels where fear and dread lay waiting to consume the weak and where the strong must fight to awaken. A thick mist swam around the scenes and figures he imagined, his mind drifted, like a leaf on a stream; it wandered this way and that and bobbed up and down. Visions appeared: warriors, Saville, then Giselle, a figure in black, Lorraine, Philippe, Theodore, Davide, and again the figure in black.

"Shaan," the black shape called softly. "Don't you know me? Shaan, wake up."

The black shape drifted for a moment, shimmered, then stopped close to Shaan.

Shaan shook his head, trying to clear his vision. The mist over his eyes slowly cleared, and the black shape became the outline of a man. His face came next, framed by long black hair held back by a silver band. The face was long and pointed, as was the nose. A big smile crossed the face, and two large eyes glistened like amber jewels.

"Well?" The face enquired.

Shaan pulled himself upright and then winced with pain as he remembered the spear in his breast. It took a few seconds for his mind to register that there was now no pain. He looked down; the spear had gone, as had his armor and clothes. He now lay in a bed of warm linen; a fire raged in a hearth opposite his bed, the flames licking upwards and the heat reaching out and warming his hands and face. The walls of the room were hung with tapestries depicting scenes of great gardens and wild animals, and a single window about the size of a small shield was set in one wall. The window was glazed with coloured glass, depicting the sun shining over a still lake.

Shaan again looked down to where the spear had pierced his side, A small scar, the size of a thumbnail, was the only indication that he had been wounded. He stroked his finger on the scar and expected to feel pain, but there was just a numbness from where the wound had healed over.

"What magic have you used today?" He asked, looking accusingly at the man in black.

"None, only time itself," and adding after a slight pause, "and a few herbs and roots have saved you this time. You were already unconscious when I brought you here and I thought it was too late, even for my skills. But your spirit is strong Shaan, the strongest I have ever encountered. Only your father came close. Now, there was a warrior," replied Gaius with a grin.

"How long have I been here?"

"Questions, questions, always the same." Gaius waged a finger at Shaan." Is it not enough that you are here?"

"Same old Gaius, answering a question with a question," retorted Shaan.

"Two months," Gaius' face suddenly lit up, "but what is time—the ticking of a clock that counts down our few remaining days?"

He paused and looked at Shaan, who tried to interrupt, "A what?"

"What?" repeated Gaius. Ignoring the question, he continued, "Remember what I taught you: time is just an illusion, a measure we can use to mark off our achievements. It does not exist; you cannot touch it, smell it, or eat it." Gaius winked.

"This is no time for lectures, Gaius. Please just answer my questions," Shaan frowned, "as simply as you can," he added slowly.

"Oh, alright," replied Gaius, "you take the fun out of everything."

"Where am I?"

"Aidenvalle."

"The Isle of Aidenvalle?"

"No, that place only exists in the world of men," replied Gaius. "Although history will claim it is there that you..."

"Stop. I do not want to know about the future, only the now." Shaan interrupted, his mood turning sullen.

Gaius turned towards the fire, warming his hands over the bright flames.

"The Queen, bring her to me," ordered Shaan. "I must see her right away."

"I cannot do that," Gaius said, turning his back to Shaan.

"Cannot, or will not?" Replied Shaan. "Bring her to me now; I command it."

"You forget, I am not yours to command," Gaius turned to Shaan, "Even if I were, I could not do it."

"Why. Surely there is nothing that the great Gaius cannot accomplish?" Shaan said it bitterly, with more than a hint of sarcasm.

Gaius looked down and walked a few paces from the bed.

"She is not in this realm."

"I don't understand," Shaan swung his legs out of the bed, "why do you talk in riddles, Gaius?" "What does that mean?"

"It was the only way," with sadness now in his voice, "the only way to save you." Gaius looked at Shaan. "If I had not brought you to another plane, then you would have died." He said this by way of explanation.

"And what of Giselle?" Shaan asked.

"She would have lost you anyway." Gaius paused and took a deep breath. "It is time that you realised that she is partly to blame for your present situation."

"How dare you, hold your tongue!" Shaan shouted, as if to block out the words he refused to hear.

"You know I speak the truth, Shaan." Gaius spoke softly. "It is time to look to the future." And with that, he left the room, leaving Shaan alone.

Shaan's head sank into his hands. It was true that Giselle had betrayed him and, in doing so, betrayed the kingdom. But could she really have been the start of his downfall?

General Tulak sat astride his huge white horse, surveying the land before him. In the distance was the city of Varsile. His black uniform contrasted with the horse's coat, with a single gold stripe down each arm and shiny gold buttons and clasps holding it in place. The scabbard of his sword was wrapped in gold twine, and the pommel shone as the sun glanced off it; however, this was no ornament, it had shed more than its share of blood over the years. Tulak has been raised in the aristocracy; he knew his worth and his direction in life. His wife was held in high esteem by those around the Queen; the Queen herself though, was another matter entirely.

The tall, beautiful, ivory towers and picturesque gardens were known throughout Dresslon as some of the finest architecture ever designed. Tulak himself came from a city steeped in history and beauty, and he appreciated fine things. It made him melancholy to think of his home and family, whom he had not seen in over a year, and the thought of crushing this city and returning home gave him a reason to fight this one last battle. He put a hand into the air and motioned for his standard bearer to ride up next to him. Behind him, twenty thousand men waited for the signal to move forward.

At the border of Dresslon, two men looked towards the oncoming army.

Daal gave a wry smile to Saris. "They seem a little underpowered, only five to one. I am disappointed."

"Let's hope the long journey here has worn them out old man. I have no wish to die today." Saris was not in a jovial mood. Unlike Daal, he did not relish battles, even though he had fought many and was a skilled warrior. Always aware that death could spring upon you from any angle and at any time. He was alert, with eyes that darted here and there looking for the next attack. He gave a nod towards the enemy.

"The legendary General Tulak, he has led his army to many victories." Saris looked along the ranks of the opposing army and then back at his. "They are many Daal; we have fought against such odds before, but that was so long ago, and we had fully trained warriors then."

"We have had time to prepare, at least, unlike the other cities that have fallen. I am sure our forces will have a few surprises in store for General Tulak."

Tulak could see the Varsile defenders in the distance. He was quite impressed with their numbers. No one, so far, had put up this much resistance and in fact, his shock tactics had proved so good that many cities had not even put up a fight, preferring to accept the invaders rather than be killed and their homes destroyed. The tactics were simple. The first few cities had been destroyed, their inhabitants killed or maimed, women taken as salves or worse, and their children slaughtered. Eventually, a few of the captives had been allowed to escape and were given time to run to the next city for shelter, where they could tell of the horrors to come. As the Bastion army approached these cities, the rulers were more than eager to send out envoys to beg for leniency and for the citizens to be spared. Of course, this was done as long as these cities were handed over to the rule of the invaders. Fear had spread quickly across the land, and Tulak's army had fought far fewer battles than had been told; such is the power of rumor. The marching had been long and tiring though, and Tulak was happy that, at least, it was at an end. Stroika had been harder than he expected, but it had fallen all the same, even if he had had a little unrequested help.

Tulak was intrigued by the green flags flying at several places in the ranks of the Varsile army. The city's colours were a red shield with a golden cross on it. Maybe they had some new allies, but whoever they were, they would fall like all the rest.

Tulak signaled his army to move forward and begin the attack. This shouldn't take long; the Varsile army was lined up in several ranks in a long line with their backs to the city walls, where they were trapped with no chance of escape and seemed too spread out to offer any solid defense. Tulak's cavalry were to go in first with the intention of breaking up the defending lines into smaller sections, and his foot soldiers would then rush in and finish them off as always. The cavalry rode battle-hardened horses that would not be afraid of any noise or swords being waved around them. Tulak unsheathed his sword and held it high into the air. This was the sign his men had been waiting for and their horses were spurred on into a gallop, the riders already brandishing long swords ready for the slaughter and sending clouds of dust up behind them. The infantry ran as best they could to keep up but were left far behind.

As the horses neared, the Varsile lines suddenly moved closer together, their shields touching and forming a solid wall. This did nothing to deter the onrushing cavalry, who could just ride through it or jump over it. With only seconds to spare, the front row of the Varsile army knelt down and picked up the three-meter-long spears that had been lying next to them hidden in the long grass. The lines behind them did the same but continued standing. The wall of shields was now like a deadly porcupine, and the riders had no chance to stop their horses in time. The horses charged onto the spears; some tried to stop but couldn't, throwing their riders, while others reared and fell sideways and all were either impaled on the spears or had their legs cut out from under them by the swords of defending troops. The riders were hacked to death by the massed ranks of defenders as they fell, and even those that tried to stand had little chance of survival. The infantry, having seen what had happened, began to slow, taking stock of the scene before them and not wishing to run headlong into the spears. Tulak, enraged, waved his sword around in circles above his head with the hope of encouraging the attack.

"Charge forward now, finish them." He shouted above the noise of the startled soldiers, who now were only edging towards the enemy. "Cowards!" Tulak pushed his horse through the ranks of his men. "With me, with me! See how they are kneeling now; they know it is useless to resist."

Indeed, the front three rows of the Varsile army had sunk to their knees, but not in fear; behind them, four rows of archers had strung their bows and now shot arrows high into the air. With a high-pitched whistling sound, they turned and arced down; the sky filled with long streaks of dark wooden death that rained down on the attacking army. The Bastion army turned and tried to run but couldn't; there were too many of them packed closely together, and now the arrows cut through them, killing hundreds in the first wave. The second wave now came, and more Bastion soldiers fell to the ground dead or wounded. The soldiers at the back of the Bastion army were scattering, allowing others to start their escape, but it didn't last long. Appearing from behind them now came another force. A thousand mounted men dressed in green silks with lances and swords came from either side of the rear of the battlefield, cutting off their escape route. They scythed through the desperate Bastion infantry, some of whom had dropped their weapons as they ran, while others were too shocked to offer any resistance. Now the Varsile army ran at their attackers, and a fierce battle ensued. Waves of arrows, along with the horse soldiers had killed thousands of enemy soldiers, and the tide had turned. The Bastion army was now staring at defeat.

After Shaan had bathed, a maid brought him food, which he ate greedily; he then drank some of the mulled wine and then went to sleep. Two hours later he awoke, rose from his bed, and dressed in the fresh clothes that had been left for him, feeling refreshed and in need of some fresh air and the chance to think.

"Now," he thought, "it is time to see exactly where I am." He had understood little of what had been said to him and still expected to see the town of Cadbury outside and his castle a short distance away.

Shaan was dressed in black leather trousers and boots, a fine pale blue silk shirt, and a black studded belt wrapped around his waist. He left his room feeling a little unsteady on his legs, the muscles unused to bearing his weight from his time in bed. He walked down the corridor and out into the courtyard beyond. Waiting for him was a large black mare, saddled and ready, just as he had requested from the maid earlier.

It took Shaan two attempts to get into the saddle; he was obviously weaker than he thought. He pulled on the reins, turned the horse, and headed out of the courtyard. There was no town or castle, as he had imagined there would be. A large meadow lay before him, and beyond that, a forest of dense apple trees. Although this may have seemed unusual to many, Aidenvalle was famed in legend for its apples and their almost magical ability to provide sustenance when required, as a base preparation for a healing tonic, or even to be made into wine.

"I may as well start there." He said as much to his horse as himself. Kicking the horse to a gallop, he set off towards the waiting trees and possibly some answers to his questions. The sun shone warmly from a clear blue sky, and it refreshed Shaan's spirit as much as his skin. Even if he found no answers, it was a beautiful day for a ride. He remembered many days like this in the past, when he had ridden out for the day with his lovely Giselle, his Queen. His face saddened with the memory of her betrayal, and he knew that he would never see her again.

"No," he thought, "I must not think such things. Someday, somehow, we will meet again; no matter what it takes, I'll get back to my kingdom again." For had Gaius not taught him that all things were possible, and had he not seen many things that other men had only dreamt of?

The only way into the forest was a narrow path just wide enough to allow him to enter on horseback. This he took, and after a few steps, it began to slope downhill, gently at first, then steeper as he went on. Shaan picked and ate a couple of apples, which refreshed him immensely, and then after a few minutes he came upon a clearing. Before him, a river ran slowly by, and beyond that, some large rocky slabs jutted up, standing proud, as they had done for a millennium. Shaan stared at the rocks. Something was not quite right; maybe it was the angle at which they were set or the colour. A thought began to materialize in his mind, but before it could form, a beam of light bounced off the stream, catching Shaan's eye and then in an instant was gone.

Shaan looked at the water; his mouth seemed very dry at that moment. Dismounting his horse, he walked to the stream, bent down, scooped up a handful of the water, and gulped it down. Shaan stooped to get another drink when something made him look across the stream. He looked towards the grey rocks; yes, there it was, a figure standing between them, or was it? His eyes strained to look deep between the giant slabs, but now he could only see darkness. Had his eyes fooled him? Had it been a shadow cast by the sun? He stood up, stretching to his full height, yet still he was unable to see anyone.

"Gaius," he called, "is it you?"

No answer.

"Don't play games, Gaius." His voice softened: "I know you're there."

Still, there was no reply. Shaan thought he heard a sound, boots on shingle, maybe? "Ah, I hear you, Gaius." He shouted triumphantly.

Shaan sprang across the stream and ran into the gaps between the rocks; he slid easily between the slabs of granite, and his feet crunched upon the shingle below. "Come out, Gaius; I have no time for games," he said to the darkness in front of him.

Shaan now stood before a cavern leading into the hillside.

"Come on, Gaius; I've much to ask and I need your help."

Still there was no reply. Shaan took a few steps into the cavern; it was almost as if the walls absorbed light, for within a few feet he was in total darkness. Then, as if to prove him wrong, up ahead he could see a shimmer, as if fire shone against a polished black surface. Shaan crept forward, quieter now in case the figure he had seen had not been Gaius after all. About twenty paces into the cavern, Shaan noticed that there was a clear opening ahead of him. The steady patter of feet echoed around the cavern, then faded and was gone, as if someone had walked off the stony floor and onto a carpet. Shaan moved on, his heart now pounding strongly; he was alert and ready to move quickly should the need arise.

The cavern now opened into a large cave; it was almost perfectly round and about thirty feet across. The cave was well lit by ten bright lanterns hung on the surrounding walls. Shaan's eyes widened, and he stared straight ahead, unable to take in the scene that lay before him. It was not the almost perfectly smooth walls of the cave or the six tunnels leading from it that had stunned Shaan, although on any other day that would have been more than enough, but the object before him. Standing dead in the center of the cave, about sixteen feet in diameter, was a table; the center ring was carved from solid oak, while the outer third was walnut. The table was highly polished and glowed in the light from the lanterns. He had seen this table before, for it was his and came from his castle.

"How did it get here? Why was it here?" A thousand questions raced through his mind, none of which he could answer. Shaan walked over to the table and placed a hand gently on it, as one would when stroking a favorite horse or dog. He walked around it, his hand never once leaving its smooth, flawless surface. Now he knew he must find Gaius and get his answers, for he could bear the torment no longer. He looked up at the entrance to one of the tunnels, then along to the next one. Which was the exit? All the entrances were exactly the same. There was not even a subtle difference between the openings to show the way back to where he entered.

Shaan had always been a logical thinker, and there were no thoughts of being trapped and unable to leave.

"I know the entrance is only a few strides down the cavern," he thought, "I'll just take each passage in turn."

Twenty steps down the first cavern, and he could see light ahead.

"First time lucky," he said to himself.

Stepping outside, he walked down towards the stream; rain was falling heavily, making ripples wash towards each bank. Now where had his horse gone? Maybe it had sheltered a little way into the forest. Shaan turned around to look at the cave. It was then that he noticed that there were no rocks here, no great slabs rising from the earth, and no other recognisable landmarks.

"Of course," he said to himself, "I came out on a different side of the cave."

He turned and walked along the river, following it around to where he thought the other entrance must be.

Shaan walked for a while but could find no other entrance to the cave, nor could he find any sign of the granite slabs. Soaked through and fearing he would never find the entrance or his black mare, he decided to walk through the forest and head back to the warmth of his temporary home. Maybe he would be able to see the walls of the building he had left a few hours ago, or at least some form of shelter from the rain, which was now coming down harder than before. A storm was brewing, and the sky was rapidly turning black.

As Shaan climbed a short slope, a stream of soft mud washed over his boots and continued to the bottom. Shaan watched its descent, then continued to the top and into the trees. Lightning streaked across the sky and lit the forest for a split second, then was gone. Shaan cursed; he did not recognise any of his surroundings and could see no place to shelter. There was nothing for it; he would have to return to the cavern and wait for the storm to pass. He turned around, but the dense forest had closed in on him, and there appeared to be trees where there had not been before. Which way had he come? He looked on the floor to trace his footsteps, but the rain had softened the ground, and none remained. Shaan cursed again. He began to run back through the forest, almost blindly; the cave surely could not be that hard to find.

After a while, he slowed to a walk, almost exhausted, cold to the bone, and aching. His body was not used to this much exercise, and he found it hard to keep his mind from the cold. Shaan sank to his knees, unable to continue. Surely, after all he had been through, it would not end here, alone and lost. Shaan blinked, clearing the raindrops from his eyes. What was that ahead? He rubbed his eyes with the back of his hand, had he imagined it? No, ahead of him, a tiny wisp of smoke rose into the air. Shaan's strength returned in a rush; he rose to his feet and staggered forward. A dozen steps or so, and he could see that the smoke rose from a small timber cabin that was almost invisible to the eye and, had it not been for the smoke, perfectly camouflaged. The cabin had been constructed with the logs running upward, so that they resembled tree trunks. There was no window or door that Shaan could see on this side, and there was no path or other indication to show that the cabin was inhabited. Shaan noted that without the wisps of smoke, the cabin would have been invisible. Without thinking about who, or what, the inhabitant may be, Shaan continued towards the cabin. He cared not if they were friend or foe; he would die out here anyway, and so he may as well die fighting for shelter and warmth.

Shaan came up to the log wall and touched it to make sure it was real. He walked around the outside of the cabin; there was no door or window on this side, and so he rounded the next corner. Yes, there was a door. He stumbled towards it, almost fell, steadied himself against the door, and beat his fist on it as hard as he could. There was no immediate reply, and Shaan was about to knock on the door again when he heard a bolt being withdrawn from within.

The door creaked open to reveal a tiny crack and small eyes peering out.

"You're early." The eyes said, "Well, come on, get out of the rain." The door opened fully, and Shaan stepped through. The face that accompanied the eyes and voice was thin and wizened. A small white beard capped the chin, and the eyes were small and oval in shape, but they glistened like polished gems. The face beamed like a small child who had found a missing toy, a look that did not quite suit it.

Dressed in a brown robe that was tied at the waist by a thin belt that buckled at the side, the man stood at about the height of Shaan's shoulders. A frown crossed the man's face. "You're early," The man seemed bothered by this.

"Early?" Enquired Shaan.

"Early." The voice repeated, as if an echo. "Never mind, can't be helped now." It continued. "Did you bring them with you?" Asked the man, "Where are they?"

"Them?" Shaan retorted.

"Them." Replied the man, the face frowning deeper, and added, "Do you repeat everything?"

The eyebrows on the face rose, "Everything." It said with a smile.

Shaan was now three questions behind and getting nowhere.

"Wait," said Shaan. "Slow down; let's take this one bit at a time. I think you are confusing me with someone else," said Shaan. "I was caught in the storm, and all I require is a little shelter and warmth, just till the storm passes."

"Till the storm passes?" The man looked at Shaan, sadness now in his eyes. "It hasn't even begun."

That was more than Shaan could bear. "You talk in more riddles than that damn Gaius." He stormed. "Please, just let me warm myself, and then I'll be on my way."

"Gaius was right," the man said, "you are still a little fiery."

"What do you know of me? I've never even been to Aidenvalle before." Shaan spoke sternly, as if chastising someone for listening to idle gossip.

"Oh, I know all about you." The man replied. "I've heard tell of your deeds, your castle, your armies, and your kingdom, but that means nothing here." He added, almost as a warning. "You won't even be considered a knight here," he continued, "you're just one man, and you're going to have to fight all the way."

"Ah, so it's a game you play with me?" Shaan looked at the man for a sign that he was right, but nothing came. "There's no war in Aidenvalle; there never has been and there never will be." This Shaan knew, for Gaius had told him on many occasions how it was the only perfectly peaceful place in the Multiverse, where everything lived in such harmony that there could never be unrest there.

"That's true at least," said the man honestly, "if only you were in Aidenvalle."

"Of course, I am in Aidenvalle," Shaan argued, "I only left…" He paused, and he didn't know the name of the place where he had been taken. "I left a few hours ago and have crossed no borders."

"Did Gaius not bring you through?" The man looked worried and said, "No wonder you're early."

Back to the word 'early,' Shaan felt sure he was being led in circles. "Please explain what you mean by early," Shaan begged, "and if I'm not in Aidenvalle, where am I?"

"Come, sit by the fire, and dry yourself." The man led Shaan to a large, soft chair and threw him a cloth with which to dry himself. "I'll make a warm brew, then we had better find out what you know."

Shaan leant back in the chair; the conversation had taken its toll and used up all the energy he had left. He closed his eyes, just for a few seconds, to try to clear his mind. The chair was so soft, he sank deep into its folds, warm and comfortable, and he let his mind drift, floating like a cloud drifting slowly across a summer sky. It wandered from Aidenvalle to Cannchester, from Gaius to Giselle. Memories washed through his mind like the sea rolling gently up the shore, each wave bringing another memory. The first time he had met Giselle was when she had tended his wounds after the battle at her father's castle. Their wedding, where she had looked so beautiful. He could see the people looking at her and how they loved her. Philippe, Bedilore, his stepbrother Kai, and his father, everyone was there, everyone except Gaius. Where was Gaius? Why had he not noticed at the time? Why now, after all these years, had he realised that Gaius had not been at his wedding?"

"Shaan, Shaan." His name drifted into his head and then faded away. "Shaan." Shaan awoke with a start; in front of him was the inhabitant of this small but extremely comfortable cabin.

"Here's your brew. Drink it up, and you'll feel much better." A mug of steaming liquid was thrust at Shaan. He took it and gazed into the thick steam, which covered the liquid below. "What's in it?" Shaan inquired, unable to recognise the sweet smell that rose from the mug.

"Herbs, spices, and a little magic." A large grin broke out across the wizened face. "Now drink up." Shaan took a sip of the liquid; to his surprise, it tasted good. He drank a mouthful, and now warmed by the liquid inside and the fire in front of him, his spirits rose. He felt almost refreshed, as if he had had a good night's sleep. He adjusted his posture, relaxing in the chair, and fixed his gaze into the eyes of his host.

"Let's start at the beginning," Shaan felt ready now to digest the information.

"Who are you, and where am I?"

"I am Bron," answered the man as he sank into the chair opposite Shaan, "and you are in the forest of Kwell, in the land of Dresslon." Bron turned away from Shaan and took a strange object from a nearby shelf. He then took a small pouch from a pocket in his robe, and out of this pouch he pulled what appeared to Shaan to be dried strands of a grass-like substance, which he pushed into a small bowl that formed the main part of the object he had taken from the shelf. The bowl itself sat on a tube about the length of Shaan's index finger. Bron picked up a taper that lay beside the fire, pushed it into the flames until it lit, then put the tube of the object in his mouth, applied the taper to the bowl, and sucked gently on the tube. The substance in the bowl flared momentarily and then appeared to go out. Smoke rose from the bowl, and Bron, looking satisfied, shook the taper putting it out, and lay it back down by the fire. He replaced the tube of the object in his mouth, sucked in the smoke, removed the tube, and gently blew the smoke into the air. Bron seemed to almost visibly relax, as if a great weight had been lifted from him. He looked over at Shaan, whose face was now one of total amazement. Shaan did not need to ask.

"It's a pipe," said Bron, in way of explanation. "A gift from Gaius. An amusing little thing, don't you think?"

Shaan shook his head slowly. He felt that the conversation was about to slip away from him again.

"Tell me what you meant by asking me if I had them." Shaan thought it best to ignore the pipe for now, asking, "and what am I early for?"

"Did Gaius tell you nothing?" Bron looked concerned.

"Nothing," replied Shaan, "one moment on the battlefield at Cadbury, the next in bed in a strange building in Aidenvalle."

"Over two cycles ago, Gaius passed through our land; he saw the carnage and death that was here. We begged him to help, but he was unable to, even his magic could not save us from the evil of Krishia. Her magic is strong, and although Gaius is great, he was unable to defeat her." Bron looked deeply into Shaan's eyes. "When he was almost exhausted, he left, promising to send a great hero who could bring an end to our sorrow."

"And who is this great hero?" asked Shaan.

"He is called Shaan of Cannchester, and he is you," Bron jabbed the pipe in Shaan's direction.

"I'm no hero," replied Shaan. "What can I accomplish that Gaius could not?"

"Legend has it that the only thing that can kill Krishia is the spear of Loris. But with that alone, you will not succeed. You will also need Lady Bella's Shield, the Helm of Othus, and the Sword, Caliburn."

"Then all is already lost," said Shaan, "for all of these artefacts are lost from this world."

"No, only from your world," scolded Bron, "and you are no longer there."

"Then the artefacts are here somewhere?" Shaan sat up a little.

"If only it were that simple," replied Bron. "They are scattered in the seven realms somewhere. You will have to venture into each realm to recover an item."

"You said there were seven realms, but there are only four artifacts," Shaan said.

"We know where not to look," said Bron. "The first realm is the cave of the table itself, the second is Aidenvalle, and the third is here. That leaves four exits to take. Each will lead to one of the objects you must seek, then you must return here before it is too late, for the final destruction of Dresslon is not long away."

"Why should I help?" asked Shaan, although he already knew.

"What else would you do?" A smile crossed Bron's face. "Lay in your bed at Aidenvalle. I don't think you would stay sane for long, my friend." He paused thoughtfully for a second. "No, you need excitement, Shaan, and besides, who knows what you'll gain at the end of this adventure?" Maybe a chance to drink from the great cup and make a wish?" Bron looked at the glowing embers of the fire. "What would you wish for, Shaan?" He asked in a soft, almost dreamlike voice, so quiet that Shaan could only just hear it, or had he only imagined Bron had said it?

"Fine, I'll help," said Shaan. "What do I have to do?"

"Nothing tonight," replied Bron, "just drink, eat, and rest, for after tonight you will know no rest for many days." Bron paused, lying back in his chair, and closed his eyes. "Tell me your story, Shaan."

"I am Shaan of Cannchester, son of Prethus, and my story is long," said Shaan.

"I've had all night," replied Bron, "so I'm ready to listen." Shaan closed his eyes and told Bron his incredible story, one that, if it had not happened to Shaan himself, he would not have believed.

General Tulak splashed water from the river over his face and body, washing off the blood of the men he had killed today and his own blood, where he had been wounded a dozen times. It was a miracle he had survived. Three arrows had pierced his body, but not any vital organs. The cuts and stabs from swords and knives had done the same. The water was refreshing, and he stood in it, waist-deep, allowing it to revitalize him. Looking around at his broken forces, he could see the weariness and despair that had crept in. He knew that he was lucky to have escaped with around a thousand men out of an initial force of twenty thousand. It would take all of his strengths as a commander to bring them back as a fighting force. How did the Varsile army get so well equipped? How did they learn those tactics, and who were the warriors in green and black who killed so many of his men?

"Aaron, I have need of you." He called to a tall, stocky man close by as he waded out of the water.

Pulling his cloak around himself while he dried, he sat by the fire and picked up the torn green flag that was lying there. "Take this flag back to Evora and tell them what has happened. They will need to send their toy back."

"She will not be happy, Lord. Not after Stroika."

"We did not summon for help before; it was her impatience. That city would have been ours in a few days, intact. Now there is little left to rule. I sometimes wonder if she even wants these cities or if her plan is something we will never know."

The hunter rose from his bed, pulled on his leather trousers and waistcoat, then sat back down on the bed, leant over, and picked up his boots, which he pulled onto his feet, and rose again. He walked over to the chair by the window, which overlooked the main street below. Glancing out, he noticed that the streets were empty as usual. Picking up the fur that lay across the chair and wrapping it around his shoulders, he crossed the room to a large cupboard. Opening the door and reaching inside, he withdrew a large bow, a quiver of white-tipped arrows, and a shiny sword, which he slipped into the scabbard on his belt. The bow and arrows he slung on his shoulders, and turning, he looked once around the room before heading out into the corridor that led to the stairs. Outside, he sniffed deeply at the morning air, and headed north.

CHAPTER TWO

Shaan had risen early. Outside, the rain had been replaced with bright sunshine, and Shaan stood, eyes closed, his face pointing up to the sky, drinking in the glorious feeling that only the sun could give. Whatever had been in the drink that Bron had given him had worked; Shaan had not felt this good for a long time. He opened his eyes, gazing into the blue sky. A solitary cloud floated by, paused as if to greet Shaan, and then drifted into the distance. Shaan smiled and returned to the cabin.

Bron had already left before Shaan had woken up; he had prepared a meal for Shaan's breakfast and left a note saying he would return later. But that was several hours ago, and Shaan was beginning to wonder if he was going to return at all.

Shaan sat down in the chair by the fire, which was now just ashes, and thought about all that had happened to him during the previous day. Maybe he was dreaming and would wake up on the battlefield to find Philippe looking over him.

The battle at Cadbury had cost him dearly; nearly all of his knights had been killed, and only eight had survived, excluding himself. The battle that had been forced upon him by Theodore, his nephew, who had sought the throne for himself and who had killed his own mother when her powers had failed to bring him the throne by magic.

Shaan thought of Saville, his sister, who was so taken by darkness that even at the end she thought that what she did was for the good. The woman who, as a girl, had shown such a fascination with the arts of magic that she had persuaded Gaius to teach her. Gaius had been so taken with her ability and quick learning that he had been swallowed up in the quickness of it all and had taught her too much without warning her of the dangers, and by the time Gaius realised what was happening it was too late; Saville had been taken by evil and was forever lost to him.

Morgau, Shaan's other sister, had fought against the dark side of magic and the danger she was to Shaan and had fled the country, although not before nearly killing him and causing him to kill one of his best and most trusted knights, Sir Ancoln. She had become known as 'Le Fay', meaning the fairy or magician, due to her addiction and proficiency in the use of magic. Cleansing herself daily, she had avoided the dark path taken by Saville until her sister herself had tricked and entranced her.

Shaan wondered what had happened to her. She had come to him the day she left, begging his forgiveness, for having broken the spell that Saville had cast on her, she now knew what she had done and what she was capable of doing. To ensure that she would not fall under Saville's spell again, she had left Shaan's kingdom to practice her art until she felt strong enough to aid him and get her revenge on Saville, but that had been the last he had seen of her.

Shaan was alerted by the sound of footsteps coming into the cabin. Looking up he saw Bron entering carrying a large bundle, which he dropped to the floor. He walked back out of the cabin and returned a few moments later with another bundle, which he placed on the table on the other side of the room.

"Good morning, how are you feeling today?"

"Much better, thanks to you." Shaan replied, looking at the bundles.

"Come over here. I have something for you." said Bron, his eyes glowing like those of a father giving his favorite son a present.

Bron opened the bundle on the floor and handed Shaan a sword. "Not of the same quality as Caliburn," Bron smiled, "but I'm sure it will come in useful."

Shaan took the sword and felt its weight, and then he swung it back and forth several times. "Not too heavy, good balance; yes, I'm sure it will come in useful." Shaan laughed. It felt good to have a sword in his hand again; he felt almost naked without one.

Bron pulled a small dagger from the bundle and handed that to Shaan as well. Shaan took it and pushed it deep into the top of one boot. This was a lesson Shaan had learned from Leon, Giselle's father, and the man who had taught Shaan the art of war while Gaius taught him the art of living.

Shaan's first act as king had been to aid Leon in defending his castle against a vast army after he had sided with the young king when the other knights had refused to accept him, even though this had been decreed by Gaius, who was known as the king maker and who had chosen the kings for over two hundred years.

The knights, as well as some battle-experienced warriors, had returned to the same place every year for thirteen years since the death of Prethus to see who the strongest and most deserving warrior was; the challenge was open to all comers, but seldom did a common man attempt it. For thirteen years, no man had endured all the tests. Shaan, who was only seventeen at the time and a man from a poor family, could not possibly be the new king, the great warrior that Gaius had prophesied. Shaan had endured the challenges and the trials and had been the last man standing before being presented with the sword 'Moonblade' that had been created by powers now unknown to the world, but the knights were split, some accepting Shaan and the majority going against him, and those loyal to Shaan had been forced to retreat to Leon's castle, where a fierce siege had taken place and after three days the castle defenses looked as though they would fall and all would be lost.

Shaan had decided then to risk all, and as he stood on

the battlement looking down, he saw Alaine of Cresswell below. Shaan knew that if he could defeat Alaine, the others would surrender, so with a mighty roar, Shaan leapt from the battlement and caught Alaine squarely on the shoulders, dragging him from his horse into the water of the moat. Shaan was the first to rise from the water; he drew his sword from its scabbard and swung it in the direction that Alaine had fallen, and with a splash, it entered the water and struck the mud at the bottom. Alaine had emerged a few feet away and now brought his own sword into play, sending it crashing down on Shaan's armor. Shaan retaliated, and the two fought back and forth across the moat while the other knights, having stopped their battle, looked on, knowing that this was the fight that would end the bloodshed. Shaan and Alaine fought for what seemed like an eternity, neither losing ground, but weariness was taking its toll, and both fighters were now finding it hard to swing the great battle swords they carried when suddenly Alaine gave a mighty blow to Shaan's chest, sending him toppling into the water. It took all of Shaan's strength for him to rise, and Alaine, seeing this, took a swing at Shaan's head.

Shaan, sensing the blade coming towards him, knew there was nothing he could do to stop it from striking home, yet in his mind he could hear himself say, "Moonblade, if you are the great sword that Gaius spoke of, then now is the time to prove it." As if in answer to his prayer, Moonblade seemed weightless in Shaan's hand as it swung up in an ark, cutting through Alaine's sword with a mighty crash as if thunder had rolled across the sky. The two halves of the broken sword fell into the moat and sank to the depths of the murky water. Shaan looked around at the watching knights to make sure they offered no immediate threat. Many stood with wide eyes; others just looked on, while a few of the knights had turned away and were making their way from the battlefield, unsure of what they had just witnessed. Shaan placed Moonblade against Alaine's throat and ordered, "Yield."

"No," replied Alaine, "I cannot, for although you have beaten me and beaten me fairly, I can only yield to another knight, as I have sworn by death that I will never yield to a common man."

Shaan thought about this; he did not want to kill Alaine, not unless he had to. "There must be a way around this," he thought, "for after this war I will need all the warriors behind me, and Alaine is by far the best." Kneeling down in the water, Shaan took Moonblade by the blade and offered it to Alaine. "Then you will knight me." Shaan said, looking up at Alaine of Cresswell. As Alaine took the sword, a voice from behind him shouted out," Now! Take the sword Alaine, kill him, and claim it as yours."

Alaine held Moonblade high in the air. Looking down at Shaan, who remained kneeling, his eyes were closed. "It is your decision; choose well, Alaine, of Cresswell," Shaan whispered.

Alaine brought the sword gently down onto Shaan's shoulder, lifted the great blade, and placed it on the other shoulder, saying, "With the power vested in me, I knight you in the name of God. Rise, Sir Shaan,"

Alaine seemed to hesitate, and slowly he sank to his knees. "King Shaan," he said softly. The knights in and around the moat all sank to their knees, accepting at last, Shaan as their king.

Bron unpacked the rest of the bundle and then proceeded to do the same to the other bundle, which was full of food, some of which he put into cupboards and the rest he left on the table. He then went over to a corner of the cabin, opened a box that lay there, and took out a sack, which he packed with the food that he had left on the table.

"This will keep you going for a while;" he turned to Shaan, "you had better be on your way."

Shaan took the bag from Bron and said, "I will not fail you." He exited the cabin; no more words being exchanged.

On his journey to the cave, Shaan recalled his conversation with Bron the previous evening, when Shaan had asked him why Krishia was attacking Dresslon. Bron had looked disturbed as he told Shaan, "Krishia desires to rule the seven realms, and the only way she can do that is by taking control of the Tower of Taal."

"Why the Tower of Taal?" Shaan had asked, even though he had not heard of it before.

"Because the tower is the gateway to the realms, and it is the only way that Krishia can get her armies through." Bron replied.

"Why not use the cave? They are not protected." Shaan thought this seemed like a logical thing to do.

"The cave is a thing of light; no evil can pass that way, but the tower is neutral ground and is open to anyone." Bron paused for a second, as if to gather his thoughts. "Since Krishia became warlike, the tower has been guarded by the Jarenn. The elite warriors of Taal, who, so legend has it, have never been beaten in war, although in reality they had not fought a war for fifty years and only a few of them had survived that time. They were now the mentors of a new army of guardians, and though the training methods have not changed, it is well known that there is no substitute for the real thing."

"At least they should be able to hold Krishia's army for a while." Shaan had said hopefully.

"Krishia's army is vast, while the Jarenn are few." Bron looked worried when he spoke these words.

Shaan came upon the stream and followed it for a few minutes before crossing. He paused on the far bank, stooped down, and picked up a piece of flint that lay near the water's edge. Then he headed towards the cave's entrance. Stepping into the tunnel, he turned, took one last look at Dresslon, scraped a cross onto the wall using the flint, then walked into the dark tunnel that led back inside. Inside the round hall that was the main cavern, Shaan again came upon the table. He took the flint and placed it on the table in line with the tunnel he had just walked along.

"At least I know where one of the entrances comes out," he said aloud as if talking to a companion. "Come on, Gaius; if you can't do some magic to help me out, at least give me some guidance." There was no reply; Shaan had not really expected one.

Shaan took the next passage and walked down its long, narrow path to the next realm of his adventure, wondering where it would lead and what help he could expect from its inhabitants.

The bar in which the hunter was now drinking was full of all the lowlifes, villains, and cutthroats that could be found on this side of town. They liked their own company, a gathering of like minds, one might say. The room was semi-dark, hiding the stains on the floor from ale and worse. The wooden seats were hard and uncomfortable; there was no padding or thought about the comfort of the patrons; there was no money to be made by buying anything of quality; the chances of such pieces of furniture being used as a weapon were high and costly to replace. An array of different beverages lined the back wall behind the bar, each one priced according to the effect it may have on you. Not all were alcohol, but some of the ingredients were only talked about in dark spaces and in hushed voices, as they were not necessarily legal, even in this town. The hunter watched, taking in everything around him. A couple too close to each other, another having angry words, four men at a table playing cards, and several loners just drinking their sorrows away. At one table, several men were in a deep discussion, was it about families, work, business, their next heist? More likely the latter in this bar. No one looked at the hunter; there was something about him you didn't want to look at too closely.

The hunter liked to drink in this kind of place because

he knew that at any second a fight could break out or someone could attack you at any moment without the slightest provocation or warning. To stay alive in this kind of place, you had to be alert, and this was the best form of training you could get. If you could survive in this kind of place, you could survive anywhere. The hunter frequented these bars to keep himself sharp, and he knew that to catch his latest prey, he would have to be at his very best, for his latest prey was a legend, probably the greatest warrior ever to live, almost a god in many people's eyes, but not quite, and it was the hunter who would prove this legend to be false. It was the hunter who would take this man's place in the order of things, yes man, for that was what the hunter would prove this pretender to be. This king of kings, whose legend had outgrown him.

"I will have your crown, Shaan Moonblade." The hunter murmured under his breath.

Krishia paced back and forth, gripping tightly onto an object in her hand, fingers whitening at the knuckles, her eyes blazing, "What are those fools doing? Can they do nothing without me?" The red train of her gown flowing out behind her, she struck out with the object at the person nearest her, commanding, "Get me a drink." She was angry. How could these imbeciles not carry out a simple task? Had she not provided them with twenty thousand men? Trained, well-equipped men, twenty thousand strong, against one city whose population was less than that, and they ran away?

Had she not already saved them from defeat at Stroika? Breached the walls, allowing them to flood in?

Glancing over at Khamel, perhaps this woman was weakening her favorite, Tulak, and perhaps she needed to do something about that. Khamel noticed Krishia's gaze and gave the Queen a smile, which Krishia returned; she was only smiling on the outside, though.

"You, boy," Krishia called out to a nearby child of about 11 years of age, "come."

The boy approached cautiously, his head lowered, looking at the ground near his feet. Krishia bent down and whispered in the boy's ear, and he turned and quickly walked away.

"Khamel, my dear girl, come! " Krishia did not have to speak loudly; her voice carried to all around her as certain peoples do. Khamel walked over to the Queen, neither too fast nor too slow, but at a measured pace, so those around her knew she was not at the Queen's beck and call, or at least to give that impression. It was a dangerous game, many thought, but Khamel was under the illusion that her presence carried some weight as her husband, Tulak, was the queen's most decorated and loved commander.

"Come, let us walk in the gardens," Krishia said softly. I wish to discuss something with you.

The gardens at Estoria were immaculate; none could rival them; they were exquisite, designed to catch the eye and the imagination. The topography was perfect; statues, ponds, exotic flowers, and shrubs lined every path, and the paths themselves were perfectly level. Waterfalls splashed into ponds stocked with brightly coloured fish, and frogs and insects chirped, calling out for mates.

Krishia walked, linking arms with Khamel; she laughed, pointed out various features in the gardens, and patted Khamel's hand from time to time until the boy caught up to them, head bowed, holding out two glasses of iced genovka (a wine and spirit mixture that was known for its light, delicate flavor but also its potency) on a tray made of pure gold. Genovka was a favorite amongst the more affluent society. Krishia took one, sipped at the contents, and nodded at Khamel to take the other. Khamel was innocent in looks but not in mind. She took the glass, raised it to her lips, and took the smallest sip she could. Krishia noticed a broad smile on her face and said, "Don't worry, my dear, I am not going to poison you, well, not yet," and she winked.

"Your majesty," Khamel exclaimed, "no such thought had crossed my mind." She lied.

"Have you heard from your husband lately?" Krishia enquired.

"I would have thought you would hear more than I, your majesty." Khamel wondered at the question: was this some kind of test of loyalty? Her mind whirled, wondering what the hidden meaning of this sudden bonding was. Caution is needed; words need to be carefully chosen, and it is important not to slip up and say too much.

"He has not written in a while; the last I heard was of the victory at Stroika, which was some weeks ago, your majesty. I am used to long breaks in letters; he is so busy on his mission to bring all under your rule." Khamel hoped the queen would accept this answer.

"Indeed, I understand he has now taken Varsile." Krishia probed.

"That is good news; perhaps he will now have time to write." It was news to Khamel; rumor around court said otherwise.

What games were afoot, wheels within wheels, plans within plans, words between words? Perhaps a chess game between Khamel and the queen, with Tulak as the prize? It was at that moment that a messenger arrived with private news for the queen, and the game was over for now.

CHAPTER THREE

Shaan emerged into bright sunshine, at first too bright for his eyes. Shielding them with his hand, he walked forward. A strange smell entered his nostrils, only slowly becoming recognizable, a smell of burning timbers and worse. Before Shaan could identify the source of these odors, a voice called out from his right.

"Daegal, Prince Daegal," the voice cried, "you're alive."

Shaan, upon seeing a man running up a path towards him, wondered to whom the man had called. He looked behind himself to see who this Prince Daegal could be, and what Shaan saw made him stand motionless as if mesmerized, for behind him was not the entrance to the cave as he had expected to see but instead an entrance to a building, a building which was ablaze and had obviously been so for some time. There was no one behind him, and Shaan wondered if someone was trapped inside. "Prince Daegal, we feared you dead." The man had reached Shaan now, his hand on his shoulder. "Come quickly; we must get you away from here."

Shaan suddenly realised that the man was talking to him. "I think you mistook me, sir." Shaan looked at the man, who stared back as if Shaan were mad.

"Oh, Prince Daegal, what have they done to you?" Was all the man could reply. "Come now, let's get you out of this place." And with that, he took Shaan by the arm and led him down the path away from the ruined building.

Shaan was taken to a nearby inn. On the way, he tried to explain that he was not Daegal, but the man would not listen and kept repeating that he was sorry that Daegal had lost his memory, probably due to some blow that he had taken during the battle. Shaan decided that it was best to keep quiet until inside the inn, where some of the locals would see that he was not this Prince Daegal and would explain to this poor soul that he was indeed mistaken. On entering the inn, Shaan was in for a greater shock. Several of the locals turned to see who had entered, and now a crowd was forming around him.

"Prince Daegal," they called. "Praise be." Others muttered. Shaan could not speak; What could he say? It was as if the whole inn was suffering some sort of grand illusion, and they all saw him as this mysterious prince. Then it came to him, it was one of Gaius's tricks. Gaius had obviously cast some spell over these people so that they saw him as someone else, and he decided to go along with the illusion, feeling that it must help him with his goal.

"I am all right; no harm has been done." He said this, trying to sound as if he knew what had supposedly happened to Prince Daegal.

The villagers stared at Shaan and asked, "What of your father?" One called out. Shaan had to think quickly; this was an unexpected question.

"I don't know," Shaan replied. "I lost him in the battle."

The man who had brought Shaan to the inn looked at him with a tear in his eye. "I am sorry, my lord, but your father is dead. I tried to save him, but it was no good; there were too many of them for me." And then, as if by explanation, "I only escaped by feigning death."

This was followed by a long silence, and then another local spoke. "What now, Daegal? Do we pursue them or let them escape back to the sea like the cowards they are?"

Shaan thought for a while, there was no real answer he could give, as he did not know the attackers or indeed why they attacked. He needed to buy a little time.

"There's nothing we can do now. We must rest and then plan an attack." He replied.

At least this should give him a chance to find out where he was and what course he should take from here in his quest. Cries of "No" and "Attack now!" ran through the crowd, and an argument ensued, but at last the more battle-wise amongst the crowd managed to explain the wisdom of Daegal's words, and the inn was returned to a more peaceful atmosphere.

Shaan persuaded most of the locals to go home and rest while he talked to the few men who remained. These men were more experienced in the ways of war, and Shaan needed to know what was happening and where he was before he could tell if he was in the right place to retrieve one of the artefacts he had been instructed to find to help him defeat Krishia or whether he should move further into this strange land.

After most of the locals had gone on their way, Shaan listened to the men who remained. It appeared that these invaders had come from across the sea in tall ships, and at first Shaan was sure that he knew who the attackers were. It was only after one man had recalled the terror that he had felt at first seeing the attackers that Shaan realised that there was no way that these men were talking about the invaders that once caused so much death and destruction in his land and who had swarmed over his own country for many years before his knights had driven them back into the sea. These creatures, for that was the only way to describe them, were very different in appearance.

Shaan listened as the man told of the strange warriors, called Chrysak, who stood almost eight feet tall, whose bodies were perfectly muscled, and whose faces resembled those of goats, with horns that stood upon their heads and sharp fangs that they used to rip the throats of any that came close enough to evade their swords. Shaan looked in disbelief, for although he had heard many dark tales during his years in Cannchester, he had never heard anything as terrifying. Shaan was beginning to hope that he was in the wrong place and that he would not need to face these barbaric creatures, but fate was to offer a cruel blow to those wishes. Jobe, whom Shaan now knew to be the one who met him at the ruins, was speaking of the attack on Daegal's home. It appeared that the leader of this pack of raiders was carrying something that Shaan needed, a shield, but this was no ordinary shield, for this one had painted on its surface the face of a beautiful woman. It could only be the shield of Lady Bella that Bron had spoken of.

"Where are these Chrysak now?" Shaan asked.

They have made camp in the valley, Prince Daegal." Jobe replied.

"Then we must take a look at them at close range." Shaan needed to see if this shield could be obtained without a full-scale battle. "We'll go tonight."

Shaan was shown to a room where he could rest. Food was brought, and he was left alone while the others prepared for the mission. The room was sparse but probably the best in the inn, as he was considered royalty by those around him, and he needed to find out why.

The room had plain wooden walls, long red drapes that had seen better days at the windows, simple paintings on the walls, and a bed covered in rough blankets that would have scratched his body had he chosen to lie on it naked. It was, however, warm, dry, and quiet.

From the window of his room, Shaan watched the moon rising slowly over a nearby hill and wondered if he had made the right decision in agreeing to help Bron without first consulting Gaius.

The hunter walked away from the tavern; three men lay dead, and another had just escaped with his life. They should have known better than to attempt to rob a man as well armed as this one was, for it should have been obvious that he was no ordinary traveler.

The fight had been over quickly; it was seldom that bandits made good fighters, most of whom were prepared only to strike at the defenseless or the old, and even though there had been four of them, they had stood little chance against a warrior of the hunter's class. The hunter had travelled many miles this day, ever onwards towards his goal. The ultimate goal of proving a legend to be fake and thus replacing Shaan's name in the history books with his own.

In Dresslon, huge clouds of black smoke rose into the air as a city blazed in the distance. Krishia's army was on the move.

The moon was now full, casting an eerie glow over the trees and bushes. Shaan and his two companions climbed down from their horses and stood in a clearing surrounded by trees.

"We had better leave the horses here and continue on foot." Jobe said, looking at Shaan as if for approval.

Shaan nodded, and Jobe took his and Shaan's horse and tied them, out of sight, to a nearby tree. Their companion, Arios, did the same with his horse. From here, they walked for a kilometer until they came to the edge of the valley, and looking down, they saw the Chrysak camp. No movement could be seen, and it was apparent that they did not expect to be attacked in their own camp by these weak country folk. The three crept forward towards the camp and then skirted around the edge. An unexpected surprise: there were no guards.

"Wait here. I want to check something out." Shaan ordered the others.

He had spotted a tent that was much bigger than those surrounding it. It was brightly coloured in reds and yellows, with flags adorning the tent poles. It looked, or at least Shaan hoped, to be the leader's tent, and not wishing to attract attention, he decided it was better to go alone.

"No, it's too dangerous," replied Jobe. "I'll come with you."

"We'll be too easy to spot; I'll go alone." Shaan repeated. "You and Arios wait here."

Shaan moved into the camp being careful not to make any noise that would wake the Chrysak and bring a painful, if swift, death upon himself. Creeping between the rows of canvas walls, listening to murmurs from within, the sounds of food being prepared, and other such nightly happenings, he reached the tent and stood quiet for a moment to hear if any noise came from within. There was none, so crouching down, he peeled back the tent's flap and peered inside. Sure enough, this was the leader's tent, for at the far end of the tent was a shield, and on the front of the shield was etched a picture of a woman's face; this could only be the shield of Lady Bella, leaning against a chair, accompanied by several spear-like weapons and other weapons that Shaan did not recognise but looked just as deadly. Looking around the tent, Shaan saw that its only inhabitant was one Chrysak warrior, who was fast asleep on a rug. The Chrysak warrior snored loudly and rolled over to face the wall of the tent. "This will be easier than I thought," Shaan said to himself.

The floor of the tent was mostly soft sand, and Shaan made no sound as he made his way around the edge to the far side of the tent. It would be so easy to kill the Chrysak leader now, as he slept, but that was not the way of a knight, and Shaan's sense of chivalry would not allow him to do this. Reaching the chair, he quietly picked up the shield, which appeared to let out a moan as if pleased by his touch. Shaan nearly dropped it again; no, it was his imagination; either that or the sound had come from another source, perhaps outside just beyond the tent's thin walls. Yes, that was it. Grasping the shield tighter, he made his way back to the tent's entrance. Again, the shield let out a moan, but this time Shaan was too concerned about getting out of the Chrysak camp to consider the possibility that the shield could make these noises.

Shaan emerged from the tent and slung the shield over his shoulder, then started towards the edge of the camp where his friends waited. "So easy," he grinned, brimming with confidence.

"No, oh no," wailed a woman's voice immediately behind him. Shaan turned around to see where the voice had come from and was met by the full force of a large club. As Shaan sank to the ground, he heard a voice that sounded like a woman crying out forlornly.

Shaan awoke with a strange taste in his mouth and the feeling of dried blood on his cheeks; his arms ached, and his wrists hurt. Blinking his eyes open, he realised that the reason his wrists hurt so much was that he was hanging from them, suspended above a pile of wood and bracken, obviously the making of a large fire. He had been stripped to the waist; a cool breeze sent a shiver down his spine.

He looked around; there were no guards and no sign of movement in the camp. Knowing that this was to be his only chance, he began to struggle against his bonds. It was no good; the more he struggled, the tighter the ropes became, and after a few moments, he stopped for fear of completely severing his wrists. At that moment, a large Chrysak appeared from the tent in front of him. "It's no good; you can't escape." The voice growled, "Now hang still; Nishian wishes to speak to you."

With that, he turned and walked back into the tent. A few minutes later, three more Chrysak appeared, this time from the tent that had housed the shield. These three were by far the biggest that Shaan had seen so far; one was the warrior that Shaan had crept past in the tent earlier.

"Welcome to our humble camp." The leader said, giving a mock bow, and turning to his companion, gave a snigger. "We've never had a male guest before. What a brave man you are for one so small; I like you therefore I will kill you quickly." He turned to the Chrysak on his right and whispered something that made him scurry off, and then turned back to Shaan. "But first, I must ask you some questions."

Shaan studied the Chrysak. He was tall, at least eight feet, as had earlier been described to him. His body was perfectly honed, a true fighting machine. He was dressed in what could best be described as a kilt with a large leather belt tied round his waist, long oddly shaped boots, presumably the feet matched the head, made of some kind of animal skin, and studded bands around his wrists.

Apart from this, he wore nothing. His dark skin glowed as if freshly oiled, and the light from nearby campfires reflected off the curved surface of his bulging muscles.

Using both hands, Nishian thrust down, embedding the shield into the sand so that it faced Shaan; the face seemed to have changed in some way; perhaps it was just the different angle it was now at.

Nishian withdrew a large knife from his belt and turned it this way and that. The blade glistened in the moonlight and Shaan assumed that it was razor sharp. Without saying another word, he drew a line down Shaan's right side, and a trickle of blood followed the blade as it made its way down Shaan's body.

"You bleed like a man; I am pleased." A smile (or what Shaan took to be a smile) crossed Nishi's face. "Some of my warriors were afraid that you might have been a god. Surely only a god would attempt to enter my camp." Now Nishian sneered, and a low growl issued from deep within his throat.

"What do you want with my shield, little mortal?" The Chrysak leader asked.

"So, your men do get scared." Shaan retorted. "And I was told that they were afraid of nothing."

"My warriors are fearless." Nishians first flew in a small ark, catching Shaan high on the side of his head. "Now, answer my question."

Shaan stared back at Nishian, his eyes glowing in defiance, not uttering a word. Again, the Chrysak struck Shaan, but this time Shaan simply smiled in return.

"Who says I am a mortal?" Shaan snarled and fixed a glazed stare on Nishian, who seemed to visibly shrink back.

"Then, shall we find out?"

Nishian turned to his left, picked up a brand from a nearby fire, and poked it into the wood below Shaan's feet. The flames rose rapidly into the air as the bracken caught first, followed by a few pieces of smaller timber.

"It was worth a try." Shaan thought to himself; He had hoped to somehow take control of the situation. Smoke rose around him, and soon he began to choke, and it seemed he would suffocate before the flames got to him.

It was at that moment that the Chrysak camp became filled with flashes of light and the sound of large explosions. The Chrysak warriors dived this way and that looking for cover, but there seemed to be none. The explosions were all around, and the bright flashes of light filled the air, blinding anyone who had not covered their eyes. The camp was in chaos, with Chrysak running in all directions, some stopping to pick up weapons, others just scattering throughout the camp. All were too busy to see what happened next.

Shaan strained to see, not only because of the flashes of light but also because of the smoke rising from the flames below him. Two blades whistled through the air, one slicing the rope binding his right hand, the other his left. Shaan leapt from the flames, and as soon as his feet touched the ground, he began sprinting from the camp, his hand reaching down to grab the shield of Lady Bella in mid-stride.

The Chrysak had never been openly attacked before and were unable to deal with the situation; this made Shaan's escape much easier. In fact, if the Chrysak had not been in such a panic, they would have realised that this was not the mass attack that they thought it was, but only a handful of locals using simple tricks of the trade.

Shaan made it to the border of the camp just in time to see Jobe and Arios galloping towards him. Jobe rode up to Shaan,

"Quick, my lord, jump up." Shaan did not hesitate but leapt in a single bound up behind Jobe, who turned his horse and galloped away from the ensuing chaos, laughing and whooping like a madman.

"I thought it may be getting a bit warm for you, sire." Jobe joked, and Shaan laughed and said back "Now I know what a roast hog feels like."

Nishian cursed. One moment the prisoner was burning, the next he had gone. What kind of sorcery was this?

"Where's my shield!" He raged as he strode through the camp back to his tent, knocking a guard off his feet in his hurry to make plans for the final destruction of these pitiful humans.

"I want this camp torn apart until that shield is returned to me. Send trackers out; I want that prisoner back." Nishian stopped and bellowed after the retreating guard, "Alive!"

The guard ran to obey. When Nishian was in this kind of rage, he was likely to execute anyone that moved, let alone those that failed him.

Shaan, Jobe, and Arios arrived back at the inn, jumped down

from their horses, and raced inside.

"Did ya see the look on their faces?" Jobe said triumphantly, "They were scared to death."

"Aye," replied Arios, "and there were only the three of us; think what a whole army can do."

"You caught them by surprise," Shaan scorned, "but next time they will be ready." He walked towards the counter. The bar was closed, but Arios leapt behind the counter and poured them all a mug of ale, which they gulped down without another word.

"We should rest now; when morning comes, so will the Chrysak." Shaan headed for the stairs. "Thank you both; you are indeed great and cunning warriors." Shaan said to the pair, who had begun to drink another mug. He climbed the stairs and entered his room.

Shaan lay the shield of Lady Bella on the bed and looked at it. It was just as he had imagined it would be. It was the size of a huge battle shield, yet it was surprisingly light, almost the weight of a small practice shield that he had trained with as a boy.

The border of the shield was edged in gold and silver, but it was not this that Shaan now stared at. It was the image on the shield itself. Staring back at Shaan was the face of a beautiful woman, far more beautiful than Shaan had ever seen (even more than his own Giselle). Golden locks fell gently around a small, slim face. Deep brown eyes looked up into his. Her small, ruby lips seemed to smile as he gazed at the vision before him. This was surprising; the face had been merely an etching before, but now it looked like a painting with perfect detailing as fine as any he had seen.

"You are hurt."

Shaan stumbled backwards; caught completely by surprise, he tripped and fell in a heap on the floor. Raising himself off the floor, he stared at the shield. Had it spoken to him, or had he imagined it, as he surely had done in the Chrysak camp?

"You must stop the bleeding." The small ruby lips moved, and the brown eyes shimmered.

The shield was indeed talking to him. How was this possible? Had he gone mad? More questions filled his mind faster than he could begin to answer them. Then he felt the wetness on his chest and remembered the wound that Nishian had caused him. Turning to a small bowl of water on the table, he took a towel and cleansed the wound before pressing the towel against it. The wound was not as bad as it had appeared now that the blood had been cleaned off, and Shaan took a piece of linen, tore it into a bandage, and tied it around his chest.

Shaan returned to the bed and looked again at the shield. This time, the face smiled at him. It seemed strange, not quite a painting but also not quite real. How could this...Shaan had seen magical things before while in the company of Gaius, but nothing quite like this. For now, he would ask no questions.

"You must rest now." The shield smiled up at him, "for there is much to be done."

"No, I must get you back to safety and continue on the other quests before it is too late." Shaan replied.

He did not consider that the shield would have no idea that he was on a quest and that she was part of it.

"Krishia will be advancing on Taal soon, and there is no time to spare." Shaan pulled on a shirt that had been left for him earlier, gathered up the shield, and opened the door.

"Stop." The shield spoke again. "You have not finished in this realm." She chastised, "Krishia can wait; you must help these people first."

"What do you know of my quest?" Shaan asked.

"Trust me," was the reply.

"If I wait any longer, then it will not just be these people who suffer, but all the people of all the realms."

He strode out of the room and down the stairs, past the entrance to the bar, and out of the door, being careful not to alert the men within. He took a horse, led it on foot a little way before mounting it, then headed off back towards the building where he had first emerged into this world.

It was only a short journey before the smoking frame of the building could be seen, and as Shaan rode on, he could see that the building had not been completely gutted by the fire and that much of it remained standing. Shaan dismounted a small distance before the door, patted his horse, allowing the reigns to drop down, and walked to where the entrance to the hall had been. He knew that just a few feet inside was the way back to the cave and then on to his next quest.

The shield, which had remained silent for the journey here, spoke in a soft, almost dreamlike voice. "If you lose this battle, it could spell a bad omen for all the battles to come."

"What do you mean?" asked Shaan.

"It is like fighting a fire; if you concentrate all your efforts on putting out the main blaze but forget the little flames going on around you, then before you know it you have many fires all blazing at the same time." The shield's voice changed and sounded sterner. "It is your choice, Shaan".

Shaan did not enter the door but decided he would look around the remains of the building before carrying on; he did not know why, but it felt like something he had to do. He climbed in through a window to avoid accidentally entering the cave. The room he found himself in seemed to have largely escaped the effects of the fire. Looking around, he could see that the inhabitants of this place had lived well, for there were many beautiful and exquisite artifacts. Shaan looked at the walls, which were hung with pictures, one of which caught his eye. This picture he had seen before, but where? Shaan looked at the picture more closely; it was of a large blue lake with the sun shining brightly overhead. Then it came to him: It was the same picture as in the stained-glass window in the room where Gaius had taken him. This was too strange to be a coincidence. Had Gaius been here? Or had this Daegal been to Aidenvalle? Shaan stared thoughtfully. His surprise was even greater when he saw the picture next to this one.

CHAPTER FOUR

Shaan rubbed his eyes and looked at the picture again. He had not been mistaken. Before him was a portrait of a family, composed of a man of about sixty years of age, a woman (perhaps a year or two younger), and a young man in his mid-thirties. There was nothing unusual about the older couple, but it was the young man that Shaan now studied. The picture was clearly a portrait of Shaan himself, either that or his exact double, but Shaan did not know the older couple. Where had they acquired a picture of him, and why was he in a family portrait with them? After all, Shaan had never been to this realm, let alone met these people.

"What do you see?" A voice behind Shaan questioned.

Shaan had all but forgotten the shield strapped to his back. "There is something very strange that I do not understand." Shaan answered, as he swung the shield from his back.

"What do you make of this?" Shaan pointed the shield in the direction of the painting.

"It is a very good likeness." The shield replied after a few seconds. "The artist caught you on a good day," she added, with humor in her voice.

"I agree." Shaan said, "The only problem is, I never posed for this picture, and I don't know these people." He jabbed a finger at the older couple.

"They obviously know you." The shield said, then added thoughtfully. "I think we should explore the rest of the building, don't you?"

Shaan took the shield and held it across his body so that she too could see where they were going. For some reason, he had settled his mind on a talking shield very quickly, and it just seemed natural. Then again, he had seen a lot of weird things in his short life already.

They proceeded down the corridor to the next room, swinging open the door. This room was much the same as the other, much as you would have expected to find it: same style of furniture, same style of decor. On these walls were full-scale portraits of all three people that Shaan had seen in the other room; only these pictures had plaques underneath.

Shaan headed straight for the portrait of himself, took a deep breath, and read the name aloud. PRINCE DAEGAL. SON OF ULRIC

"Well, what do you think now?"

"I think that it is no wonder that the villagers think you are Daegal." Replied the shield honestly, "Although I think there is more to this than just coincidence."

An hour later, Shaan had explored the whole building, or what remained of it after the fire. He had discovered nothing else to his advantage. The rooms were similarly decorated; a few more pictures were here and there, but none to point to the origins of the owners, and there were no clues as to who this Daegal was or why he resembled Shaan so much.

"Well, what now?" Shaan's question was directed at the shield.

"As I said, it is your choice." The shield spoke softly now: "You must either put out the small fire now or deal with a much larger one later."

"How come you know so much about warfare, my lady?"

"I have had, as my master, many great leaders in many realms," the shield stated proudly. "Being a part of war seems to have been my purpose in life; I wish it had been different." She let out a sigh.

The hunter had travelled for two days now and had come to the town of Marlborough. Strolling down the main street, he had a feeling that something was wrong. The people looked sad, almost in a state of depression; they walked limply, heads bowed to the floor. Nobody spoke; they just went about their business or sat on the side of the road, staring blankly into the distance. Some had tears in their eyes, including some of the men. The hunter was puzzled, wondering what could possibly have caused them such distress.

The hunter lay his bags on the floor of the tavern and ordered a glass of ale. The ale was served without a word, and so the hunter threw some coins onto the counter, which the barman collected up and placed in his purse.

"What has happened to bring such sadness to a whole town?" The hunter asked.

The barman looked at him as if he were insane. Surly he must have heard.

"The king." The barman said, "You must have heard."

"Heard what? I have been on the road for many days and have not had time for idle chatter."

"Then I must be the bearer of grave news." The barman looked up into the hunter's face, who was at least a foot taller than he was.

"The King is dead. He died defending the country against the evil Theodore and his witch mother. But not before destroying the whole of Theodore's army and killing Theodore himself."

This was indeed bad news; not only did all these people believe this rubbish about Shaan, but by getting himself killed, he had denied the hunter the chance to show them the truth. There was only one thing to do. He must travel to Cadbury and check out this story for himself.

Moroc was tall and handsome. He was dressed in a sand-coloured shirt and tan-coloured breeches tucked into brown leather boots. He took out a small dirk, sliced off the man's left ear, and tossed it to the waiting hounds, one of which caught it in mid-air and swallowed it whole. The man winced but did not scream out, as the dirk was razor sharp and did not immediately cause pain, at least not for a few seconds anyway. Then the man screamed but was quickly silenced by the dirk passing through his thin shirt and into his heart. Moroc let the prisoner fall to the floor, turned away from the prone body, and left the room.

"Well, did you find out where he is?" Krishia asked, her long black hair cascading over her shoulders.

"Not yet" was all Moroc could reply. He had been disappointed with the way the interrogation had gone.

"What about the last prisoner, did he know nothing?" Krishia quizzed. "Maybe I should talk to him." She looked across at Moroc. Moroc did not return her gaze but remained in deep thought.

"Not another one? That's the third one you have killed today." Krishia snapped.

"They are weak, these people of Dresslon," Moroc replied, sarcasm in his voice.

"Most people are weak when stabbed with a blade." Krishia shot back. "Maybe they just do not know." She added quietly, almost to herself.

"I'll kill them all if necessary." Morocs anger was rising. An expert at torture and Krishia's number one, he should have found the answer by now.

"I have a better idea." Krishia was already moving towards the door. "Sophia."

"Not that witch; she will be the downfall of us all."

Moroc already knew that he had made a mistake with that comment. Krishia raised her hand, and in a moment, Moroc was on the floor in agony.

"Your insolence will be the death of you." Krishia said as she hurried from the room.

It took a few minutes for Moroc to be able to get to his feet and a few more before the pain subsided. He knew he had been lucky that time and vowed to keep his thoughts to himself in the future.

Shaan spun around, his sword flying from its scabbard. It was not something that he had heard, but rather a feeling that he was being watched. The shield had also sensed something and had become instantly as light as a feather, turning itself on Shaan's arm so that it was ready to protect from any attack. There was no one in the room, but someone was definitely close by, maybe just outside in the hallway.

Shaan adjusted his stance, ready to attack or defend, as necessary.

He crept forward, opened the door, and moved silently into the hallway. He stopped and listened. A sound? No, just his imagination. No, there it was again. The sound came from the next room, the sound of movement, very quiet, but Shaan had heard it.

Shaan pushed open the door and ran into the room, sword held high and ready to strike quickly, but was stopped immediately in his tracks by the man sitting in the chair. The occupant of this room was dressed all in black; a band of solid silver framed his jet-black hair, and jewel-like eyes stared at Shaan. It was a man Shaan knew well.

"Gaius!" Shaan exclaimed.

"Shaan!" Gaius replied, mimicking Shaan's surprise and raising his eyebrows mockingly.

"Where have you been?" Shaan asked.

"I have been nowhere; it seems it is you who have wandered," Gaius replied. "I thought you were resting, and when I returned, you had gone."

"It is just as well that I did. There is little time to spare." Shaan said, "Krishia's army has moved against Dresslon already."

"I know," Gaius retorted, "but I have not had time to tell you what must be done."

"I have met Bron, and he told me everything. "I must act quickly to retrieve that which will aid in the fight against Krishia."

"You acted too quickly; I fear." Gaius's face turned to look out of the window. "There was a set route to take, an order in which to visit each realm if the outcome was to be assured. Now I feel the wheel of chance turning; random events have been set in motion, and now the destiny of all the realms is left to fate."

"How could I have known?" Was all Shaan could say.

"All is not lost; it will be just like the old days when you conquered a kingdom and drove evil from the land, only this time it will be a little harder." Gaius turned back to Shaan. "I understand you are having a little local trouble."

"That's an understatement. Just when I thought how easy things were, that's when the Chrysak were introduced to me. These creatures are..."

Shaan was cut short.

"Chrysak, did you say Chrysak?" Gaius asked with urgency in his voice.

"I did. "You know of them?"

"Indeed, I do, Shaan; there is no time to lose. You must act now before they gain a foothold, or you'll never stop them. They are worse than a plague; once they have a settlement established, they will rape the land and kill all but a few, whom they will keep as slaves or for sport." Gaius rose to his feet. "I'll keep you no longer, my friend, for to delay would mean disaster."

"You must help." Shaan followed Gaius towards the door.

"What help would I be? I am no warrior." Gaius had passed through the doorway; his voice seemed to echo as if he were walking down an empty hallway.

"The locals, Shaan, they are your army. They know the ways of war. Use their skills well." And the voice had gone.

Moving through the door, Shaan called, "Gaius, Gaius." But it was no good; he had vanished.

"I guess it's just you and me." A voice drifted up from Shaan's side.

"What?" Shaan said it as if in a daze.

"Let's go, Shaan. Listen to Gaius's words: "Time is short." The shield's voice entered Shaan's head like a war cry.

"You are right, let us go and talk to Arios and make plans for war."

Sophia sat with her legs crossed and her back straight. She was proud of her position as mystic and soothsayer to the greatest sorceress the land of Bastion had ever known. Her long red hair flowed over her lithe body and lay cascading about her on the floor. Hair that, when she stood, still reached the floor. Sophia waited for her daily visit from the Queen. She knew what the Queen would want, not because of her powers but because for the last two weeks she had asked the same question over and over. "Where is Bron?" Sophia would cast the runes but always get the same answer. "I cannot tell yet." It was not that Sophia's powers were weak; they were not, but the runes were, at best, a guide and not an exact science, and, at best, they could give only pointers to specific objects. No, the runes could not tell. They served a very different purpose. The runes could, if you knew how to read them, tell you the order in which events would happen, what action to take to ensure that result, and what to do to change the outcome. Up until now, the queen had taken the advice well, and city after city and land after land had fallen to her. Now it seemed that she had become obsessed with this Bron and expected specific answers that the runes could not or would not give her.

Two guards entered the room, one on either side of the door, and a few seconds later the Queen strode in.

Krishia stood before Sophia. Sophia had not risen; she was the only person in the whole of Bastion who could have done this without being immediately killed. She was too precious to Krishia, for now anyway.

"Your majesty." Sophia spoke quietly, almost in a whisper, but loud enough for even the guards to hear. "What is your question?"

"Where is Bron?" was the expected reply.

"You know the runes cannot name places, your majesty." Sophia tried not to sound stern, but it was really becoming very tiresome, and she wished that Krishia would ask something new.

"Let's try it another way." Krishia's eyes lit up; an idea had just come to her, and she now knew how to ask the question and get a clue as to the whereabouts of the allusive Bron.

"What route must I take to find Bron?" She asked almost triumphantly.

Sophia dipped her hand into the large velvet bag and pulled out three small flat stones, onto each of which was carved a symbol. She laid the rune stones on the woven cloth in front of her.

"There is a journey indicated here, a journey over mountains to a place of nature. Here is what you seek, but beware, a warning of overcaution is shown. You must act quickly and directly; delay could cost you everything."

"Which mountains? And what do you mean by a place of nature?" Krishia asked calmly.

"As I have explained," Sophia replied, "I cannot be specific, but I believe that the place of nature will be a forest or lake of some kind. Your cartographers should be able to locate the possible alternatives for you."

"Of course. Thank you once again, Sophia; you have once again proven your worth to me." Krishia nodded at Sophia and turned to leave.

"One more thing, your highness." Sophia called before Krishia had fully turned away. "The last stone I chose, it's a warning." Sophia stopped, as if she had thought better of revealing this information.

"Well, continue, Sophia. A warning that..." Krishia prompted.

"That even in victory, you will face defeat." Sophia said, looking down.

"Ha! We will see about that." Krishia glided from the room, laughing aloud. "We will see."

The sun was high by the time Shaan returned to the inn. People were going about their business, buying, selling, swapping stories, and the like. As Shaan passed, they stopped, bowed, then continued with their activity. Shaan pushed open the door to the inn and walked inside. He was tired now and needed to rest. He wished he had brought some of the brew that Bron had given him a lifetime (or so it seemed) ago. The inn was empty except for the barman, who was preparing for the upcoming trade. Shaan nodded a greeting and headed for the stairs.

From inside his room, Shaan could hear people talking. The voices were those of Arios and Jobe. He stood for a while and listened, but the talk was nothing unusual, just that of two friends catching up, so Shaan swung open the door and walked in.

"Sire." Both Arios and Jobe rose from their seats, heads bowed. "Good morning, gentlemen. How are you?" Shaan asked politely.

"We are well, sir." Arios answered for both of them. "I hope you don't mind us intruding, we were waiting for you to return. We believe it is time for action."

"Indeed, it is." Shaan replied. "Go and fetch your best warriors and tacticians, and meet me here in two hours." A huge smile crossed Jobe's face, and he slapped Arios on the back.

"Let's go, my friend. Today will be marked forever in the history of our people. Today we will win a great victory."

Shaan lay on the bed, the shield next to him, and fell immediately into a deep sleep. It was something he had taught himself to do before a battle, for he knew that, come the battle, he would need all his strength and alertness to stay alive, let alone to have victory.

The hunter looked up towards the nearby hills. Sitting on one, shrouded in a thin veil of mist, was a castle. The castle had several high towers of ornate design from which huge flags flew. A golden glow shone out through the mist, and the hunter knew that this was the castle of gold, Cannchester. As he approached the castle, he could see the sun shining off the many windows, whose construction had been designed specifically to give off a golden glow. It must have been an impressive sight for an attacking army. A castle of pure gold, it was no wonder that very few had challenged her occupier, for the owner of this castle must be enormously powerful, with large armies to defend it.

"Yes, an imaginative design." The hunter said to himself.

As the hunter came closer to the castle, he could see that the drawbridge was lowered and that there were no guards at the entrance. Very unusual; surely a castle of this magnitude would have guards on duty.

The hunter passed under the portcullis and towards the main building.

The door was open, and he walked inside uncontested; there were no signs of anyone. The entrance halls were grand, the walls were adorned with paintings, the floor was covered in blue carpet, exquisitely crafted furniture lay here and there, and indoor trees and plants added to the beauty.

Walking down a corridor, he could see the entrance to the great hall, and his pace quickened as if he were worried that whatever was in there would be gone before he arrived.

As he moved into the inner chamber, for the first time he saw the ring of armored men. In his surprise, he stumbled, almost falling, his sword clattering against the stone archway that served as the entrance. Before he had had time to right himself, eight swords had been drawn and eight knights advanced on him.

Marcus was not a handsome man; in fact, he would be considered less than pleasing in the eyes of many women, but he had power, and that of course made him attractive to some.

He was also quite short, and like a small dog, this made him vicious and aggressive when confronted. On this day he was dressed plainly, not wishing to be recognised as a warrior of Bastion just yet. This was to be a secret mission, one that did not cause another war front to develop, just yet.

Marcus, followed by a dozen of his best men, headed towards Kwell, where he had been assured Bron was to be found. Why his sister was so desperate to have this man under her control, only the gods knew. Anyway, he was pleased for the opportunity to take an expedition away from the main battle zone for a while. Even Marcus sometimes grew weary of the killing, and this was going to be easy. Just him and his twelve men against the army of Kwell seemed like a poor choice, but, after all, Sophia had warned them against being overly cautious, so Marcus had decided to take only a few men, ride quickly to Kwell, capture Bron, and ride quickly out again. No prolonged battle and no chance of injury to himself. That was the way he liked it, causing pain to others at no risk to himself.

Shaan was alone, kneeling before the alter in the towns small church, he prayed as he always had before a battle. He prayed for victory in battle, protection for his men, and most of all, forgiveness for the killing he must do today. The meeting had gone well; plans had been made for where to attack, where to defend, what surprises lay in store for the Chrysak, and what to do if all was lost. The warriors had left to prepare their traps, sharpen their weapons, and kiss their loved ones good-bye, some for the last time. Shaan's thoughts turned to his loved one, Giselle. Where was she? Was she alive? Had she returned to the nunnery? And what of his knights, had they returned to Cannchester to restart the dream that was lost?

The door to the church swung open, and Shaan emerged looking sullen. He took his scabbard from the hands of the page and buckled it around his waist. Then he took up the shield of Lady Bella and held it before him.

"We will fight well today," he exclaimed.

"I know." She replied, a gentle smile coming to her face. "Do not fear, Shaan; I will not let any harm come to you."

A horse awaited Shaan, and he climbed into the saddle, drew his sword high into the air, and proclaimed.

"Warriors, today you take back what is yours. Together, we will drive the invaders back to the sea with such fear cast into their hearts that they will never again attack this fair land. Today and forever, victory is yours."

With this, a great cheer rang around the town, and Shaan, with his new army, set forth to the battlefields once again.

Khamel was distressed; she was looking to do damage control. What had happened, and how could it have happened? It must have been something in the wine.

The morning after her walk with Krishia, she had awoken in her bed; her head was fuzzy, and when she tried to turn to her side, she felt something stopping her. She was shocked, who was this man? How did he get in her bed, and where was her nightwear? The man grunted, opened his eyes, and smiled. With that, Khamel sprang from the bed, grabbed her gown for a nearby chair, and covering her naked body, she backed further away from the bed. Reaching out, she grabbed a brass candlestick from the side table.

"Get out!" she screamed.

Unfortunately, that brought a servant rushing to the room in time to see the naked man climbing from Khamel's bed.

"Sorry, my lady, I didn't mean to..." The maid uttered it sheepishly.

The man pulled on his pants, brushed past the maid while pulling his shirt over his head, and left.

"Are you alright, my lady?" The maid asked.

"Out, get out," was the reply.

And now, now, there were whispers and rumors that could only have come from the maid unless this man had chosen to spread the gossip himself. What was she to do? Why? Why did this happen to her? If and when Tulak finds out... she refused to think of the consequences. She would confront Krishia herself for the answers.

Krishia, dressed in white and adorned with golden bracelets and necklaces, stared out of the window, watching the groundmen work. She had been waiting for news from the front lines, especially from Varsile, where the city walls had still not been breached.

There was a commotion outside her door, a woman was raging, demanding access, and a guard was remonstrating with her. The door burst open, the woman managing to get halfway inside before being pulled back, the guard throwing her to the floor just outside of the doorway. Raising his hand to strike the intruder, the guard looked over at Krishia, who moved her hand to signal him to stop.

"Let her up."

Khamel struggled to her feet; her face was red as much with embarrassment as it was with rage.

"Ah, the Lady Khamel, how lovely to see you again. Do come in". Krishia smiled, but the sarcasm in her voice could not be mistaken. "To what do I owe the pleasure?" Waving her hand, the door slammed shut.

"You, you drugged me, and..." Khamel could hardly get the word out.

"Oh, that's what you are upset about?" Krishia smiled, "Yes, of course I did, my dear girl; you are much more useful to me now."

"You admit it? How dare you, I..." She was cut off mid-sentence.

"You, will do as I say." Krishia said sternly: "Once you have learned to,"

"Guard!"

The guard rushed in, ready to defend his queen with his life.

"Take her below, throw her in with the thugs that were brought in last week; they should be happy to get some female company."

"You can't do this to..." Khamel was hauled away by the guards and taken to the dungeons.

The hunter spread his arms wide, keeping them well away from his weapons; even he would have had trouble drawing his sword against the advancing foe.

"I come in peace." He spoke quickly, fearing that talking any slower would have disastrous results. "I did not mean to startle you, gentlemen."

"Who are you that would disturb our mourning?" One of the knights asked.

"Just a pilgrim, looking for some answers." The hunter replied.

"You are well armed for a pilgrim." Another knight proffered.

"These are dangerous times, even for a pilgrim."

The hunter moved his left hand very slowly to the buckle of his belt, releasing the catch and allowing the scabbard to fall to the floor. Next, he let the bow slide from his shoulder.

"I mean you no harm, friends."

He hoped they had not seen the dagger tucked into the top of his boots; not that it would be much use against eight fully armed men, but it was the best he could do in the present circumstances.

"We are sorry, pilgrim; it seems that we have lost our sense of trust. Forgive us. Come, you must be hungry."

The knight, who now spoke, sheathed his sword, followed by his companions. "Would you break bread with us, friend?" he continued.

"Thank you, yes." Replied the hunter.

He was indeed hungry, and this was an ideal chance to find

out what had happened here, for these knights must surely be the remains of Shaan's army. A meal was already on the table; it seemed that the knights had been close to eating before the hunter burst in on them. He was shown to a chair in a room adjoining the great hall.

"I apologise for disturbing your gathering." The hunter said honestly, for he had genuinely not known that the knights were in the hall when he had rushed in.

"And we apologise for our treatment of you, sir." A knight rose to his feet. "But since the great battle, we are all weary and have not yet regained our trust in our fellow man." And after a short pause, "I am Bedilore; this is Berel, Lyonell, Meneduke, Marrake, Philippe, Galwraith, and.."

"And I am Thomas." Said the youngest of the knights, rising from his chair, "At your service, sir."

"I am pleased to make your acquaintance, gentlemen. I have heard so much about all of you, particularly you Galwraith." The hunter nodded in Galwraiths' direction, "Although much must be the stuff of old barman's tales, eh."

"I am not sure to which tales you refer, sir, but I also believe a few of our adventures may have flowered a little." Galwraith said, winking at the knight next to him.

"Tell me, sirs, why do you gather here?" The hunter inquired.

A sad look crossed the faces of the knights, and there was a moment's silence before Philippe spoke.

"We gather daily and wait for a message."

"A message from whom?"

"From the king, of course." Philippe spoke sternly. "You have chosen a new king?" The hunter was surprised. "So quickly."

"No, it is a message from King Shaan that we await." Lyonell spoke for the first time.

"But is Shaan not dead? Slain by Theodore?"

"We have seen no body, and until we have proof, we will hold our faith that Shaan will return to us." Lyonell continued. "If Shaan were dead, we would know. Gaius would come to proclaim the new king, as he always has. Until then, we will wait."

The hunter had never known such devotion, from the lowest people to the greatest knight. Maybe there was more to this Shaan than the hunter had first thought.

The meal continued in silence for a while until the hunter spoke again.

"Please tell me about King Shaan; I am intrigued to know more, more than just the tales and legends, but to know the truth behind the man and why everyone who knew him or knew of him was so utterly devoted to a humble man of low birth."

"I hope you are in no hurry, sir, for this is a long story, one which, if you do not already believe, will make you believe in magic, demons, destiny, and, above all, love." Sir Galwraith rose to his feet. Slamming his goblet down onto the table, he began to tell the fantastic story from beginning to end. From Prethus and Igraine to Shaan and Giselle.

CHAPTER FIVE

The view ahead was breathtaking. From these high hills, the forest of Kwell looked as beautiful as anything Marcus had seen; even he could appreciate its tranquility. He breathed in, the pure air filling his lungs and energizing is soul. He held it there for a few seconds, then slowly released it. Motioning to the flag bearer next to him, he reached across and took the standard. Driving the shaft into the soft earth, he proclaimed,

"I take this land in the name of Krishia, Queen of Bastion, and Conqueror of all." He looked over to the flag bearer again and said, "I think I will retire here, Lars. What do you think?"

He did not wait for Lars to answer, but instead, kicked his horse on, and headed into the thick green mass that was the forest of Kwell.

Shaan sat upright and proud on his steed. From here, he could survey the advancing Chrysak army. The Chrysak had no need for subtle battle plans; after all, they were, they believed, the greatest warriors in the world, so onward they marched, never fearing that these mere humans could possibly harm them.

As the Chrysak army reached a piece of the valley that had trees lining each side, Arios looked over at Shaan, who, without expression, gave a small nod. Arios lowered the flag that he had been holding aloft, and instantly, a mass of white-tipped arrows flew from beyond the trees, cutting down a dozen of the goat-headed warriors. The rest broke into a run, not ordered or controlled, but a stampede for cover and the safety offered by the surrounding trees. The few horse riders kicked their horses into a gallop and rode quickly on without looking back. In front of them, they could see some of their attackers, and it was on these that their attention was focused, so much so that they rode headfirst into the next trap.

It had only been a few hours since Jobe and his men had finished their work here. First, they dug a huge pit about two meters deep that spanned the width of the track. Then they filled it with water diverted from a nearby stream. Next, they covered the surface with a thick layer of oil, which was then covered with a thin layer of dust and leaves so that to any unsuspecting rider, it would have looked like solid ground.

All but a few of the Chrysak riders were now scrambling for the edge of the pit, having been thrown from their mounts either when the horses had fallen into the pit or when the more aware had stopped dead; their riders, unable to cope with the sudden change of direction, had been thrown helplessly into the strange mixture. None of these bemused Chrysak would make it out of the pit, for the brand that Jobe held in his hand was tossed into the pit, a blue flame spreading across its entire length in the blink of an eye and engulfing all before it. The Chrysak in the pit died a horrible death at the hands of this beautiful but deadly sight. The remaining riders turned their horses into the forest and made their way around the flaming pit, but when they reached the other side, there was no sign of their tormentors.

Nishian reined in his horse, pointed his head skywards, and let out a deafening roar.

"Kill them, kill them all. Women, children, all of them." He raged. "Burn their homes and kill their cattle. Do not leave a trace of their miserable existence."

The battle was looking more even now, and Shaan turned his horse and headed to where the next confrontation would take place.

Marcus spun round, his hand flying to the hilt of his sword just in time to see a pheasant break cover and fly a little way into the distance. That was as far as it got before an arrow sent it crashing to the ground. At least one of his men would be eating well tonight. Marcus visibly relaxed, returning to his correct position in the saddle. He was getting more than a little edgy; they had seen no one since they had entered the forest an hour ago, and although this was exactly what Marcus had wanted, it was a bit too quiet for his liking. He now felt that they were being watched, as if a thousand eyes peered out from behind every tree, and from every bush, the sound of scurrying came rushing to his ears. His men seemed not to notice as they continued to chatter aimlessly amongst themselves. Maybe it was just his imagination after all, but was he willing to take that chance?

Stopping his horse, he waited for his band of men to pass. He ordered the trailing two men to take up position here and wait to see if they were being followed. Four more men were sent to scout the surrounding land to see what dangers lurked in this ever-darkening forest. Marcus and the remaining six would continue, knowing that at least they would get some warning before an attack came. Marcus cursed the soothsayer, Sophia; it was her warning against being overly cautious that had put them in this position. If Krishia had listened to him, he would be here with a whole battalion and not just a few men. Marcus swore that when this war was over and Sophia was no longer needed, then it would be him that took her head.

The Chrysak warriors were now not more than two kilometers from the town, and Shaan knew that if they were to stop them, it would have to be here. The battle was about to start for real. There was to be only one more trick, and then it was back to the old ways. Sword against sword, spear against spear The Chrysak still outnumbered Shaan's army, but nothing could be done about that now. This last plan must work and work well, or all would be lost. Jobe and his men had lined up on foot in front of the advancing Chrysak, while Arios had taken a dozen men on horseback to one side of the clearing and Shaan had taken a dozen more to the far side, where, hidden by trees, they awaited their chance to change the course of this battle in their favor. They did not have to wait long. Twenty arrows with small explosives strapped to their shafts were fired into the advancing Chrysak pack, and just as in the rescue of Shaan in the Chrysak camp, the goat-heads dove for cover. Some panicking, others confused. Meanwhile, Shaan's men had spurred their horses into action and bore down on the disarrayed invaders; swords drawn, they cut through the Chrysak army, killing warrior after warrior as they charged. By the time they had passed through the attacking ranks and emerged from the other side, many of the Chrysak lay dead or dying. Shaan and his men turned their horses and headed back into the fray, now supported by Arios, Jobe, and their men. The battle proper had begun.

Marcus trotted his horse along the stream, allowing the cold water to refresh his steed's tired feet. To the right rose a grassy slope leading up to a hill with rocky outcrops. To the left, the forest had receded a little, making Marcus feel a little more comfortable. Ahead, the stream turned a corner, disappearing around the hill, and it was from here that the sound of splashing could be heard. As Marcus rounded the corner, he could see the man bathing in the cool water. The man was small and thin, with a white beard capping his tapered chin. This had to be his prey, and so Marcus kicked his horse on. At the sound of the approaching horse, the bearded man looked up and hastened to the edge of the stream, having only time to pull his brown robes over his head before Marcus was upon him. He swept by, knocking Bron to the floor, brought his horse in a tight circle, jumped to the ground, and pulled Bron to his feet roughly by his robes.

"We meet at last, little man." Marcus grinned; this had indeed been as easy as Sophia had predicted, and maybe he would not kill her after all.

"Sire, sire. We have discovered a cabin in the forest." One of the men that Marcus had detailed to search the area rode towards him from out of the cover of nearby trees.

"Good. Let's go, old man." Marcus pushed Bron up the muddy slope towards the log cabin. "Let's see what secrets you have to hide, my little friend."

Inside the cabin, Marcus and his men began to tear the place apart. They were not sure what they were looking for, but if Krishia wanted Bron that badly, then he must have something particularly important. Bron looked on helplessly, unable to stop the pillaging of his home.

Shaan's blade swung this way and that, taking one Chrysak through the throat and another in the chest, acting like a huge scythe, cutting down the invading weeds. Only a few Chrysak now remained. They had been caught out completely by the battle plans of Shaan's army. Totally demoralized by the wholesale slaughter of their comrades, they had been unable to regroup and now fought with the will of warriors who knew that they were doomed. The only real resistance came from Nishian himself, who, when last Shaan saw him, was being attacked by three of Shaan's men, all of whom now lay slain. A sword came swinging at Shaan's head, which he easily parried and then thrust out with his own sword, instantly killing the opposing warrior. Only five Chrysak remained standing now, and Shaan signaled to Jobe. Jobe raised his battle horn to his mouth and blew. At that, Shaan's army fell back, breaking off their attack, and moving a short distance from their foe. The Chrysak did not follow but remained where they were, swords held in defensive positions, waiting for the new trick that was to come. What death had these barbarians in store for them?

"Well, finish it then." One of the Chrysak called out.

"Why do you play with us?" Another is called fearfully.

At least if they were to die, let it be quick.

Shaan looked over at Nishian. Both warriors were covered from head to toe in the blood of their enemy. Nishian became aware of what Shaan had in mind. This whole battle had taught Nishian a great many lessons, and he bowed his head to Shaan, sheathed his sword, and turned and left the battlefield. The few remaining Chrysak warriors did the same, each in turn bowing and leaving. The battle was over. There was no point in mindless slaughter, and besides, Shaan needed some survivors to return to the Chrysak's home land to tell of what had happened here so that the Chrysak would be more fearful of invading other lands in the future and may themselves be fearful that these barbarians would want to take revenge by invading their homeland and taking them as slaves. It had not occurred to the Chrysak that another race could be this powerful before, and now they had to change their way of thinking and prepare for any possible invasion of their land.

When the Chrysak had gone (followed by a few men to make sure that they set sail), Shaan looked at Arios from some distance away, and Arios looked back, a small smile crossing their faces. Arios gave Shaan a halfhearted salute, which was all he could manage to get from his aching limbs; Shaan did likewise, and though they were separated by the expanse of the battlefield, each knew what the other was feeling and what he was thinking.

Shaan looked down, remembering the shield of Lady Bella. She had taken many blows and had saved Shaan's life on more than one occasion during the battle. He expected to see her battered and buckled, but there was not a mark. There was no indication that they had ever been in a fight, let alone a full-scale battle. The lady of the shield looked up at Shaan and winked but said nothing.

"Thank you." Shaan whispered.

Back at the inn, the celebrations had started. Men hugged their women and children, laughed, and told stories of their heroic deeds, while others comforted those who had lost their men and reassured them of how bravely they had fought and of the cause for which they had died.

Shaan slipped away from the party and headed to the stable to saddle a fresh horse. It was time to leave, for he had no time to celebrate this victory. Krishia's army must be well advanced by now, and he knew there was much to be done.

"Where do you go, stranger?" It was Arios; Shaan must have been tired, for he had not heard him enter the stable.

"Stranger is it now?"

"Well, you're not Prince Daegal, that's for sure. I know that now. "Not that he was not a great warrior; he was, but you do not act like him, my friend." Arios paused then continued, "I will forever be in debt to you, my friend. Anything you need, wherever you are, just call and I will come." Sadness came to the warrior's eyes. "We will miss you, whoever you are."

"I am Shaan, and I too will miss you, my friend. But I must leave now; there is much I must do. If I can find out what happened to your Prince Daegal, then I will send word to you. Say farewell to the others for me." Shaan said as he climbed into his saddle. "Take care of yourself, Arios."

And with that, Shaan rode from the stable and disappeared into the night.

CHAPTER SIX

Marcus and his men had all but stripped Bron's little cottage, but they had found nothing that seemed of value. In fact, they had found no indication as to why Krishia should be so concerned about this pathetic little man at all. It occurred to Marcus that he had not heard from his out-riders for a while, and he ordered the remaining guards to scout around outside to see if anyone approached; this also gave him time to be alone with Bron and perhaps make him talk a little.

"Now, my friend," Marcus said in a soft voice, "why would a powerful sorceress be after a worm like you?" As he spoke these last words, his hand shot out, striking Bron and sending him crashing to the floor.

"Talk to me, worm," he spat, and while doing so, he kicked out at the prone figure, sending him sprawling through the door to lie in a heap on the damp grass. Blood dripped from a gash on Bron's face, and his ribs hurt as he tried to catch his breath. He was unable to do that before another blow came up into his chest, this time rolling him over and over. Marcus drew his sword and held it high in the air.

"I grow tired of this game; I think I will tell Krishia that you tried to escape and that one of my guards killed you." Marcus gave a little smile. "The worst thing that will happen is that Krishia will put the guard to death, and at least you will be of no more concern to her."

Bron struggled to his knees just as the blade came arcing towards him. There was a loud crack. The blow that should have cut through Bron's neck never came, and as he looked up, he saw that another blade had intercepted it just before it made contact. Bron looked up into Shaan's eyes.

"Ha! What kept you?"

Shaan did not reply to Bron but instead looked straight at Marcus.

"Shall we dance?" Shaan said with a grin.

The two swordsmen pulled away from each other, their swords scraping as they did so, sending a shower of sparks onto the kneeling figure that was Bron.

Bron, ignoring his pain, quickly executed a sideways roll to escape the battle zone. Shaan turned his sword in a tight arc, bringing its full weight towards his opponent's head. Marcus barely blocked the blow, but in doing so, he turned full circle and sent his own sword flying towards the now defenseless Shaan. The sword ripped through Shaan's shirt, grazing his skin. Shaan did not look at the wound, but he knew it was there; he could already feel the trickle of blood running down his stomach. As he pulled back a little, he raised his sword and waited for Marcus to make his next move. Marcus jumped towards Shaan and slashed downwards, a blow that would have been a winner against any other fighter, but Shaan was not just anyone, and before the blade had travelled half its distance, he had dropped to one knee, parried the blow, and sent his own blade upwards while at the same time executing a perfect roll to bring him back to a standing position. This move had taken Marcus completely by surprise, and now he stood with blood gushing from a wound in his side.

Shaan raised his sword and touched it to his forehead, then aimed it at Marcus again. "That's one each," he smiled.

Marcus could not hold back his rage any longer. A great roar issued from his throat, and at that, he spun quickly, his sword flashing round to find Shaan's head, but Shaan had dropped his weight, allowing the oncoming sword to pass over his head, his own blade shadowing that of his opponents. At the last instant, he altered the angle of his blade in such a way as to send the other flying through the air out of control. It landed a little way from them, point down, and swayed back and forth in a most undignified manner.

Marcus stood with eyes wide; he had never been beaten in swordplay before and at that moment swore that he never would be again.

"We must leave you now, but I am sure we will meet again," Shaan said, giving a mock bow and leading Bron off into the forest.

"Come, my friend, I do not believe that it is safe in Kwell for you at the moment."

Marcus had disappeared into the forest, so pausing only for Bron to collect a few things and stuff them hurriedly into a red sack, the two made off towards the caves. On the way, they passed the body of one of the outriders that Shaan had met on the way to Bron's cottage. From behind them came a shout, and both Shaan and Bron broke into a run, and without saying a word, they had raced down the muddy bank and splashed their way through the stream. Halfway up the other bank, Shaan could hear Marcus shout, "Kill them. A thousand pieces of silver to the man who gets their heads."

Looking over his shoulder, Shaan could now see two men running towards them; he turned and drew his sword.

"No, Shaan, quickly this way," Bron called from a short distance ahead.

"You go on; I'll hold them," Shaan replied.

"There is no need," urgency now in Bron's voice, "Hurry, Shaan."

Shaan paused for a second, then turned and chased after Bron. Up the hill they ran, into the entrance to the caves.

"Go on, Bron, save yourself," Shaan urged.

The men were almost upon them now, and Shaan assumed a defensive stance.

"It is alright, my friend," Bron spoke softly, no sign of panic in his voice. "Watch."

The two attackers had reached the cave's mouth and rushed forward. The men flared brightly for a split second and were gone.

"In the name of God," Shaan began.

"In the name of good, at least," Bron cut in. "I told you, only good may pass this way."

Shaan looked out of the cave in time to see Marcus walking off into the forest, no doubt also amazed at what he had seen.

"What are we going to do to keep you safe? I need to take you somewhere." Shaan asked Bron.

There was no reply, and when Shaan turned around, he found that this was because Bron was no longer there. Shaan was getting used to this sort of thing now and decided to continue to the central cave, and if Bron were not there, he would continue on his adventures.

It was late, and the hunter had retired, having been given a room to stay in. He lay thinking of the tales that the knights had told and wondered if they could possibly be true. If they were, then maybe, just maybe, the hunter was severely misjudging this Shaan Moonblade. He was still not convinced, but at this stage he was ready to analyze the information that he had gained before destroying the fake legacy of this so-called king.

In the halls below the sleeping chambers, Philippe was in conversation with Bedilore.

"Why did you tell the pilgrim that it was you that had returned the sword to Arielle?" Philippe asked.

"Because, my brother in arms, we still do not know much

about this traveler, and if he were to spread our stories, then all would know that it was you who had knowledge of the swords whereabouts, and if some person who, shall we say, had desires to be a king found out about this, he may attempt to get this information out of you, and this could be the downfall of us all," Bedilore replied.

"But now it will be you that they chase," Philippe looked worried for his comrade.

"Yes, but the worst they can do is kill me." "For I will never be able to reveal the sword's location because I do not know where it is."

Philippe nodded. This made perfect sense, although he wished that it had not been Bedilore who had to carry this burden for the rest of his life.

"Do you think that we will ever see Shaan again?" Philippe changed the subject.

"I do not know, but I hope that he has found peace wherever he is."

Shaan walked slowly down the next passage to whatever realm he would find there. He had not seen Bron again and had decided to leave the Shield of Lady Bella in the safety of the caves. At least if anything happened to him, then the forces of light would have one ally in the fight against Krishia. The wound on his stomach was not as bad as it had looked, and already the blood had dried, leaving a thin line where he had been cut. Shaan hesitated at the mouth of the cave, remembering what had happened to the two men that Marcus had sent after him, and then, with a deep breath, he stepped through.

Water rushed upon Shaan, going up his nose and into his open mouth. Panic began to set in, then in realization, he closed his mouth and kicked hard, swimming up to the surface of the water. Breaking out into the air, he took in a large gulp and then began to cough and sputter violently. He reached out with his arms, pulling himself to the bank, and clawed his way out of the water. Shaan lay on the bank, coughing up the last of the water that had entered his lungs. When his eyes had cleared from tears as much as water, he looked out over a lake. It was just as well that he could swim; otherwise, he would have drowned there and then. This was most unexpected. Of all the places that he had thought he would end up; a lake was not one of them.

Although it was a warm day, Shaan began to shiver. He stripped off his shirt and hung it on a branch to dry. He pulled off his boots and tipped out the water inside. Next Shaan unbuckled his belt, took his sword, and leaned it against a nearby tree.

Then he lay down on the soft grass and closed his eyes. He dreamt of days gone by, of Cannchester, of his knights, and of Gaius. In all his life, it seemed as if he had never known peace or tranquility, but he was experiencing it now, here on this soft bed of grass in a world that he did not know. "Surely there can be no evil in this place, and at least here my task should be a little easier," he thought. The sound of laughter drifted into Shaan's dream state, and then it was gone. Shaan dreamed some more about Cannchester and the wondrous things that Gaius had shown him. Again, the laughter came to his ears, but this time he awoke with a start. Someone or something was moving in the bushes behind him. Rolling sideways, he pushed off with his feet, diving towards the sound, and in an instant, he had brought its body hard to the floor.

Shaan rolled over so that he was sitting on top of the now-wriggling body. He raised his hand to strike down against the struggling mass, but just in time, he managed to stop his fist from smashing into his new foe's face.

"Well, what have I got here then?" He asked.

"I'm Hetti, that's what I am, and I'll trust you to let me up, ruffian," the squirming girl replied.

"And what might a Hetti be?" Shaan inquired about holding the girl tighter so that she could not escape.

"I am. Hetti. That's my name, now let me up."

"Not until you tell me what you are spying on," Shaan studied the girl. She was about fifteen years old, with blonde hair, blue eyes, and thin red lips. She would make a beautiful woman one day.

"Let me up, sir, I beg you. This is a most undignified position for a girl of my standing to be in."

"And just what is your standing?" Shaan again questioned his wriggling captive.

"Let her up or I will surely take your head." Shaan could feel the cold steel against his throat. Shaan rose up off the girl and looked straight into the eyes of his assailant.

The eyes that stared back were bright green and sparkled in the sunlight. The face around them was framed in red hair that cascaded all the way down to the waist. The body under the head was slender, but not thin, and well curved. Shaan found it hard to return his gaze to those bright eyes, but when he did, he could not again look away. He was completely entranced by this wonderful sight. The blade at his throat forgotten, Shaan just stared at the hypnotizing eyes.

"Who are you?" demanded the vision in front of him.

"I mean you no harm, but when I heard the movement in the bushes, I thought that someone was about to attack me."

"I asked who you were," the woman repeated.

"I am Shaan," Shaan said with a smile, and as he spoke those words, he stepped quickly forward, turned in a circle, his arms moving in an arc. When he had completed his circle, it was Shaan who held the sword and not the woman. He turned the sword blade down and drove it into the earth. "And I mean you no harm," he repeated.

"You are very quick, and I suppose it was Hetti that sneaked up on you."

Shaan nodded towards Hetti. "Well, we have already met, young lady; now tell me, who is your beautiful friend?"

"This is the Countess Rebecca," Hetti replied, giving a small curtsey in Rebecca's direction. "And I am her lady in waiting."

Shaan looked back at Rebecca. "I am most pleased to make your acquaintance, my lady."

"You still have not told me who you are," Rebecca said.

"I did, my lady. I am Shaan, and I am at your service." Shaan gave a low, sweeping bow and flashed a huge smile at the Countess.

"I mean, what are you doing on my land?" She paused and added, "I see that you have swum in my lake and no doubt poached some of my fish for your lunch."

"On the contrary, madam, I have not eaten in a while, and the reason I am wet is because," Shaan hesitated, and after a slight pause, "I slipped and fell into the water, and I was just resting a moment while my clothes dried out."

"I do not believe that for a moment," Rebecca shot a cold glance at Shaan. "But I think that your clothes should be dry enough by now, and I would be pleased if you would be on your way."

"There is nothing more I would like, but I am afraid that I am a little lost. If you could point me towards the nearest town, I would be most grateful."

"Where are you headed?" I know the area well enough." Rebecca replied.

"I am not sure, my lady. Maybe north, maybe not." In fact, Shaan did not know which way to go, but it was clear that he should be on his way. He turned to pick up his sword.

"Wait. You are bleeding," Rebecca commented without emotion.

Shaan looked down. The wound that had been caused by Marcus had opened a little, and although it was not a deep wound, it was indeed bleeding quite profusely.

"I suppose you got that when you slipped as well?"

"It would appear so," replied Shaan.

"Come, I will see that you have it dressed before you move on," Rebecca said.

She pulled her sword from the earth, turned, and walked away without saying a word.

"Well, come on then," called Hetti as she followed after the Countess.

Shaan shrugged, pulled his shirt from the branch where it hung, and strode after the others.

The room in which Shaan now sat was beautifully decorated and had plush carpets on the floor. Around the edges of the room were various cupboards and small tables, on which sat ornaments of different shapes and sizes. The table in front of him was covered in an intricately woven cloth, and dishes of deliciously-smelling foods were now being placed upon the table. His wound had been cleaned and dressed. The Countess had been persuaded by Hetti to allow Shaan to join them for a meal before moving on. Shaan had told Hetti a short tale of his adventures while his wound was being attended to by another member of Rebecca's staff, and Hetti had, after a while, rushed to tell the Countess, who was eager herself to hear a few more accounts of this man's life.

Rebecca had emerged from another room, changed, and was now dressed in a gown of such a fine fabric that it seemed to flow and ripple like a small pond whose waters were blown by a gentle breeze. The gown was coloured red, with an intricate pattern weaved on one shoulder and down the entire length of one side in golden thread. If she had looked beautiful before, then now Shaan was unable to find any words that would describe her. She sat down at the head of the table and motioned to the waiting staff to begin serving the meal.

"I see the new shirt fits you well, Shaan," Rebecca said for the first time.

"Yes. Thank you; the other was beginning to look a little worse for wear," Shaan said.

The Countess had had one of her staff bring him a new shirt after he had washed it, as she did not want him at her table in a ripped, not to mention dirty, shirt.

"Hetti tells me that you are a great adventurer, Shaan. Pray, tell me some of your stories in payment for your meal," the Countess demanded.

"Well, I am not much of a storyteller, my lady; Gaius was the one for that, but I will do my best," and Shaan began to tell Rebecca and Hetti of some of his adventures when his Knights had ridden the land fighting evil and bringing peace to the villages, towns, and cities of his country. He told of Galwraith and the green knight, of the quest for the sacred stones, and of the treachery of Theodore. As he told these tales, it seemed to Rebecca that she had entered a dream world and that if she closed her eyes, she could clearly see all that Shaan had spoken of as if she were there herself. The meal continued, and Shaan talked on while both Rebecca and Hetti listened to his stories, laughed at his jokes, and asked questions about all of the things of which he had spoken. The meal ended, and still, the women listened, neither of them wanting the conversation to end. They talked until evening came, when Shaan mentioned that it was late and he really should be moving on, as he had to find a place to stay before it got too dark.

"I had not realised how late it had become. I am afraid that we have kept you talking far too long," Rebecca said. "I cannot let you walk out into the night, Shaan. Would you care to stay here until morning? I can have someone make up a room for you."

"It is very kind of you, Countess, but I do not want to put you in any trouble," Shaan said honestly.

"It is no trouble; after all, it was us that kept you talking for so long," and at that, Rebecca clapped her hands, and page appeared at the door.

"William, have Lisa make up a room for our guest," Rebecca ordered.

"Yes, ma'am," William turned and hurried to carry out his task.

"Thank you, Countess," Shaan said.

"Please call me Rebecca. You make me feel so old when you call me Countess."

"Very well, Rebecca," Shaan replied, and they smiled at each other.

"Tell me about yourself now, Rebecca," Shaan asked, leaning back in his chair.

CHAPTER SEVEN

"What do you mean, the king who will be king?" Krishia thundered.

Sophia looked up at the raging Queen as she admitted to herself that the runes were acting strangely today.

"That is what they say, your Majesty. These three stones were drawn from the pouch at the same time. One mentions a king, the other mentions someone who will be king, and the third is a joining rune, therefore, they speak of the king who will be king."

Sophia tried her best to make some sense of it all, but she could not get away from what the runes were saying no matter from which viewpoint she looked at them.

"So, what you are saying is that the king who will be king has changed the course of events in Kwell and is now gone from this realm. Then this man must be Bron," the queen declared.

"No, I do not think so. I have a feeling that a new force is at work here," Sophia always trusted her instincts in these matters and was usually right.

"Is Marcus alive?" Krishia asked.

"Yes, but he has lost all but two of his men."

"Damn fool," Krishia cursed, "such a simple task, even one of my serfs could have carried it out."

The curtain that hung over the doorway to Sophia's room was abruptly shoved aside, and Moroc rushed in.

"We have a big problem, your majesty," Moroc said in angry tones.

"What is it now?" Krishia shouted, her voice full of venom.

"Talmarc," Moroc muttered between clenched teeth.

"And what of Talmarc?" Krishia asked, "It is just another city like all the others. What could possibly be a problem with Talmarc?"

"Jarenn," Moroc did not think that he needed to say more; after all, the legends of the Jarenn warriors were well known. Krishia had other ideas.

"Must I do everything myself?" She raged and pushed past Moroc and raced through the corridors of her castle, calling for her chariot to be made ready. She would take care of these Jarenn once and for all, and maybe then, just maybe, she could trust in these fools that she had commanded to do something for herself.

Khamel lay in her bath, her body bruised and battered; her purple and yellow skin told the truth, and she was broken. When she had been pulled from the dungeon by Krishia's guards, she had expected death and was surprised to find herself delivered to her home, even if unceremoniously dumped on the steps.

She would never again challenge the Queen, not even to utter a curse under her breath while alone.

The hunter's journey was coming to an end. He had ridden relentlessly for two days on his way to Trevena. The sun was rising, and it cast an eerie golden glow over the ruins of the castle that lay before him a little way into the sea. The tide was high, but the hunter knew that in a few hours the sea would retreat, revealing a causeway to the castle. He dismounted from his horse and led it slowly through the shallow waters, allowing the salt water to refresh its tired legs.

So, this was where it had all begun. Where Prethus had invaded the Duke of Dumnonia's castle, taken his wife, and given life to Shaan. Later, Gaius had come and taken the child as his own. The hunter could almost feel himself being caught up in the magic of this place and had to chastise himself; after all, he did not believe in magic and all that nonsense. There was always a logical explanation, and the hunter had never seen anything to make him believe different. All these legends and tales of sorcery were the words of dreamers or drunken men used to con someone out of another drink. No, no magic; just men against men, sword against sword. That was the way that empires were forged.

He sat and watched the tide roll away. What was he doing here? Why travel all this way in search of answers that he knew did not exist?

This was a new feeling for him. He had never suffered from self-doubt before, always knowing the direction in which his life was going. Until now. Until this Shaan had entered his life. Why had he been drawn to seek Shaan out? For the first time, he realised that he did not know why he was doing what he was doing. Only that he must. All this thinking was muddling the hunter's mind, and he was beginning to wish he had never embarked on this adventure in the first place.

Two hours later, the water level was shallow enough to allow the hunter to lead his horse over the rocky causeway towards the castle. Even though it had been severely damaged by many battles, it was still one of the grandest that the hunter had seen. Approaching the main entrance, where a portcullis would normally have barred his way, the hunter could see that the left-hand gate was open and hanging from its huge hinges, and that the right-hand gate was missing altogether. Passing through, he entered the courtyard. Most of the walls inside the castle were intact, and it was obvious that the castle was in better condition than it had appeared from the outside. Leaving his horse to wander on the castle grounds, the hunter made his way into the castle proper.

Once inside, he strolled down a long corridor, passing many rooms but not venturing in. It was as if he were being drawn to a room at the very end of this passage, a room where he would find the answers that he sought. At last, coming to the final door, he turned the knob, swung open the great oak door, and stepped inside. The figure sat in a large, comfortable chair, looked up, and smiled.

"Welcome Johnathan . I have been waiting for you."

And the great oak door closed behind him.

Shaan reached the bottom of the stairs. He still did not know in which direction to travel, but at least now he was fully refreshed. He could hear the sound of arguing coming from the room opposite the stairs. It was the Countess Rebecca and two men. Shaan was not one for prying but could quite clearly hear what was being said.

"You will accept our offer," one voice said.

"You know what will happen next time we visit," another, harsher voice said.

"Never," This time it was Rebecca who spoke in a defiant voice.

"Oh, but you will," said the first voice again. "Show her Gant."

The sound of glass smashing filled the room. Gant knocked more objects off a table and then looked at Rebecca.

"It won't just be your possessions that we break," Gant said, raising his hand to strike Rebecca. The hand, though, did not travel any distance, its path being blocked by Shaan's own.

"I believe the lady said no," Shaan said. "Now, I think you should leave."

"So, you have hired yourself a bodyguard. Well, it won't do you any good," Gant snarled. "Get him, Mal."

Mal was already on his way, jumping towards Shaan, but he

was too slow. As Mal swung at Shaan, he ducked, his own fist lashing out and catching Mal full on the jaw. Mal's body was hurled over a nearby table to land in a crumpled heap on the floor. Shaan followed this attack by slamming his elbow back into Gant, who immediately doubled over. Shaan rose from his crouching position, his knee rising up as he did so to catch Gant in the face. Gant fell back, blood pouring from his nose.

"I ask you again, sirs, please leave," Shaan said.

Gant and Mal rose from where they had fallen and stumbled to the door.

"We will be back, and you had better reconsider," Mal said threateningly to Rebecca. "And we have not finished with you yet," he snarled at Shaan.

When they had gone, Rebecca turned to Shaan.

She looked drained. "I do not know who you are or what you want, but thank you."

"Who were those two?" Shaan enquired.

"Just a little local trouble. They caught me unawares, that's all," Rebecca avoided giving a direct answer to Shaan's question.

"Do you often have local trouble?"

"It is very hard for a woman on her own," Rebecca answered. "Since my husband died, it seems that everybody thinks that they can just walk over me, and I am tired of being pushed around."

"From the way you handled me yesterday, I would say that no one would be able to push you around, my lady."

"Handled you indeed. You disarmed me in a second," the Countess looked ashamed, "if my husband had been alive, he would have died laughing."

"Maybe you're just out of practice, my lady. If you would like, I could spar with you for a while," Shaan offered. "Besides, it looks like you could do with some help here."

Then Shaan realised that he was forgetting the point of his being here. How easy it was to forget in the company of this beautiful woman. Shaan also remembered his Giselle, who, in another realm, waited for him, or did she? Perhaps she thought him dead, or maybe she hoped that he did not return so that she did not need his forgiveness for her treachery. Shaan recalled how he had found her in the arms of his best friend and how, deep in the forest, he had been unable to kill them as they slept. It had been their treason that had destroyed his faith in man and, in doing so, brought an end to his kingdom. It was becoming clear to Shaan that he had blamed everyone for his downfall except the true culprits, for in his love for both Giselle and Davide, he had found it impossible to accuse either.

Have I been so blind for all these years? Shaan wondered.

"I think I should be moving on, Rebecca; I have already taken up much of your time." Shaan turned to the door, "But I do think that you should hire a bodyguard."

Shaan stepped through the doorway.

"Wait. Will you be my bodyguard?" Rebecca pleaded with sadness in her voice.

"I cannot, my lady, for I have much to do here." Shaan continued his way to the main entrance.

"Please!" Rebecca caught Shaan by the arm, and he turned to face her, looking straight into those bright eyes. Rebecca moved towards Shaan, his arms reaching out to embrace her, his face moving ever closer to hers.

"No. No, my lady," Shaan pulled back suddenly. "I cannot."

"I am sorry, Shaan. I did not mean to...," Rebecca started.

"Oh. No, Rebecca, it is not you. Nothing would please me more, it is just that...," Shaan stumbled for words, "just that I do not want you to think badly of me, my lady. For you are the most beautiful and intriguing woman that I have ever known, and I do not want to endanger our friendship."

"I would never think that of you, Shaan. I wish you would change your mind and stay."

"I wish I could, but there is something very important that I have to do here. Something that, if left undone, will destroy all that we know and love," Shaan walked away from Rebecca, pain in his heart. "Hire the best men you can; I do not want to see you get hurt."

"Think of me," Rebecca called, "I'll be thinking of you."

These words rolled through Shaan's mind as he walked down the long path that led to the gate of Rebecca's mansion.

Two hours later, Shaan had reached a small town. He still did not know which of the objects he would find in this realm, but at least the choice had been narrowed. He knew that it was not the shield of Lady Bella, and he also guessed that it was not the sword, for he felt sure that that was still in his own realm. That left only the spear or the Helm of Othus. Perhaps by walking around the town and maybe visiting a few bars or markets, he may hear of a legend or story relating to one of the objects.

Shaan could hear the sound of voices and commotion coming from a little way off and headed in that direction. The noise came from a small marketplace. People were busily going about their daily chores, buying, selling, and haggling loudly. Nobody paid any attention to the newcomer. All manner of goods were on offer here, and Shaan decided to browse the various stalls. There were traders selling food, jewelry, and the like. In one corner of the market, an old woman had set up a stall telling people's fortunes, and in another, an old man was selling medicine. Shaan stopped at a stall where a great many weapons were on display. He picked up a broadsword and turned it this way and that.

"A fine weapon, sir. Finest in the land," the vendor said. "Made of the strongest steel."

Shaan smiled, put the sword back on the rack, and moved on. The blade had been much too heavy and would have made the sword exceedingly difficult to wield in battle. If this was the finest example of weapons made in this realm, then they either had a lot to learn or had not had much experience in war.

Shaan continued to walk around the market, making polite conversation with some traders and listening to others, but he never heard one word that would aid him on his quest. The people here were too busy carrying out the ordinary tasks of living day to day to worry about stories and legends.

Across from the market was a bar, and it was in this direction that Shaan now walked. On entering the bar, he ordered some ale, the day was hot, and he had not had a drink since leaving the mansion that morning.

"That will be two cromms, sir," the barman held out his hand.

Shaan fished into the small leather pouch that Bron had given him. It contained various types of coinage that Shaan might need on his journeys. He dug out a coin and gave it to the barman. The bartender tossed a few smaller coins back to Shaan as change.

Shaan sipped at the ale. He had tasted better, but the lukewarm liquid did its job of quenching Shaan's thirst.

"Ain't seen you around these parts before." A woman had joined Shaan at the bar. Leaning on one elbow, she peered into his eyes.

"You got time to spare?" She winked at Shaan in a most unladylike fashion and wiped her nose on the sleeve of her dress.

"I beg your pardon, madam," was all Shaan could reply.

"Madam, well, I ain't heard that one in a long time," the woman laughed. "Madam indeed."

"Leave the customers alone, Rosie. How many times do I

have to tell you?" The barman yelled. "If they are wanting your service, I'll call you, like I always do."

Rosie headed off, like a scolded dog, back to her chair.

"Sorry about that, sir," the barman said to Shaan. "Can't resist a handsome face; that's her trouble."

"Quite a busy town you've got here," Shaan said to the barman.

"Always busy for the Mullen," the barman replied.

"The Mullen. What's that?"

"Everyone knows what the Mullen is. You must be from far away, sir," the barman looked surprised. "The Mullen is the great festival of giving. It is what keeps us all alive and gives us the protection of Rani."

Shaan was about to ask what or who Rani was but decided better of it.

"And when is the Mullen?" He enquired instead.

"The Mullen starts tonight with the choosing, and then at noon tomorrow we have the giving," the barman smiled, a look of almost relief crossing his face.

"Ya best not be messin with the Chosin, sir. Folk round here don't like strangers getting involved," this was an obvious warning and set Shaan's mind to work.

What was so special about this choice? And what was the gift? At first, Shaan thought that it was merely a festival, but now he was not so sure. Shaan decided that he would stay and see what occurred here.

Shaan had spent the rest of the day wandering around the town. No one had mentioned the events to come, so he thought it best not to ask too many questions. The sun had faded and the moon was beginning to peak from behind a thin veil of clouds when Shaan heard the commotion in the streets. He rushed from where he had been sitting in the bar out into the dusty marketplace, as did all the inhabitants of the bar. The marketplace was already full of people; more came from all directions. It seemed that all the townsfolk were gathered here for the choosing, and now Shaan would see what all the fuss was about.

The crowd had formed a half circle around a hastily built stage, on which now stood a dozen figures. Shaan could not see clearly from his position, but it appeared that most of the figures on the stage were children or teenagers. It seemed that some kind of selection was taking place as every now and then a child ran from the stage into the arms of its waiting parents, who would hug and kiss it and carry it or lead it away from the stage and presumably back to their home. This continued until there was only one child remaining, and it stood on the stage, eyes looking down. Shaan was sure he had heard a sob. Not the kind of noise you would have expected from a winner. Before he could query this with the man standing next to him, a great commotion had broken out over the far side of the crowd.

"Make way. Make way!" a voice bellowed. "I have the one."

A cheer broke out, and the child on the stage looked up and leapt from where it stood into the arms of its family. Meanwhile, the man who had shouted had reached the stage and climbed on, carrying a huge bundle over his shoulder. This was no ordinary bundle, though; this one wriggled and kicked. The man dumped it on the floor, pulled out a knife, and cut the drawstring on the sack. A body from within pulled this way and that until it was free. Casting the sack into the crowd, it made a break for freedom. It was a useless effort; the man caught it by the arm and pulled it back to the middle of the stage.

"This will ensure our safety for a long time," he said.

The crowd cheered, and Shaan pushed his way through to get a better look. He was now quite near the stage and could see that the child that was being held was Hetti, Rebecca's maid. Tears ran down her face, and it was obvious to Shaan that she feared for her life.

"Let her go," he shouted as he tried to mount the stage. "Release her."

The people around him pulled Shaan back. He struggled violently against them, but there were too many. Hetti screamed, but Shaan barely heard her as the blackness overtook him.

"I warned you not to interfere, sir," the barman said as he let the club in his hand relax now that it had done its work.

CHAPTER EIGHT

The ropes around Rebecca's wrists were beginning to bite into her flesh, and a thin trickle of blood was making its way down her right arm. How long she had been hanging she did not know, but it must have been a couple of hours, and she ached from head to toe. From the hall, she could hear the sound of approaching footsteps. She closed her eyes and tried to reach out with her mind. She thought of Shaan and wished that he was here now, and she called to him with all of her remaining strength. Rebecca had never had the gift, unlike her mother, and she knew that it was a useless act, but all the same, she had to try.

Gant entered the room. "How are you feeling today?" He asked with mock concern. "Those bracelets really suit you."

He reached up and stroked at the ropes that were now stained red. Rebecca opened her eyes and spat full into Gant's face. Gant replied by striking Rebecca hard across the cheek, which reddened immediately. Although the blow stung, Rebecca refused to acknowledge it, and her face still carried a look of defiance.

"You still don't get it, do you?" Gant pulled Rebecca's hair, forcing her head back, and he pushed his face into her neck, kissing and biting at the soft flesh.

"You are mine now," he laughed as he drew a shiny knife from his belt.

Holding the knife to her throat, he whispered, "And you will do as I say," and then, as if he had not noticed it before, he touched the silken fabric of her garment.

"What a lovely dress, Rebecca," he said as the blade in his hand flashed sideways, cutting a shoulder strap as it did.

One side of the dress fell forward, revealing Rebecca's left shoulder.

"What have we got here then?" Gant moved his lips to kiss the exposed flesh.

Pulling slowly at the material of the dress, Gant heard a satisfying ripping sound, and the more he pulled at the cloth, the more he could see of Rebecca's body. Slowly, as if teasing himself, he tore at the cloth, following its path with his tongue.

Rebecca's mind raced. Not this, anything but this, but there was nothing she could do to prevent Gant from performing any act that he wished.

Gant now had half of Rebecca's breast exposed and was about to finish the job when Mal burst through the door holding a rope. Gant turned, cursing, but when he saw what was on the end of the rope, he could not stop himself from breaking into a great roar of laughter.

Mal pulled violently at the rope, sending William tumbling to land in a heap on the floor.

"Up doggy!" laughed Mal. "Show our good friend Gant how you beg!"

Mal pulled on the rope, which was bound tightly around William's neck. William coughed and sputtered, tears streaming from his eyes.

"Let him go; he is just a boy," Rebecca pleaded.

Mal turned to face Rebecca, his face twisted with rage.

"I told you what would happen. Now you leave me no choice," Mal spat as he took the knife from Gant.

"No!" Rebecca screamed.

"No!" The sound of a woman's scream awoke Shaan with a start. He rolled over and tried to sit up. He could not; this was because his hands were tied behind his back.

"Shaan, you're alive," was the sound of Hetti's voice.

Shaan twisted around as best he could and saw Hetti sitting across from him.

"I thought they had killed you for sure," she said.

"It would take more than a tap on the head to kill me," Shaan smiled at Hetti, "I have a king-size headache though."

"What are you doing here?" Hetti asked Shaan.

"More to the point, what are you doing here?" Shaan reversed the question.

"I guess I am the chosen one," Hetti replied.

"I gathered that. But for what have you been chosen?"

"It seems that I am to be the new bride for Rani," Hetti said, matter-of-factly, as if Shaan should know what she was talking about.

"And just who is Rani?" Shaan asked.

"Rani is the lord protector of these parts, or at least," Hetti hesitated, "if we do as he says then he will not kill us."

"Great protector," Shaan sighed. "What happened to his last wife?"

"He probably got fed up with her," Hetti spoke in monotones.

"And what does he do when he gets fed up?"

"He eats his old wife and then makes the townspeople find him a new one." Again, Hetti seemed to think this was quite natural.

"How long has this been going on?" Shaan tried to wriggle into a more comfortable position.

"As long as anyone can remember, certainly long before I was born," Hetti replied.

"We have to stop it," Shaan said.

"Oh, you'll get your chance." Shaan had not seen his captor enter the room, "just like the count did."

"The count?" Shaan quizzed.

"Rebecca's husband," Hetti this time said, "nearly succeeded as well."

"Rebecca's husband fought Rani. What happened?"

"Rani killed him." Hetti looked at the dirty floor. "Three years ago, now."

"It was good sport," the barman joked. "Rani was really angry after that. Swore the next man to challenge him would be killed very slowly, hacked to bits piece by piece. I reckon it's your lucky day," and the barman broke into hysterical laughter and turned and left the room.

Shaan looked at Hetti, a tear now trickling down her cheek. "Do not worry, it will be alright."

"You cannot win, Shaan. Rani is an expert with all manner of weapons. You must escape, run away, and don't come back," Hetti cried.

"If only." Shaan tugged at the ropes. "It looks like we are in this together."

The wind blew gently down the main street of Talmarc. All was quiet, at least for now. The armies of Bastion had been driven back to the wastelands and had made camp.

Saris, tall and muscular and dressed in the green silks of the Jarenn, spoke to the older man next to him.

"Not a bad day's work, Daal."

Daal, a man at the end of his years, scorned his younger partner.

"When you reach my age, you will appreciate what a day's work is, my boy."

Despite his years, Daal still possessed the posture and body of a man half his age. Standing tall and proud, his fine white hair and beard waving in the breeze.

"I wonder why they retreated so easily." Daal said thoughtfully.

"They have heard of your savage reputation," Saris slapped the old man on the back.

"Me, I am just an old man," Daal replied in a soft voice.

"Tell that to the twenty men you killed today," Saris said, pushing Daal in the direction of the nearest bar.

"Now you know that I do not drink," Daal said.

"Ah, but I do," Saris said as they entered the bar.

The barman had already poured a glass of ale by the time he reached the counter, and Saris reached out to take it but stopped abruptly.

"Look at this Daal."

Daal looked at the glass of ale. At first, the liquid seemed to ripple and then wash from side to side. A few seconds later, a loud thumping sound could be heard from outside. Saris and Daal ran to the door. When they reached the street, it was packed with the townsfolk, who had all come out to see what these strange noises were.

"Look! Up in the sky," a young man pointed upwards.

Saris followed the man's outstretched arm, and what he saw made him doubt his own senses.

The thumping noise was now almost unbearable as the dragon's wings beat slowly, straining with each stroke to keep its huge bulk airborne. Its head looked this way and that, and it let out a high-pitched screech.

This noise shattered the windows in every building in the vicinity of the town center, sending shards of sharp glass raining down on the masses gathered in the streets.

People were now running aimlessly, trying desperately to escape this terrifying sight. It was of no use. As they ran, the dragon spat out a huge flare of orange and blue flame, instantly turning twenty people into burnt cinders. Next, it turned its attention on some houses, which exploded into a mass of burning timbers. There was no escape for either buildings or people as the dragon flew back and forth across the town, setting buildings ablaze and burning up men, women, and children where they stood.

A few of the men had armed themselves and gathered together in the street with Saris and Daal, and when the dragon saw this, it flew towards them, stopping a little way off. With a great thud, the dragon landed and slowly walked to where the men stood.

A great barrage of arrows and spears flew at the beast, but all bounced harmlessly off its armor's thick scales. The dragon grunted a few short roars as if it laughed at the puny attempts of its attackers. Reaching out with its long neck, it snapped its jaws around one of the men, lifting him high in the air before tossing him skyward, catching him in its mouth, and swallowing him whole. This caused the men to break ranks and run in different directions, and Saris and Daal ran with them, knowing that they could not hope to beat such a formidable creature.

As they ran, the dragon spewed searing flames after them, killing many before they had made it to safety.

Saris and Daal had made it to the edge of the town and ran a little way into the wasteland, where, throwing themselves to the ground, they rapidly covered themselves in the sand and debris, hoping that the dragon would be unable to locate them. They had to escape and make it back to Taal to warn the others, or all of Dresslon and beyond would suffer Talmarc's fate. It was becoming all too clear that they were up against more than just the armies of Bastion in this war. Had Krishia found a new ally? Or was she even more powerful than anyone had dreamed?

Within an hour, the whole of Talmarc had been burned to the ground and all its inhabitants slaughtered. It was several hours later than that when Saris and Daal gingerly rose from their hiding place, surveying the towns ashes, before moving quickly off into the night.

The sun was at its highest point and shone brightly down from a blue, cloudless sky. The huge amphitheater stood, as it had done for centuries, in the desert, an hour's ride by chariot from the town. Its walls were bleached white from an eon of brilliant sunshine. Inside the amphitheater, the seats were full, not just of the town's folk but also of the nomads that inhabited the desert.

At a rough guess, Shaan would have said that there were at least a thousand people gathered here. He looked all around for a means of escape or maybe some surprise help from the crowd, but neither seemed likely. Shaan and Hetti had been escorted to the middle of the amphitheater's arena and were now guarded by four armed men. The men were dressed in ceremonial outfits, but their weapons were all too real, and it had been made clear to Shaan that if he tried to escape, both he and Hetti would be killed where they stood.

Their only hope of survival now lay with Shaan. If he could defeat Rani, then they would be allowed to go free. This seemed the best solution, and Shaan was not afraid to take Rani on; after all, he had had a lot of practice of late and felt sure that he could beat any man in a fair fight.

All of a sudden, the crowd became quiet, so quiet that Shaan could almost hear his own heartbeat. A man in a robe of purple with silver symbols marked on it began to chant a strange rhyme. The crowd seemed to be hypnotized by the rhythm and began, as one, to sway from side to side, and a low hum issued forth from some of them. Shaan stared into the crowd; some of the people who had not been caught up in this mass hysteria looked terrified. Panic was setting in, but they were too afraid to move. Abruptly, the chanting stopped, and a gasp issued from the crowd. To Shaan's right, a huge billow of smoke rose into the air, and slowly it drifted away. As it cleared, Shaan could make out a shape from within. The more the smoke thinned, the clearer the image became, until the giant figure of Rani was all that remained.

Rani stood ten feet tall and had, at first, the appearance of a man. Then Shaan noticed the third arm, and there would have been a fourth, but where it should have been there was only a stub. Hetti saw that Shaan was looking at this and whispered to Shaan, "The count."

She did not need to say any more. It was clear that Rebecca's husband had gotten close enough to cause Rani a lot of pain. This raised Shaan's hopes a little, but not much. Rani was an impressive sight. In one hand he held a spiked club, in another a huge double-bladed sword, and in the third a sharp-bladed spear. Shaan wondered what the fourth hand would have held had it still been attached.

As Rani walked towards the waiting guards, Shaan looked closely at his opponent. Ranis' face at first appeared normal, and at first Shaan could not make out what it was that seemed to be different. It was the eyes. Rani had two eyeballs in each socket, which he could move independently, and thus was able to see in all directions at once. There would be no sleight-of-hand battle tricks that would catch this foe out.

When Rani reached the guards, his voice boomed out.

"What is this? I demand a bride, and you present me with more objectors."

"I am sorry, Lord," the man in the red robes came running up.

"But we only live to serve you, and this man has threatened us all with destruction," he paused to take a deep breath, "and we need judgment."

With this, the crowd cheered and cried out for the death of Shaan. Not because they hated him, but because they were afraid that Rani would wreak terrible revenge if anyone dared to question his power.

"Ah, what do we have here? Do you question my power? Do you dare challenge my right to rule over you?" Rani leant his head towards Shaan. His foul breath almost made Shaan vomit.

"I question the right of anyone to rule with fear and death as their powers," Shaan answered.

Rani roared with rage, striking Shaan across the head as he did, sending him sprawling to the ground.

"No one questions me," Rani roared, as much to the crowd as Shaan. "No one."

Rani looked at the stump where his arm had been.

"Ah. Now I remember. I will take you slowly. Every cut will be a masterpiece. Every drop of blood will be savored, and then," he paused, "you will die," and with that, Rani smiled a huge smile and addressed a nearby attendant.

"Bring him a choice of weapons."

Rani turned to Hetti and pointed the spear at her. He scraped the blade along her cheek.

"Excellent. I am sure we will be very happy," he said, then laughed. "For a while anyway."

Hetti wanted to scream, but she refused to give Rani the satisfaction and thrill of knowing that she was scared; instead, she looked defiantly into his eyes.

Shaan was given the choice of three weapons. A sword that was only half the length of the one that Rani wielded. A chain with two spiked balls on the end, it was also not much use unless Shaan could get in close, and the third weapon seemed even more useless than the rest; it was a silver ball about the size of Shaan's clenched fist, and he could see no use for it whatsoever.

"What is your choice, little mortal?" Rani teased, knowing full well that none of these weapons would be of any use to Shaan.

Shaan chose the sword; at least he knew how to get the most from this weapon, even if it was short.

Rani looked almost bored and said, "Always the sword. Do you mortals only know the use of one tool?"

Shaan thought it was an odd choice of words, 'tool' rather than 'weapon'.

"It will do the job," Shaan said.

Rani turned his spear over and rammed it into the earth. "I pity you," he said to Shaan.

With his now spare hand, he took the silver ball, pressed a panel on its side, and tossed it towards two guards a short distance away. There was a small explosion, and when the smoke had cleared, the two guards lay dead.

"You would have beaten me had you chosen wisely," Rani chuckled.

The two remaining guards dragged the bodies, or what was left of their dead comrades, away, and Hetti was taken to the perimeter of the arena by the man in the purple robes.

"It's just you and me now," Shaan said as he dived to one side, grabbed the sword, and swung it at Rani.

It was a useless act. Rani was too quick, and his own sword crashed against Shaan's, sending it spinning across the arena. Shaan ran to pick it up, expecting Rani to be hot on his heels, but he was not. Rani just stood and waited for Shaan to return.

Shaan again attacked, and again his sword was sent flying. This time Rani followed up this move with a stab from the spear, catching Shaan in the shoulder. The club whistled over Shaan's head as he just managed to duck under its swing. Shaan again picked up his sword, only this time he circled around Rani, trying to make him make the first move. He did not have to wait long. Rani swung the huge broad sword at Shaan's head, causing him to jump to one side, and as he did so, Rani again stabbed out with the spear, this time catching Shaan in the thigh. Shaan cried out in pain and stumbled to the floor. As Rani swung the club down, Shaan rolled away and the weapon slammed into the floor, causing a large dent to appear and a cloud of dust to rise into the air. Things were going badly, and Shaan could not think of any way to improve his odds.

"I am disappointed in you. I had thought that you would have put up a little resistance as all these people are here to cheer you on," Rani jeered. "Yes. I know that they secretly want you to win. I am sorry, but I am going to have to disappoint them."

"Not if I can help it," Shaan leapt forward, his sword burying itself in Rani's side, then he rolled away again, avoiding Rani's swinging blade.

Rani looked surprised but did not let the pain show. He dug his spear into the ground and took hold of Shaan's sword in one hand. Deliberately and with great showmanship, he slowly pulled the sword from his side, smiling as he did so. Rani was determined that the crowd would see that he was not badly hurt.

"And now, you will die," Rani declared.

Rani lifted up his huge broad sword and advanced on Shaan, who, weaponless, was now doomed.

The crowd had gone quiet, too quiet, in fact, and Shaan could feel the hand of death on his shoulder. Suddenly, Rani stopped and stared at Shaan. No, not at Shaan, but beyond him.

Shaan looked around, and there, about ten meters away, stood a man in the outfit of a hunter. A bow was in his hand, and an arrow already strung was pointing at Shaan.

"Shaan Moonblade. "I have come a long way for you," the hunter called.

Just when he thought things could not get any worse, they did. This was all Shaan needed. Would he be beheaded or shot through with an arrow?

The hunter lined up his arrow and, in a flash, with a great whistling of wind, the arrow flew towards Shaan, passing directly over Shaan's head and catching Rani in the left eye.

Rani screamed; it was probably the only time he had screamed in his life. He grabbed at the arrow, tried to pull it from his skull, and fell to the ground. With a last roar, he died, the arrow still buried deep in his brain.

The silence was unbearable. No one dared speak, least Rani rose up and struck them all down. Minutes seemed to pass when all at once a great cheer came from the crowd and people came leaping over the boundary wall, running up to Shaan and the hunter. At first, Shaan feared that they might finish what Rani had started, but they did not; they were delighted and hoisted both Shaan and the hunter high into the air.

"Thank you," Shaan called to the hunter.

"Do not thank me, thank Gaius," the hunter replied. "That arrow was meant for you until he convinced me otherwise."

Then his voice was drowned out by the crowd as they were swept away in a victory dance.

CHAPTER NINE

As Shaan and Johnathan , the hunter, rode to Rebecca's rescue, Shaan recalled what Johnathan had told him. How he had at first set out to kill Shaan and then, after his meeting with the remaining knights and his journey to Trevena, where Gaius had confirmed what he had been told by the knights and also told him of the great evil that threatened the world, how he had changed his mind and decided to aid Shaan.

The weather was worsening as they rode. It had become colder, and a mist now blew across the countryside. Shaan's rage was growing, and he swore to himself that if anyone had hurt Rebecca in any way, he would make them pay dearly. His thoughts were with the Countess now, and he longed to be with her.

The mansion came slowly into view, and Shaan and Jonathan kicked their horses on to greater efforts.

The double doors lay open, allowing a gentle breeze to drift into the elegantly decorated bedroom. Rebecca lay on the bed, having been cut down from where she had hung. Her hands were still tightly bound, and her dress lay in tatters around her. Her eyes were red and stinging from the tears she had cried. Although she had tried to disconnect her consciousness from the body that Gant had invaded, she had found it impossible. Her mind was blank, and she was not even sure that she wanted to live any more.

The door to Rebecca's room opened slowly, and Gant entered.

"Hello, my lovely," Gant grinned. "I hope you are rested."

He walked over to where Rebecca lay, sat on the bed next to her, and ran his rough hand up and down the exposed flesh of her body.

Gant leant over to kiss Rebecca on the lips, but as he did so, something moved and caught his attention. He was certain that he had seen a figure moving outside, and he rose and walked onto the balcony. Looking down into the grounds, he strained to see through the mist.

The soft, white veil of mist swirled this way and that, and then, as if pulled back by some unseen hand, it revealed a figure. Standing dead still and leaning on a huge double-bladed broadsword, the figure stared up at Gant. At that moment, not a sound issued from the world. It was as if all the creatures, even nature itself, waited, afraid to utter a sound in case some great god destroyed it.

"Mal. Mal!" Gant shouted in fear as he ran from the room and down the stairs.

Rebecca wondered what it was that could scare Gant this much. She rolled over to the edge of the bed and slowly worked her way into a standing position. She made her way onto the balcony and gazed down at what had terrified Gant so much. She prayed that she was not dreaming. She was very weak but managed a faint call.

"Shaan. Shaan,".

Looking down into the grounds, she watched the mist swirl around a figure. She blinked and looked again, but this time only the mist remained.

"No," she cried. "No, I was not dreaming. This cannot be."

Mal came running into the hall, almost colliding with Gant.

"What is it?"

"He's back." Gant grabbed Mal by the shoulder. "I thought you said that Rani would take care of him."

"Who's back?"

"That stranger, the one who broke my nose," Gant said.

Mal brushed Gant aside. Rushed to another room and emerged with two swords, handing one to Gant.

"He won't be so lucky this time," Mal said, and then shouted up the stairs. "Reece. Jorgan. Fuzz."

Three men appeared at the top of the stairs, weapons at the ready.

Outside, the men began their search for any sign of Shaan, but after a few minutes they had found nothing. They gathered together on the lawn.

"Gant's been dreaming again," one said. "Scared of his own shadow," another laughed.

Gant threw a punch at Reece, who easily dodged it.

"That's enough," Mal snapped.

"Looking for someone?" Shaan's voice echoed through the mist.

The group all turned as one, and there, shrouded in mist, stood the almost ghostly vision of Shaan, leaning on his sword with a blank expression on his face.

"Aghh, he's mine," Reece declared, beginning to draw his sword from its scabbard. Before it was halfway out, an arrow had smashed its way into his skull, and he was dead before his limp body hit the floor.

A second and third arrow took Jorgan and Fuzz before they could react.

"Just me and you now, boys," and Shaan lifted the great broadsword and advanced towards the terrified duo.

Gant turned and ran, leaving Mal to face Shaan alone. He raised his sword and swung it hopefully at Shaan, but it fell well short of its target. Shaan continued to advance, closing the distance between him and Mal. Mal swung again, and this time Shaan met Mal's sword with his own. The huge broadsword, which had been Rani's, smashed through Mal's own blade and continued on its path, cutting through Mal's clothes, then his skin, and finally coming to rest buried deep in his bowels. Mal slumped forward, causing the blade to go deeper into his body. Shaan pulled the sword free and turned to follow Gant, leaving Mal to fall to the ground in a pool of his own blood.

Gant ran blindly through the mist, stumbling and then tripping over some unseen object on the floor.

"Curses," he thought and struggled to his feet.

He tried to run and found that he could not, as he had damaged his ankle in the fall. Gant limped and half-hopped as he tried to get to safety, but it was no use. He could hear Shaan gaining on him.

"Gant!" Shaan shouted with such force that Gant, almost involuntarily, stopped and turned to face him.

"It wasn't my idea." "Mal made me," Gant whimpered.

"I am going to kill you," Shaan growled.

"No. Please no," Gant begged. "Anything. I'll do anything."

"Then die," a voice from behind Gant said weakly.

Blood suddenly spurted from Gant's mouth, and the tip of a sword's blade appeared through his chest. Gant fell forward to reveal Rebecca, her hands shaking as she let the hilt of the sword slip from her grasp, allowing Gant to complete his fall to the ground.

"Rebecca!" Shaan shouted, dropping his sword, and running forward to sweep her into his arms. "Are you alright?"

"I am now," she proclaimed. "I am now."

While Rebecca bathed, Shaan and Jonathan removed the body of William and buried him in the woods, where Rebecca said that he had spent most of his free time. He loved the woods and the beauty that nature provided. Next, they took the bodies of Gant and Mal and their henchmen and burned them on a huge pyre along with all of their possessions. Rebecca did not want any trace of them left on her land.

Rebecca had not told Shaan all that had happened to her, fearing that he would no longer want her. She had scrubbed her body for an hour but still felt dirty, as if she would never remove the smell of Gant from her skin. She vowed that no man would ever have power over her again. This is what she swore on her life. She would learn to fight as well as any man. Better than any man.

When Shaan next saw her, she stood straight, shoulders back, was dressed not in an elegant gown, but in burgundy-coloured leather breeks and a waist coat, and had a sword strapped to her side, held in place by a thick studded belt.

"I want to be with you, Shaan. Always," she declared.

"And I you," Shaan replied, "but I cannot take you. Where I must go and what I must do will be very dangerous, and I am not even sure that I will survive."

"Then I will die with you," Rebecca said, and she meant it.

Shaan stared into Rebecca's eyes, reached out, and took her in his arms.

This time, when their lips met, Shaan did not pull away. It was time to stop living in the past and hoping for reconciliation with Giselle, for he knew in his heart, as he had always known, that this would not happen. It was time to start living for him again and to forge a new life out of the ashes of the past.

Rebecca, Shaan, and Johnathan rode back to the town, leaving Hetti in charge of the mansion. The staff, having been released from their captivity, would begin the task of cleaning up and returning the household to normal now that all the excitement was over.

As they rode down the main street of the town, it was clear that the townsfolk had not been slow in taking revenge on those who had betrayed them. Hanging from hastily erected scaffolds were the bodies of several men, one of whom Shaan recognised as the barman who had clubbed him as he had tried to rescue Hetti.

The people came running out to meet them, shouting gleefully as they did so.

"They are back", "the warriors return", and "the new lord is here."

Shaan did not understand the last shout and turned to Rebecca.

"What do they mean, the new lord is here? Who is that?" He enquired.

"It is Jonathan," she smiled. "He killed Rani; therefore, he is the new lord."

Jonathan laughed aloud. "Me, a lord," he laughed again. "Well, I never."

"They live by the warriors' code here," Rebecca explained. "Rani killed the old lord to become ruler, and now you killed him so...

"So, I am indeed Lord," Jonathan said in mock triumph. In reality, he did not want this; he preferred others deal with all this ruling business and let him get on with his life. "Well, let's see what privileges we get."

A man stepped from the crowd. "Welcome back, sir," he said,

looking at Jonathan. "A feast has been prepared for you and your companions."

He then led the three to a large house on the outskirts of the town that was the residence of whoever the lord was at the time.

The feast was one of the grandest that either Rebecca or Jonathan had seen. All of the townsfolk attended, and all had happiness written on their faces, for they were more than pleased to be under the rule of this newcomer now that Rani was out of the way.

All kinds of food were served, and the wine flowed like water. Dancers danced, jugglers juggled, and magicians performed tricks, many of which Shaan had been taught as a boy, but all the same, he laughed and pretended to be amazed with the rest.

During the feast, Shaan talked to many people. He had been interested to find out how one man had managed to overcome a whole town. As the story of Rani's arrival and how he challenged the old ruler to battle, and after that, how the townspeople tried to get rid of him, unfolded, Shaan began to think that maybe Rani had had supernatural powers. It seemed that no matter what traps or schemes the townsmen had thought up, Rani was always one step ahead. Never falling into a trap, always knowing who had tried to kill him and reeking revenge on them. But then again, how had Jonathan managed to kill him? Rani had been taken completely by surprise, and it had seemed almost too easy. Shaan then noticed a portrait of Rani in full battle dress. The trousers and jacket had leather straps inlaid with strips of metal wrapped around them, and on his head sat a steel helm. In his hands he held various weapons, and at this time all four were present.

Shaan had inquired as to why Rani had not worn this armor when he fought him and had been told that after the first few battles Rani had stopped wearing the armor, declaring that he did not need it to beat such weak people as these.

The crowds had gone now, and only Rebecca, Shaan, and Jonathan remained. They sat, relaxing, in one of the smaller rooms of the house.

Jonathan spoke to Shaan. "And where do we go from here?" It was a question to which Shaan had no answer.

"I think it is getting late and that we all need some rest," Shaan replied.

Jonathan looked at Shaan and then at Rebecca,

"Of course. I think I will retire now and leave you two alone."

"I did not mean..." Shaan started.

"Of course not," Johnathan winked at Rebecca, "but all the same, I am tired," and he rose and left the room, bidding the others goodnight.

Rebecca came over to where Shaan sat and settled into his lap, wrapping her arms around him.

"Are you tired?" She spoke softly.

"A little. I have had a hard day," he joked.

"Come then," she said, rising and taking Shaan's hand so that he followed her out of the room and up the stairs.

Rebecca led Shaan to one of the many bedrooms and took him inside.

"What do you think of this one?" She asked.

"It is the most beautiful in the house," Shaan replied. "I am sure that you will sleep well here."

Shaan turned to leave. "I will be in the next room if you need any..."

Rebecca put her hand to Shaan's lips to stop him, and without a word, she pulled him to her, enfolded him in her arms, and kissed him. They sank to the bed, their lips never parting.

"You can't talk to me like that," Marcus raged. "I am the Queen's brother."

"You couldn't even catch an old man," Moroc taunted. "Look at you, call yourself a warrior?"

Marcus turned with anger burning in his eyes. He reached down to where his sword hung.

"Go on. Just give me one excuse," Moroc snarled.

Marcus withdrew his hand. He knew that Moroc could easily beat him and decided that it would be best to get back at him in another way, and besides, there was no one else in the room to see that he had backed down.

"Where is Krishia anyway?"

"She is resting," Moroc answered. "We have to make our way directly to Taal and take the tower."

"And when will our Queen decide to join us?" Marcus said sarcastically.

"When she is ready," Moroc shot Marcus a warning glance. He should be careful without Krishia here to protect him.

Sophia put her hand into the bag and pulled out a rune. Wyrd, the blank stone It was the seventh time that she had pulled this stone from the many others in the bag in seven attempts. Wyrd, the stone of fate, Wyrd is the stone of destiny. The fate of mankind had been decided, and nothing could alter that now. Sophia had no way of knowing which side would win, but now she knew that certain wheels had been set in motion and that certain paths were going to cross.

Shaan had awoken in Rebecca's arms. Carefully, he rose from

the bed so as not to wake her. He dressed quietly and left Rebecca to sleep. It was clear that she needed it after all she had been through.

He wandered the corridors of the house seeking Jonathan. Looking inside many of the rooms, he was nowhere to be found. One door attracted Shaan's attention more than the others. The door had a plaque on it, on which a strange design had been inscribed. Shaan pushed open the door and stepped into the room. This was without doubt the armory. Hanging from the walls were all manner of weapons and shields, likely the trophies of Rani's battles, Shaan decided. Then he saw it, at the far end of the room was Rani's armor, lying on a bench of gold.

Shaan ran his fingers over the armor. How cleverly it had been made. Each leather strap had been inlaid with a band of steel, just as Shaan had seen in the portrait. The straps had been sewn on to the clothes at precise angles, which would deflect any incoming blade and turn it away from the body. The design of the jacket meant that there were no visible gaps through which a blade could pass, and the collar on the jacket was high to protect the neck, and this, as well, had a steel band running around it. The helm itself was made of a metal that Shaan did not recognise and was designed to fully protect the head. Shaan tried it on and peered out through the eye slits. It felt comfortable and seemed to be a perfect fit.

At that moment, Jonathan entered the room, saw Shaan wearing the Helm, and thought to himself, "I might have known where to find you."

Shaan turned to Jonathan. "Well, you were right."

"What do you mean? Right about what?" Jonathan asked.

"About me being here," Shaan replied.

Johnathan shook his head and thought, "What kind of magic is this?" "Now he reads minds."

"How do you do that?" Shaan asked.

"Do what?" Jonathan looked puzzled.

"Speak without moving your lips."

"I am not," Jonathan replied, and he wondered, "Am I losing my mind?"

"No, you are perfectly sane, my friend, but, it is a great talent that you have," Shaan's smile was hidden by the helmet.

"What talent? and how did you know what I was thinking?" Jonathan was getting angry now at the game that Shaan was playing. "If he does not stop, then I am going to flatten him," he thought to himself.

"There is no need for us to fight," Shaan said. "I only said you had a great talent."

"Behind you, quick," Jonathan thought.

Shaan span around, ready to defend himself, but there was no one there.

"In the name of God, you can read minds."

Shaan turned back to Johnathan , pulled off the helm, and threw it to the floor.

"No wonder Rani could never be tricked. The helm has some strange powers. I could hear your voice without you speaking," Shaan said as he stepped back from the place where the helm lay.

"So that's what Gaius was on about," Jonathan said. "This must be the Helm of Othus".

"What's that?" Shaan looked puzzled.

"Gaius said that you were looking for some artefacts and that one of them would let you know your enemy's plans. I thought that he referred to a map or some similar object, but now I understand. This is it, Shaan. The object you need from this realm"

Johnathan reached down and took the Helm of Othus and held it out for Shaan.

Shaan refused to take it. "No," he brushed past Jonathan and out of the door.

On reaching the bedroom that he had slept in the night before; he noticed that Rebecca had awakened and was sitting up. He ran to the bed and put his arms around her.

"Can you swim?" He asked.

"Yes, I can. Why do you ask?" was the reply.

Back at the lake in the grounds of Rebecca's mansion, three figures dove into the clear water and swam down to the entrance to a very special cave.

CHAPTER TEN

"So, it is true," Rebecca said, running her hands along the smooth surface of the round table.

"I thought my lungs were about to burst," puffed Jonathan, and he gave Shaan a slap on the back.

"Are you warm enough?" Shaan looked at Rebecca, where water was dripping from every part of her clothing.

"I feel alive and refreshed," she replied, tossing back her head, and sending a shower of tiny droplets of water cascading across the table.

"What's this?" Rebecca asked, her eyes coming to rest on the shield.

"This is the shield of Lady Bella," Shaan picked it up and looked into the beautiful face. "Hello, my lady."

The shield said nothing but stared back at Shaan. He knew that she would not talk in front of the others. Not yet anyway.

Shaan replaced the shield on the table. The hunter put the two sacks he had been carrying on the floor and sat on the table, his hands resting on his thighs.

"I don't suppose you have any dry clothing, do you?" He quizzed Shaan.

Shaan looked down at himself. His clothes were in rags, and the bandages around his many wounds were torn and stained.

"We must be moving on; time is running out," Shaan said, and he began walking towards one of the entrances.

"Not that way. Follow me!" Johnathan had jumped to his feet and was heading off in another direction.

Rebecca stood watching the others. "Well, one of you make a decision."

"Why that way?" Shaan asked.

"Why not?" Johnathan replied. "Come on," and then he was off at full pace down the passageway.

Shaan looked at Rebecca, shrugged his shoulders, and followed.

The Countess ran to catch Shaan, slipped her hand into his, and together they strolled, like two teenage lovers, after the hunter.

When they emerged from the caves, it was spitting with rain, but the sun could be seen peeking through the thin clouds, and it was clear that it would not be raining for long. The crunching of their footsteps on the gravel reminded Shaan of the sound of a marching army, and as they slipped between the giant granite slabs, he thought of battles past, both won and lost. Rebecca's voice woke him from his daydream.

"Where are we?" she asked.

Jonathan was about to answer her when Shaan spread his arms wide, turned to face her, and announced in a loud voice.

"Welcome to Aidenvalle," and a huge smile crossed his face. He looked around at Jonathan. "Why here?"

"You need rest and medicine. We need food and dry clothes. Where else could we be sure of finding them?" And he smiled at Shaan. "And... Gaius told me that I must bring you here."

"Why would Gaius want me here?" Shaan said as much to himself as to Jonathan.

"That I do not know, but it must be important whatever it is," Jonathan replied.

"I guess we will find out soon enough," Shaan said as he marched off down the slope and waded across the shallow stream.

The others followed, and after a while they all emerged out of the forest and into a green meadow. The rain had stopped now, and the sun shone down as if to greet them. In the near distance, they could see the building where Shaan's adventures had begun. A short while later, they were there. Pushing open the great wooden doors, they stepped inside and were immediately greeted by two of the staff.

"Welcome back, sire. Gaius awaits you," one said, leading the three to a room off to one side of the entrance hall. The maid opened the door and ushered them inside.

The pointed face looked up as they entered, and the amber eyes sparkled like those of a child upon seeing a particular toy that it wished to play with.

"Shaan," the figure in black proclaimed as if taken by surprise, and then a smile appeared as he continued. "You look terrible."

"Nice to see you too, Gaius," Shaan said, not in the least offended as he realised that he must indeed be a frightful sight.

"Johnathan ," Gaius nodded towards the hunter, "and?"

"The Countess Rebecca of Patreaux," Rebecca said, announcing herself with a small bow.

Gaius nodded again but said nothing. He looked across at Shaan.

"We need to speak, alone," Gaius said, and he spoke to the maid who was still at the door. "Show our guests to their rooms and have some food prepared," he ordered.

The maid curtsied. "Sir," she replied, and then to Rebecca and Jonathan, "This way, please."

When Shaan and Gaius were alone, Gaius's expression darkened.

"How are things going, Shaan?"

Shaan held out some of the shredded pieces of his shirt. "Same as always," and he gave Gaius a little smile. "It will be alright. I have a good feeling about this."

"She is very pretty."

"Gaius!" Shaan seemed surprised. "I did not think that you noticed such things."

"Do not lose your way, Shaan," Gaius warned.

"She helps me, Gaius. She is my reason now. She cleared my mind, and now I know why I fight and why I must succeed. I think I love her, Gaius."

"And Giselle?" Gaius stared at Shaan. There was a long, awkward pause.

"Why were you not at our wedding, Gaius?"

"I think you already know that. I tried to warn you, but you were so full of this, love, that you were blind, and I did not want to see the destruction of your world," Gaius leaned towards Shaan and pointed a finger at him. "I'll not let you do that again."

"You mean Rebecca?"

"I do not know yet, but if I find that she means you harm, then I will have no option but to act this time," Gaius rose to his feet. "But this is not why I had Jonathan bring you here."

"I already know that," Shaan said.

"I have to show you something," Gaius motioned for Shaan to follow him. Through the twisting corridors and down a spiral staircase they went, eventually arriving outside a door marked with a wooden cross.

Gaius took Shaan by the shoulders and looked into his eyes. "In here is something that I should have shown you years ago, and now it is too late."

"Too late for what?" Shaan asked.

Gaius said nothing, but quietly and gently opened the door. Shaan stepped through.

The room was plainly decorated and had bare walls. Against one wall was a bed, and on the bed lay a man. Shaan stared at the man, who stared back.

"So, we meet at last," the man said weakly; a wheezing cough followed his words.

Shaan tried to answer but could not, for the sight before him had rendered him speechless. On the bed lay a man who was the exact image of Shaan.

"Daegal," Shaan whispered the name. He looked closer at the man and then turned to stare at Gaius, again unable to speak.

"Yes, it is Prince Daegal," Gaius paused, "your brother."

"My brother?" Shaan could not believe this. Was he dreaming?

"A long time ago, when the world was young, I knew that a king would be born of magic. A king who would unite a country A man asked that I grant him a wish, and in return, I commanded that what was conceived of that magic would be mine. That man was Prethius. I had expected a boy, but Egraine brought forth twins. Not knowing which was the chosen one, I took them both, and in order to ensure that one survived, they were separated. You were fostered by Ector, and Daegal by Ulric."

"Why did you not tell me, Gaius?" Shaan asked.

"You had a destiny to fulfill."

Shaan kneeled on one knee beside Daegal. "If only I had known."

"We would have been great friends, you and I," Daegal said quietly, his voice straining to get the words out.

"Yes, yes, we would." It was plain to Shaan that Daegal was dying.

Daegal closed his eyes and lay his head on the soft pillow. Shaan looked at Gaius, who said nothing but shook his head slowly from side to side. Shaan rose and led Gaius outside the room.

"Save him, Gaius," Shaan begged.

"I cannot," Gaius replied.

"But you saved me. There must be a way, Gaius."

"No. When I saved you, it nearly cost me my life. I told you, Shaan, I have no magic left. I am weak, and it will take a long time before I am strong again. It was all I could do to bring him here after he was mortally wounded in his fight with the Chrysak." Gaius gazed at Shaan; his eyes seemingly alight with fire.

"You are the last now, Shaan."

"The last what?" Shaan was puzzled.

"The last son of light. The last son born of magic. The last hope for mankind," Gaius said as he raised his arms high in the air. A ball of bright light flew from Gaius's fingertips and struck Shaan, and then Gaius was gone.

"Gaius. Gaius!" Shaan looked all around him, but his mentor had vanished.

Shaan could no longer feel any pain from his injuries, and he quickly pulled back one of the bandages. All traces of damage were gone. It was as if he had never been in a battle. He felt as if he had slept for a week and was completely refreshed.

"Gaius, what have you done?" he wondered. Rushing back into the room, he could see Daegal lying still on the bed. Hardly daring to touch him, Shaan reached out. The body was cold, and Shaan knew that Daegal had died. Shaan closed his eyes and prayed for his lost sibling.

"Now I fight for two, my brother," Shaan pledged.

Rebecca and Johnathan were eating when Shaan entered the room. Rebecca could see that Shaan was clearly disturbed.

"What's wrong?" she asked.

"Nothing. We must leave in the morning," Shaan said solemnly.

"You're the boss," Jonathan waved a chicken leg at Shaan. "Come, eat."

Shaan sat opposite Rebecca and rested his elbows on the table.

Rebecca reached across and took hold of Shaan's hand. It was cold to the touch. "You seem troubled," she commented.

Shaan squeezed her hand but remained quiet.

Marcus brushed aside the flap on Moroc's tent and stepped inside.

"How long before we make it to Taal?" He asked.

"A few more days, if we do not meet any more resistance," Moroc answered.

"Good. I will go and see Sophia and find out what the runes have to say."

"We don't need advice from her," and after a pause, "besides, I have not seen her in days," Moroc said.

"Where is she?" Marcus demanded.

"She said she was going to meditate in the hills. Who knows with these witches?" Moroc said sarcastically.

"And you let her go?"

"I have more important things to think about," Moroc shot back. "Come. Learn," he beckoned to Marcus.

Moroc led Marcus into another section of his tent. A map was spread out on a table.

"What's this?" Marcus asked.

"This," Moroc spread his hands over the map. "This is the key to victory. From this map, we can see not only the location of Taal but also its strengths and weaknesses. The best positions for our weapons and the ideal place to draw them out for a battle," and at this he slammed his fist onto the icon of the tower. "I have them now."

In the great hall, the Jarenn sat at the crystal table. Legend had it that the table had been carved from a single emerald of immense size. The table itself measured ten feet in diameter, and a strange green fire seemed to emanate from its core. The walls of the hall were also made of crystal, only this was clear, and the light from the table danced and swam within, giving the hall an eerie glow.

"Dragons have been extinct for a thousand years," a soldier was saying.

"I know what I saw," Daal argued. "I may be old, but I am not senile."

"Maybe some other beast, perhaps a Griffin?" the man suggested.

"Fifty feet long and spitting fire?" Saris entered the conversation. "It was no Griffin."

Just then a man, even older than Daal, entered the room, and all became quiet. This was Ling Chuan, believed by many to be at least three hundred years old.

"It would appear that we have quite a problem here," Ling Chuan stroked at his long beard that came almost to his waist. His hair, like his beard, was silver gray, and he wore the ceremonial robes that befitted his position. His clothes were green, as with the other Jarenn, but had strange black designs woven into the fabric. Around his waist was a golden sash.

"Jason and Benn, take your men and set up the perimeter defenses. Hulum and Nasim, you are in control of internal operations. Perus, you take care of the zones. If they make a breakthrough or we are attacked in another realm, then you must seal the entrances any way you can. We must not allow

Krishia to enter any realm but her own."

The commands were given, and Ling Chuan settled into his seat at the table. The commanders rushed to their tasks, and men hurried after. When the room had again become quiet, Ling Chuan stood and addressed the remaining Jarenn.

"Many of you have never seen a battle before, let alone fought in one. To those of you who are young and just emerging into manhood, I say it is perfectly honorable to be afraid. The older warriors, those who have been to war, are no doubt already afraid. This is natural. It helps us cope with the stress that our bodies now feel. The fire burning within each of you now reaches a peak, and we must use this fire to consume all that opposes us. We will succeed; we must succeed, for the fate of all of humanity rests with us."

With this, a huge cheer rang around the room as Jarenn after Jarenn rose to his feet, each man chanting his sacred name. "Jarenn. Jarenn. Jarenn."

The night had turned cold, and Rebecca had pressed her body close to Shaan's in order to keep warm. He had been quiet all night and refused to tell Rebecca what troubled him. Now as he slept, she watched him, as if guarding him from whatever danger threatened. She wiped the beads of perspiration from his forehead as he tossed this way and that, and all at once he sat up in bed crying "No," then immediately laid down and fell back into his tormented sleep.

It seemed that she had not slept at all that night, and as the sun rose, Shaan's eyes flickered open, and she pulled him to her, kissing him gently and enfolding him in her arms.

"I love you," she whispered in his ear.

"Will you wait for me?" he whispered back.

"No. I'll not wait," she replied. "I am coming with you. We will not be parted again."

"It is too dangerous," he cautioned.

"I am still coming," she said, then put her hand to Shaan's lips to stop him from arguing further and ran her free hand through his hair.

Jonathan had risen early and had already packed provisions for the coming journey. He was eating a large breakfast when Rebecca and Shaan joined him.

"Good morning. Sleep well?" he inquired.

"Do you ever stop eating?" Shaan teased.

"I must keep my strength up, and besides, we don't know when our next good meal will be."

Shaan and Rebecca joined in the meal, and the three made polite conversation as they ate. After breakfast, they bade the staff farewell and set off for the caves on foot, not wanting to abandon their horses in the forest and all deciding that it would be unwise for one of the staff to follow them in order to return the horses.

In the cave, Shaan marked the table opposite the entrance where they had come in. He now knew where all but two of the exits went.

"Which way now?" asked Jonathan.

"I think the left," Shaan replied. It did not really matter; both would need to be taken in time anyway.

They all proceeded down the passage that Jonathan had indicated and, on reaching the entrance, came to a halt.

"After you," Shaan joked.

"Why me? You're not scared, are you?" Jonathan made a sweeping bow and motioned Shaan forward.

"Not at all, but if it's another lake, I would rather you swim back in and tell us first. That last one came as a bit of a surprise, I can tell you."

Jonathan walked through the mouth of the cave only to re-emerge a few moments later.

"The water's fine, come on in," he smiled, then disappeared again.

"After you, my lady," Shaan said to Rebecca.

"Why, thank you, good sir," she replied with a mock curtsey.

Finally, Shaan himself walked through into the next realm, and when he did, he could not believe his eyes. The sky was orange, and, with a loud crackle, huge sheets of lightning passed by overhead every few seconds.

"What kind of magic is this?" he asked no one in particular.

"It's beautiful," Rebecca stood, transfixed by the wondrous scene before her, "I have never witnessed such a sight in my life."

"Nor I," Shaan said.

It was a long time before they felt able to pull their eyes away from the sky and begin their journey into this strange land.

CHAPTER ELEVEN

The view stretching out before them was as beautiful as it was daunting. Reaching upwards towards the sky on both sides were the mountains, unclimbable, their sheer faces rising for hundreds of feet. Ahead lay a rocky path, the red dusty floor trailing off into the distance as far as the eye could see.

"I guess we do not have a choice of direction here," Jonathan was the first to speak; even so, he still stared up at the strange vision above him.

"We may as well move on. I think we have a long journey ahead of us," Shaan said, looking down at the bags that Johnathan carried. "How long will the supplies last?"

"Three days at best. I did not think that we would have trouble finding some source of food," Jonathan replied. "Shall we return to Aidenvalle for more supplies?"

"No, we do not have the time," Shaan said, taking one of the bags from Jonathan, which he slung over his shoulder and then set off along the dusty path. "You coming?" he called to the others.

It was two hours later when Shaan came to a halt. The view ahead had not changed, and if it had not been for the cave's entrance receding in the distance, they would have sworn that they had not moved one step.

"We should rest for a while," Shaan said, dropping his bag to the floor.

"About time too," Jonathan sighed.

Rebecca had already seated herself on a smooth, flat rock that lay by the side of the path. She had not complained, but it was clear to the others that she was not used to this prolonged trekking. She wiped her brow on the sleeve of her blouse. The white material darkened as the sweat was removed from her forehead. Next, she removed her leather waistcoat and lay back against the smooth wall of the cliff face. Closing her eyes, she imagined the comfortable surroundings she had left behind. There was no going back; she knew that, but it was nice to imagine.

Shaan came and sat next to her. "Hot?"

"Just a little." Rebecca smiled at him. "I am getting a bit tired of the view, though."

"I know what you mean," Shaan replied, staring off into the distance. "I am sure that I can see a slight curve in the path ahead. What do you think?"

Rebecca looked, straining to peer through the vapor of heat rising off the track. Then she too noticed what Shaan had seen.

"I think you're right."

Johnathan had pulled a skin of water from his bag and was taking a drink. After he had had a couple of mouthfuls, he inserted the plug and tossed the skin to Shaan, who handed it to Rebecca, and having taken a drink, she handed it back to Shaan. When both had drunk enough, the skin was tossed back to Jonathan, who returned it to his bag. They rested without conversation, all three still looking in wonder at the incredible sky. A short while later, they were again making their way down the never-ending path. It was an hour later before anyone spoke.

"You were right, the path is beginning to bend," Rebecca said to Shaan.

Sure enough, there was a definite change in the track's direction. It was gently curving away to the left. The rock face had changed too; it seemed to be getting lower, and Shaan was sure that the sides were not so steep. Another hour had passed, and the track's curve had become so severe that for the first time, Shaan could not see what was ahead.

It was time to rest again, and as they sat, they speculated on what they would find.

A low rumbling noise suddenly came to their ears, and Rebecca turned to Shaan.

"What's that?" She asked.

"I do not know. I can't tell where it is coming from," Shaan replied.

The rumble echoed off the surrounding cliff faces. It grew louder, and this time the floor beneath them began to vibrate.

"What's happening?" Rebecca asked with urgency in her voice.

"Come on. Hurry!" Johnathan had grabbed Rebecca by the hand and was pulling her along the shaky path with Shaan in hot pursuit.

As they ran, they were showered with dust and stones descending from all around them. The rumble turned to a roar, and the stones turned to rocks, and as they ran, they looked up. The cliffs themselves seemed to be shaking with terror at this great sound, and they cast larger and larger pieces of debris onto the fleeing trio. A bolder smashed into Shaan, sending him sprawling to the floor, but he was up and running again in a second; there was no time for feeling pain at the moment. With a great crack, a large section of stone, twenty meters in length, broke away from the cliff and came hurtling towards them.

"Let's go, come on!" Jonathan shouted as he quickened his pace.

The others had not needed this advice and had also sped up. With seconds to spare, they made it to relative safety as the huge slab crashed down only meters behind them.

"That was too close," Jonathan panted, as they ran on.

"I can't go much further," Rebecca was breathing hard, her heart beating fast.

"Just a little more," Shaan said. "Listen."

The roar had returned to a rumble, and even this was subsiding now. The rocks had turned back to dust, and the three slowed their pace.

"I think it's over," Shaan said at last after having drawn in several deep breaths.

"You're right," Jonathan confirmed. "You alright? I thought you had it when that boulder struck."

Shaan looked down at himself. "I would appear to be."

Rebecca was leaning up against the rocky wall, sucking in as much oxygen as she could.

"Am I glad I met you two?" she said sarcastically. "Beats weaving any day."

The men laughed at this, and Rebecca joined in, but only for a few seconds before she became quiet. She raised her arm and pointed.

"Look," was all she could say.

The others turned to face the direction in which Rebecca now pointed. In the distance stood a building, but this was no ordinary structure. It was by far the largest that any of them had seen. Even from this range, it was a magnificent sight. The huge dome that was its center arched hundreds of feet into the air, and high towers that seemed to touch the sky rose from the ground on all sides. From these, walkways stretched out to join the main structure. The perimeter of the building's grounds seemed to be shimmering, as if light reflected from a mirror.

"I guess we know where the trail goes to now," Johnathan said.

"I have a bad feeling about this," Shaan said, taking a step towards the building as if this would make the view clearer.

"How can anything so beautiful cause us harm?" Rebecca said, and she took off down the track.

"Women!" Jonathan said, and set off after her.

Shaan followed on, carefully studying the surrounding cliffs. He was sure that he had seen movement in the shadows a little way ahead. He caught up to Jonathan and expressed his fears.

"I have not noticed anything, and I am sure I would have," Jonathan whispered back. Even so, he decided to be extra vigilant from now on.

An hour later, they realised that they had been wrong about the building. It was not hundreds of feet high; it was at least a thousand, and they were still an hour's walk away.

Krishia lay on a bed of soft down covered with sheets of the purest silk. She did not move, apart from the slow rising and falling of her chest as she breathed. The handmaidens, specially chosen, tended to her needs as she slept. Cleansing her skin and fanning her body so that it stayed cool. Ten guards had been posted at the door, and none but the handmaids were allowed to enter the chamber, not even Marcus.

"I must see the queen," he demanded, but the guards did not reply, nor did they move away so that he could pass.

"You know who I am. Let me pass, now!" Still, the guards failed to react. They just eyed him, and Marcus knew that if he had tried to push his way through, he would have been cut down as if he had been a peasant.

"You are all imbeciles, and I will see to it that you lose your heads when Krishia awakes." Marcus raged as he stormed off. He had not travelled all this way to be treated like this. Yes, they would all pay.

As he rushed through the corridors, he came across two female servants.

"You two, come with me; I have need of some entertainment."

The servants giggled and followed Marcus to his room.

Shaan stared into the blue and white sparks that flew from post to post. This was the strange, shimmering light that they had noticed. From a distance, it had appeared solid, but now they could see that the effect had been caused by this strange phenomenon. Jonathan reached out, then thought better of it. Picking up a rock, he tossed it into the sparks, and with a small flash it was gone.

"A magic wall of some kind, we will not be able to go this way," he said.

He had not been surprised or shocked; he had seen a great many strange things during his travels, and this was just one more.

The valley had widened, and it was possible to walk around the perimeter of the building, or at least as far as they could tell, for it curved away as far as the eye could see. They started to work their way along the boundary, hoping to find a way inside the wall, and they had not moved far when a scurrying noise caught their attention. As one, they turned towards the source of the noise, but all that they saw (as an indication of what had made the sound) were a few particles of debris falling to the ground behind them. Again, the scurrying was heard, only this time coming from the opposite direction. They turned to face the new noise, but again, there was no visual evidence.

"Whatever it is, it's all around us," said Jonathan as he pulled an arrow from its quiver and made ready to fire.

Shaan and Rebecca drew their swords and assumed defensive stances. Then the whole valley became alive with noise as a hundred voices called their battle cries and every ledge and outcrop of the surrounding mountains became crowded with moving figures, whose shadows neither Shaan nor Jonathan could make out.

"We have company," Jonathan said.

"That's very perceptive of you," Rebecca shot back. "Now tell us something we don't know."

"I don't see you coming up with any bright ideas," Jonathan retorted.

"This is no time to argue," Shaan interrupted. "This way," said Shaan, and he was off, running along the dusty track.

The others chased after him, but as they did so, more and more figures appeared above them. Long ropes now cascaded down the cliff face, and the black figures followed like spiders, landing silently before taking up positions surrounding the trio.

"What do we do now?" Johnathan asked, not expecting a reply.

As if in answer to the question, the black figures drew their weapons and advanced. Shaan could still not make out what creature attacked, as they were dressed from head to toe in black cloth and masks hid their faces. If he was going to die, then he wanted to know what had killed him.

"We mean you no harm," he said, as if he thought the three of them stood any chance at all against so many.

With that, the attackers raised their weapons and charged, howling like banshees, and Shaan, Jonathan, and Rebecca prepared to die. Suddenly, from behind them, there was a crackling noise followed by a loud pop and a voice calling. "Quick. This way."

Shaan risked a look behind him. An archway, framed by blue light, had appeared in the wall. The voice again called. "Run."

Without thinking what or who was behind the wall, they ran, half stumbling, half falling, through the archway with death at their heels. As the last one made it through, with a pop, the archway was gone. Shaan could see the black figures on the other side of the wall, but they made no attempt to breach it; obviously, they knew what powers the wall had.

"We do not get many visitors," a gravelly voice said.

Shaan looked up into the eyes of their rescuer, or rather, would have done if this had been possible. The face that he now stared at had a nose, mouth, and ears but no eyes. Where these should have been, there was just smooth skin. This person had not lost his eyes; he had never had any in the first place.

"Do not fear; you are perfectly safe while the shield wall is up."

"The what?" Shaan asked.

"The shield wall," the man replied. "You just came through it."

"Who are they?" Shaan pointed at the shadowy figures through the wall. Then he realised how stupid he was being; after all, the man could not see what he was pointing at.

"They are the Myrina. The cursed ones," the gravelly voice said. "I am surprised that you made it through. Come now, we must go inside."

A great door marked the entrance to the building, reaching many meters into the air. As they approached the door, it opened, not swinging inward as Shaan had expected but sliding to one side.

"Welcome to Elendor. I am Tramen."

"I am Shaan, and this is the Countess Rebecca."

"Rebecca," Tramen interrupted. "And the hunter, Jonathan. Yes, I know."

"You know?" Shaan repeated.

"Of course. "Now may I offer you some refreshment?"

"How do you know?" Shaan asked.

"That is not important," Tramen added. "Now, some refreshment?" and he ushered the three towards another door.

While Shaan talked to Tramen, Rebecca and Jonathan took

time to look at them. The room they were in stretched away into the distance, and they could just about make out the far side. The walls curved upwards and out, and from these, at strange angles, jutted structures and gantries that were possibly more rooms. In the center of the room was a pedestal, and from it an orange glow emanated, but they could not make out what was on the pedestal from this distance.

"What is that in the center of the room?" Rebecca asked.

"Truth" was all that Tramen said in reply.

Tramen led them into another room and told them to wait. The room was furnished with large, comfortable chairs and low tables made from a material that Shaan did not recognize. He ran his hand along one smooth surface.

"What do you make of this?" he said.

Both Rebecca and Jonathan studied the table.

"It's not wood or metal, that's for sure," Rebecca commented.

"It's like nothing I have ever seen," Jonathan added. "And have you noticed something strange about the room?"

"No, what?" Shaan looked around, but everything seemed normal.

"No windows," Jonathan said.

"I still do not follow what you mean."

It was Rebecca who picked up on the clue. "There are no windows, but it is still light in here."

"Exactly. It's light in here, but there are no lamps or candles burning."

"Then where is the light coming from?" Shaan asked.

Jonathan looked up. "Look, the whole ceiling glows, more magic?"

"This is indeed a strange place," Shaan said quietly.

At that moment, the door slid open, and drinks were brought

in. The tray held out to Shaan contained three glasses, each filled with a yellow liquid, and though he was not sure what the liquid was, he took a glass anyway.

"Thank you, Tramen," he said.

"I am not Tramen. I am Risanne."

"I am sorry. Thank you, Risanne," Shaan said. "Are you Tramens' brother?"

"No. Why do you ask?" Risanne was puzzled by Shaan's question.

"You look like you could be twins."

"Twins, what are twins?" Risanne asked.

"Never mind." Shaan could tell that he was getting nowhere with this conversation.

Rebecca and Jonathan each took a glass, and Risanne gave a slight nod and left the room.

"Was that my imagination?" Shaan looked at the others and rubbed his chin.

"If it was, then I have gone mad also," Rebecca said. "I could have sworn that that was Tramen."

"Stranger and stranger," Jonathan remarked thoughtfully. He sniffed at his drink. "Smells good."

"After you," Rebecca raised her glass to Jonathan.

"Good health," Jonathan upended his glass and drained its contents. "Tastes as good as it looks."

Shaan took a sip of his drink. "Not bad," and he, too, emptied his glass. Rebecca lifted hers to her lips and tipped the liquid into her mouth. As she did so, she noticed Jonathan wince and then fall to the floor.

The army of Bastion had set up camp within sight of the tower of Taal. Saris looked out on them from the top of the tower. Through the scope, he could see clearly into the heart of the enemy base. They were perhaps an hour's march from Taal, and Saris knew that the time had come. He left the lookout post and made his way inside the tower. Passing many landings, which marked the different levels of the tower, he eventually arrived at the ground floor. In a room adjacent to the stairs, he found Daal.

"I must leave now," Saris said.

"They are here already?" Daal asked.

"They are here."

"I am glad; I hate waiting." Daal put his arms around Saris. "Take care, my son."

"I will, Father, do not worry; I will be back soon," Saris promised, and he turned and left the room.

He had never known his father worry for his safety before. After all, had his father not taught him all that he knew? Had his father not made him the best of the Jarenn?

In the courtyard, his comrades waited, already in their saddles. Saris mounted his horse, pulled on the reins, and steered his way through the gateway and towards the Bastion camp. Ten Jarenn warriors followed after. From the ground, they could not see the camp as it was hidden by the low hills that surrounded the tower. This was to be to their advantage, as the enemy would not be expecting an attack. Indeed, had it been the other way around, no doubt the Bastion army would be preparing to defend from within the safety of the tower. Ling Chuan had known this, which was why he had ordered the attack to take place. Saris did not know why he had volunteered for what was obviously a suicide mission; he only knew that it had been the right thing to do. The others were all volunteers, and they all knew their fate. Saris took his squad along the planned route that would lead them behind their target. It was when they arrived at their destination that he spoke for the first time.

"I hope Jason and Benn are all set up," he said to the nearest member of his group.

"I also" was the reply.

Saris brought his horse to a halt and addressed his men.

"You all know what to do." "We cannot fail here, for the future of all will be decided on how well we perform."

"Saris," a young Jarenn spoke, "I am proud to fight alongside you."

The man was called Hal, and he was the son of Saris' best friend. He was also Saris' personal student. Saris nodded but did not reply directly to Hal.

"All of you will be remembered forever for your deeds today. Remember who you are and what you represent, and may the gods receive your spirits," then he drew his sword, held it high in the air, and with a loud battle cry, he kicked his horse on. "Jarennnn."

Moroc was emerging from his tent when he heard the cry, and he turned to face the direction from where it came.

"What's this?" He raged. "To arms, to arms."

The Bastion army had only set up camp two hours ago after a day's forced march and was not expecting to be attacked. Its soldiers ran this way and that, taking arms from where they were stacked, but for some, it would be too late. Saris' men came storming into view, ten against a thousand, but they had the advantage of surprise, and the flaming balls of oil-soaked cloth that whirled around their heads were sent spinning deep into the heart of the camp. Tents flared up as the balls struck home, and fire quickly spread as the flames leapt from one piece of cloth to another. Due to the location of the camp and its huge population, the tents had been positioned close to each other, and it was now clear that this had been a very bad idea.

The enemy army was in disarray, unsure whether to attack the invaders or put out the raging fires. With every second of indecision, Saris and his men wreaked more havoc. Moroc was rushing this way and that, trying to bring some order to the chaos.

"What are you doing?" he shouted. "Kill them," and to another group, "Pull the tents down, make a fire break."

Saris' men brought their swords into play, slashing in all directions, cutting the enemy down, slicing heads and limbs from bodies. The ease of their attack was at an end as they had reached a part of the camp that was not ablaze, and the bastion here was prepared for them. The first Jarenn killed was shot in the neck by a well-aimed arrow; the second by a spear in the side. Another's horse was swept from under him as its legs were taken from it by two long blades wielded by a pair of huge warriors, who then moved in to finish its rider, and a particularly acrobatic warrior had leapt up behind one Jarenn and slit his throat as he tried to escape.

"Let's go. Come on!" Saris shouted, and the remaining Jarenn spurred their horses towards the border of the camp, braving the stabbing and shooting of a hundred Bastion weapons as they did so. When they emerged from the camp, only three remained, and these struck out for Taal, leaving the camp in uproar behind them.

"The lookouts, where were the lookouts?" Moroc was incensed. "Bring Captain Derrey to me."

A few minutes later, Derrey was standing before Moroc.

"Explain." One word from Moroc had the captain trembling.

"Well, sir, there were a few lookouts."

"A few. "A few!" Moroc stormed.

"You said that they would not attack," the captain spat back, and then wished he had not.

Moroc's blade flashed from its scabbard, and in an instance, the captain's head lay on the floor.

"Anyone else who cannot do their job?" Moroc growled, "Now clear this mess up."

Saris, Hal, and Brett rode at full speed, but they were making no headway against the chasing pack. Twelve Bastion horse soldiers had managed to mount up during the chaos and were in hot pursuit, and in another few minutes they would be on top of the Jarenn. Hal chanced a glance over his shoulder.

"We are not going to make it, my friends," he shouted above the clatter of the horses' pounding hooves.

"Just a little while longer," Saris shouted back.

"I don't think we have much time," Hal replied.

"There, beyond that outcrop," Saris pointed ahead.

In an instant, they had passed the rocks, followed closely by the chasing pack. Then, as the pursuers passed the outcrop, there was a great swishing sound, and two saplings sprang upright from where they had been tied, the wire strung between them decapitating the leading four riders. A hail of arrows quickly dispatched all but one of the others; this remaining man had been thrown to the floor as his horse had reared at the sound of the trees being released from their bonds. In seconds, he was surrounded by green-clad Jarenn with a blade held at his throat.

"What shall we do with this one?"

"Finish him," Jason said.

"No, wait," said Saris, who had turned his horse and had now joined his comrades.

"You're getting soft, Saris," it was Benn talking this time.

"No. I think we should let him return to his people with a message," Saris said.

"What do you have in mind?" Jason asked.

CHAPTER TWELVE

Tramen and Risanne entered the room and walked over to where the prone figures lay. Taking hold of Jonathan's arms and legs, they carried his unconscious body from the room. When the door had slid shut behind them, Rebecca's eyes flickered open. She scrambled her way over to where Shaan lay.

"Shaan, can you hear me? We have to get out of here." She whispered.

Shaan did not respond; the drug had worked well. Rebecca rolled him over and tried to wake him, but she could not. At that moment, she heard footsteps approaching the door; she rushed back to her previous position and lay down with her eyes shut. The door opened, and the two men reappeared, this time taking hold of Shaan before disappearing again. Rebecca knew that if she was to escape, it had to be now. Jumping to her feet, she ran over to the door, stopping a few paces from it. She studied the door and its surround, but there was no handle. How did it open? She knew she had to work fast, but how was she going to escape? She reached out and walked towards the door. To her surprise, it opened, sliding silently aside. Rebecca dashed to one side, fearing that Tramen was about to come in. After a few seconds, she took a gamble and peered outside; there was no one in sight. Rebecca slipped out of the door and around the corner. From here, she could see the main entrance, and she was just about to make a run for it when it began to open. There was only one thing for it. Rebecca ran down the nearest corridor, hoping to gain some time to think. From in front of her, she could hear footsteps. What to do now? She headed for the door opposite to where she stood and prayed it would open in the same way as the others. It did. She entered the room, and the door slid closed. The footsteps drew closer, passed the door, and faded away down the corridor.

Looking around the room, Rebecca saw that she was in some kind of office. Boxes were piled in stacks around the room, and here and there long cylinders stood on end. A white table in the center of the room caught her attention, upon which was a white box about twenty centimeters in length. Curiosity got the better of her, and she walked over to the desk. The surface of the box was smooth and reflective, and there was no indication of how to open it, but Rebecca was learning fast. She placed her hand on the box, and the lid opened. Inside were two cubes.

Taking one out, Rebecca examined it, turning it over and over in her hand. The cube had buttons on two of its sides and what appeared to be a small glass plate on one side. Rebecca pushed one of the buttons; the box let out a high-pitched squeak, and the glass plate lit up. The combination of these surprised her, and she dropped the cube; it fell to the floor, bounced once, and then lay still. The plate had stopped glowing, and the cube was now silent. Rebecca stooped down and scooped it up, but before she could re-examine it, a loud wailing sound came from the corridor outside. They had discovered that she was missing.

The tapping of footsteps could be heard coming down the corridor; they stopped outside the office door. Rebecca crouched down behind a pile of boxes, too afraid to even breathe, as slowly the door opened. Risanne stood in the doorway, then, after a moment's pause, took a step into the room.

"Rebecca, it is no use hiding."

Rebecca did not make a sound. She held her breath and hoped that Risanne was bluffing. He was not.

"The boxes offer you no safety." "Come now, it is for your own good."

Rebecca decided to try and shift into a more comfortable position, but in doing so, she lost her balance, falling forward and sending the stack of boxes tumbling over. Risanne rushed towards her, the door closing behind him as he did so. As he approached, she rose to her feet and made to draw her sword, but she was too slow, and a hard fist smashed into her jaw and sent her crashing to the floor.

"I am surprised at you. I thought that you would understand."

"Understand what?" Rebecca asked, blood running from the corner of her mouth.

"The need for sacrifice After all, do your people not worship Rani?"

"Do not confuse fear with worship," Rebecca snapped. "Besides, we do not have that problem anymore."

"Do not think that the same will happen here," Risanne warned. "Now... you will come with me."

"No, I will not," and she tried to dart past Risanne, but another blow sent her back to the floor.

"Have it your way," Risanne raised a foot, ready to smash it into Rebecca's face.

Without warning, Risanne was sprawled on the floor, the black shape that had appeared from nowhere landing on top of him. Light glinted off a flashing blade, and a spurt of blood rose high into the air.

"This way, quick." The black-clad figure grabbed Rebecca's hand and hauled her to her feet.

Then it was gone, climbing quickly and without effort up a rope and into a hole in the ceiling from where it had emerged. Rebecca looked down at the limp body of Risanne, then up to the dark hole above. She had nothing to lose, and without hesitation, she took hold of the rope and pulled herself up and into the darkness. The portion of the ceiling that had been removed to make the hole was replaced, and Rebecca found herself in complete darkness on her hands and knees.

"Follow me."

She could not see the person who spoke to her, but she moved in the direction of the voice. After a short distance, a bright light burst in upon them, this time immediately ahead, as another panel was removed to create a hole, and it was through this that the shadowy figure squeezed through. When Rebecca had, in turn, passed through the hole, the panel was put back in place. This time they were in a lighted passage that was a little higher than before, and they were able to rise to their feet, although they still had to stoop down. Rebecca's rescuer was about to move on when Rebecca called out.

"Wait. Who are you?" She asked.

"That is not important."

"It is to me. I owe you my life," Rebecca said.

"You owe me nothing. I did not come to save you; in fact, I had no idea that you would be in the room."

"Then what were you doing?" The Countess was becoming curious.

"That is no concern of yours," was the reply, in a manner that Rebecca took to indicate that no more questions should be asked.

"Then at least tell me who you are."

A loud sigh escaped from the masked figure, and it pulled the hood from over its head to reveal a woman in her early twenties, her dark hair cropped short at the back with a short fringe at the front.

"I am Mari, now, can we go?" She said as she stuffed the hood into the folds of her clothing.

"Thank you, Mari," Rebecca said.

Then they were moving again, through the twisting passages that lay above the heads of those that sought them. As they moved, Mari told of the battle against the Lucians and how the Myrina had been able to infiltrate the city of the Lucians by moving around in the voids in between the various levels of the building.

"But how did you get into the city?" Rebecca asked.

"You will see," Mari replied.

After fifteen minutes, they came to a halt. It was a dead end; there were no panels in the wall to remove, and the only possibility seemed to be down.

"Now listen closely. We have to go down into the city, and if we don't move fast, Lucian will detect us. Do as I say and don't ask questions, and we will be out of here before you know it," Mari said, and then she took off her jacket and handed it to Rebecca.

"Wait, we have to rescue my friends; we can't just leave them here."

"Put this on," Mari commanded; it was not a request.

"What for?" Rebecca asked.

"I said no questions. Do you want to get out of here or not?" Mari hissed.

"Of course I do, but I do not understand."

"The Lucians do not see in the same way as we do; they sense colours," Mari offered as an explanation.

"I am still not sure that I understand," Rebecca looked puzzled.

"Everything they see is made of coloured shapes. They cannot see fine detail, and they cannot see color. " Mari looked at Rebecca and formed the word with her lips.

Rebecca filled in the missing word with "black?"

"Right, now put the jacket on," Mari said. "And these," she continued, taking her trousers off.

Underneath her clothes, Mari had on a black long-sleeve shirt and long leggings. She replaced her boots and gloves and pulled the mask over her head. Rebecca had pulled on the trousers and jacket, her own black boots finishing the outfit.

"I'm ready," Rebecca announced.

"Not quite." Mari pulled up her shirt to reveal a black undershirt. Taking her knife, she cut through the thin material, and with a tug, it came free of her body. This she wrapped around Rebecca's head so that only her eyes showed.

"Sorry about the smell," she said with an unseen smile, "it's been a tough day."

Mari looked down at Rebecca's hands. "If you hear any Lucian coming, put your hands inside your jacket, and whatever happens, don't move."

"What?" Rebecca could not believe her ears. "Don't move?"

"Trust me," Mari said, removing the panel in front of them. She leaned through the hole to make sure that there was no Lucian in the corridor, then she dropped through the hole, landing silently on the floor. Rebecca followed, not quite as quietly, her feet making loud slapping noises as they hit the ground. Mari was already a short way ahead, keeping close to the corridor's smooth wall, and Rebecca chased after her. The corridor curved gently to the right, and it was impossible to see what lay more than a short distance ahead, Mari slowed her pace to allow her to listen for any sign of danger. After a while, the curve straightened out, and their path was now blocked by a door.

"This is the tricky bit," Mari said.

"What's on the other side?" Rebecca asked.

"It's not what, but who," Mari turned to Rebecca, "now remember what I said, if we run into any Lucians, don't move; don't even breathe more than you have to."

Rebecca nodded to show that she understood and took a deep breath to steady her nerves. "I hope you're right about this."

Pressing against the wall, they edged forward; the door opened, and they stepped through. Now they had a choice of two directions to go in, but Mari did not hesitate and immediately turned right and made off in that direction. After a short distance, she came to a halt.

"Why have you stopped?" Rebecca whispered.

"Listen." Mari put her finger to her lips.

Rebecca could hear nothing at first, but then, after a few seconds, she heard it too. The soft padding of footsteps coming towards them is getting louder and louder.

"Down," Mari whispered, and she immediately dropped into a crouch, pushing herself harder against the wall.

Rebecca did the same, and together they waited for their fate. Around the bend came the two Lucians, walking briskly and with purpose. They marched up to where the women crouched and stopped. One of the Lucians cocked his head to one side, listening, his foot only a hair's breadth from Mari's.

"What is it, Yarmus?"

"I thought I heard something," Yarmus said.

"I cannot hear anything." replied the other Lucian.

"Maybe you are right," Yarmus paused for another few seconds then continued down the corridor. It was two minutes after this before Mari rose to her feet.

"Right, let's go," and keeping low, she set off again.

Rounding the next corner, they came upon a corridor lined with doors. Mari stopped in front of one of these and motioned to Rebecca to follow. They stepped inside the room, and the door slid silently closed behind them. Mari pulled off her mask and used it to wipe the sweat from her forehead.

"That was close," she said to Rebecca.

"It's a relief to get this off," Rebecca said, removing the cloth from around her head and gasping for clean air; the smell was indeed not pleasant. "Where to now?"

"In here," Mari said, opening a grating in the wall.

"What's in there?" Rebecca asked.

"It's the air ducts for the city."

"Air ducts. "What are air ducts?"

"You don't know much, do you? The air ducts carry fresh air around the city. We use them to move around undetected," Mari explained.

"Then why have we risked capture by using the corridors?"

"The ducts are not all interlinked, and occasionally we need to use more... conventional routes," Mari pulled herself into the duct. "If we stay here much longer, we will be detected."

Rebecca knew that Mari was right and climbed in behind her. Mari allowed her to pass, then swung the grating shut behind them.

"A little bit further and we will be out of the city. Stay close and be as quiet as possible." With that, Mari pushed past Rebecca and crawled along the metal floor of the duct.

"Hold on. What about my friends?" Rebecca called.

Mari stopped and looked over her shoulder. "Friends?"

"They were drugged and taken away by Tramen and his cronies." I don't know where he took them, but we have to rescue them."

"What do you mean, we? Look, I didn't expect to have to rescue you when I entered that room, and you ruined my plans, but we made it. Now if you think I'm going back in there now that they are on full alert, you are crazier than you look," Mari hissed.

"Then I'll go alone."

"You won't make it past the first Lucian on your own," Mari warned.

"Then help me," Rebecca pleaded.

Shaan snapped awake, his eyes opening suddenly, his vision blurred. He became aware that he was laying on his back on a hard surface and that his arms and legs were tied to the corners of whatever he was lying on. His vision cleared, and he looked around as best he could. To his right, a few feet away, lay Jonathan, tied in the same way but still unconscious, although he did not appear to have been harmed in any way. To Shaan's left was empty space as far as he could see, and the same view greeted him when he looked down towards his feet, but in pushing his head backwards a completely different scene awaited him. Shaan remembered when they had first entered the city and the strange pedestal that Rebecca had pointed out to him; now, from close up, he could clearly see what they had strained to make out from a distance.

On the floor stood a small disc that glowed orange from within. Rising up from this were two thin struts of shiny metal, both of which had moon-shaped curves cut into them at the top, and suspended from these cuts was an object that Shaan sought. Measuring what Shaan gauged to be two meters and made of wood with pure silver entwined around it, the shaft of the spear reflected the orange glow of the dais. At one end of the shaft hung a white ribbon, while the other end was tipped with a razor-sharp blade of approximately thirty centimeters in length, and it was from this that small droplets of a shiny red liquid fell into a receptacle below. This was it, the spear that bled, or most certainly an incarnation of that spear. The spear that killed the Son of God, the spear of Longinus

A groan came from Shaan's right, and he turned his head in that direction.

"I don't know what was in it, but it was good stuff," Jonathan said.

"Sure had a kick to it," Shaan replied.

"Are you injured?" Johnathan asked.

"Only my pride."

"And Rebecca?"

"She's not next to me, I thought she was on the other side of you," Shaan said with concern in his voice.

"No, nothing here," Jonathan said, casting a sideways glance in that direction.

"If they've harmed her, I'll...," Shaan started.

"I do not think you are in a position to do anything," a voice cut in.

They had not heard Tramen approach and were startled to hear his voice.

"We have not hurt her, but she, on the other hand, has killed one of us," he continued. "Not to worry, we will soon have her back in our safekeeping."

"Safe. "I dread to think what you would call dangerous," Johnathan said in a tone that summed up his feelings.

"Do not be alarmed; soon you will be at one with God and your spirit will be free from the evils of this world, for you, Jonathan, are one of the lucky ones," Tramen said with the voice of a preacher.

"I'd rather be cursed," hissed the hunter, and he struggled with his bonds, but to no avail.

"What do you want with us?" Shaan asked calmly.

"As I said, you have been chosen to become one with the Lord."

"If it's all the same to you, we'd rather not," Shaan said hopefully. "Besides, we really have to be going now."

"Shaan," Jonathan whispered, then said louder, "Shaan!"

"What?" Shaan swiveled his head around but did not need his question answered. Forming a circle around them and the dais, where hundreds, if not thousands, of Lucians were all spaced out evenly about four feet apart as if on parade,

"It is time," Tramen said.

From out of the ranks of those gathered there came two Lucian priests, dressed in long, flowing robes similar to those that Tramen now wore. They carried between them an ornate stand, which was made of fine strands of metal and reminded Shaan of some intricate spider's web. On the stand was only one object, a ceremonial knife. The handle of the knife was as intricate as the stand, and on the end of this was a large blood-red crystal. The stand was placed next to Tramen, and with this done, the two priests retired. Shaan and Johnathan renewed their hopeless struggle against the bonds, but both knew that the end had come.

"Gaius. If you can hear me, I could use some help about now," Shaan muttered under his breath, but there was no reply, and no magical aid was forthcoming.

Oblivious to their struggle, Tramen had begun the ceremony and was uttering the words and incantations of the ritual he had been taught as a child, using the ancient language of his forefathers. Words that seemed to rise and fall like some strange song, both beautiful and disturbing at the same time, and as he did so, he waved the knife in front of himself, caving strange symbols in the air. A low hum came from the others assembled there, as if in chorus to Tramens's singing. Shaan had stopped struggling and was lying quite still, seemingly hypnotized by this almost enchanting song, his mind drifting, remembering every detail of the last few days and the brief time he had had with Rebecca. Beautiful Rebecca. Without conscious thought, he smiled as he recalled the love she had brought to him. At least he had known real love before he died.

Tramen had come to the end of the ceremony and now held the knife high in the air and spoke aloud the final words that spelt death to his helpless victims.

"Now take these most glorious sacrifices in your name, Lord, and protect us as we live only to serve and worship your greatness," and with this he lowered the knife and rested it on Shaan's neck, but before he could draw the red line that would release Shaan's blood in a hideous sacrifice, a shout came from the rear ranks of the Lucians.

"Fire. Fire!"

Tramen looked around; sure enough, a great plume of smoke was slowly drifting across the room from one of the corridors. The whole mass of the crowd moved as one in the direction of the smoke, some running to investigate and others just moving to get a better view of what was happening. Tramen strode purposefully into the throng, issuing orders as he went. Suddenly, an explosion accompanied by a loud bang shook the room. Another smaller one followed. This sent the Lucian's into a frenzy of activity, rushing here and there, shouting commands and instructions to one another so that everyone was involved in the mayhem in one way or another, so much so that it seemed that Shaan and Johnathan had been forgotten. This was just what Rebecca and Mari had hoped for when they started the fires that were causing all the commotion, and no one noticed when a panel was lifted in the ceiling above the captives and two black figures descended towards the dais, cutting the prisoners' ropes and aiding them as they clambered up into the roof space and the panel was closed behind them. Without a word, the two figures were off, in a crouching position, darting across the twisting pathways, ducking under overhanging pipes, and leaping over obstacles that lay in their way. Shaan and Johnathan followed; this was no time to ask questions. After what seemed like an hour but was probably only a few minutes, they stopped, panting as they leant against a wall, bent over with their hands on their knees, gasping for breath. Then one of the black-clad figures pulled at the cloth that concealed its identity and, with a huge smile, looked at Shaan and said, "Now we're even."

"Rebecca!" Shaan shouted with surprise and stood up to rush to her side.

He was immediately sent back into a crouching position as his head made fierce contact with the ceiling above him. Laughing, Rebecca kneeled beside him, flinging her arms around his neck, kissing his lips.

"Who's your friend?" Johnathan said, looking over at the now-unmasked Mari as she ran her fingers through her short black hair.

"Johnathan , Shaan, meet Mari. We owe her everything," Rebecca said.

"Glad to meet you," Jonathan gave Mari a smile.

"As am I," Shaan said.

"Save the niceties for later; now they're going to be really mad," Mari chided. "We'd better keep moving," and with that, she turned from the others and began to walk away.

"She doesn't say much," Rebecca whispered and nudged Shaan in the direction that Mari had gone.

"How come the drink did not affect you?" Johnathan asked.

"Because I did not drink it," Rebecca said smugly. "I spat it out when I saw you fall."

Moroc had decided not to execute the sole survivor of the men who had chased the Jarenn scum from his camp; instead, he would think up some exotic torture or suicide mission for him at some later date; after all, he had brought a message back with him. It had been a warning to withdraw his troops or face the same fate as his men, a warning that the powers of light would strike his men down at every turn and a warning that there would be no survivors from his army; all would be destroyed and none left to tell the tale. It was this that had enraged him so much that he had gathered together a band of men to ride to Taal and plant their standard at the feet of these so-called 'guardians of the way.' Proof that no one could halt the fire that was the Bastion army. A fire that would cleanse and unite the realms for all time, and as he climbed into his saddle, he felt a sense of power, a wondrous dark power, as if nothing and no one could harm him or his men. He lofted his standard high into the air and nudged his horse forward. He would not ride fast but would walk his horse right up to the gates of the tower so that all could see he was invincible.

CHAPTER THIRTEEN

Mari had led the others through seemingly endless passages, and now they had slowed, coming to another seeming dead end.

"Mari, how do the Lucian read our minds?" Rebecca asked.

"I too have been wondering that," Shaan added. "When we first met, Tramen knew our names without us telling him."

"And he knew where I was hiding," Rebecca continued thoughtfully. "But how come they don't know where we are now?"

"They can't read minds. Tramen must have touched one of you. In that way, he became in tune with your mind for a brief time and knew what you knew. As for knowing where you were hiding, I think it must have been a lucky guess."

"Where can we get some black clothes like yours, Mari?" Shaan reached out and touched Mari's arm, having been told by Rebecca that Lucian couldn't see this colour or lack of colour.

"You don't need any; we will be out of the city in a few moments," she replied.

"Yes, we do. We have to go back for the spear. It is the reason we came here."

"Go back? You are as insane as she is," Mari pointed at Rebecca. "Look, I have gotten you this far, and that's more than I bargained for. Now we must leave the city; they'll be on their guard for a long time after this. You have put my plans back days, possibly months, so if you'll just come with me, maybe I'll survive to make another attempt."

"Another attempt at what?" Johnathan wondered.

"I came to steal a key," Mari explained. "If I had succeeded in my mission, then my people would be able to reclaim what is theirs."

"And what is that?" Johnathan enquired.

"The city. It was our home before the Lucians came," Mari said, her eyes closing as she remembered how they had invited the Lucians into their city, taking pity on them because they were blind.

At first there were only a few of them, then more and more came until they outnumbered the Myrina and took their homes from them. Mari had been only five at the time, but she remembered it as if it were yesterday, when her family and her friends' families had been cut down by the Lucian's strange weapons, and how, after they had fled, the Lucian had erected the shield-wall around the city to stop them from returning. Suddenly she snapped out of her dream and back into a reality that she did not wish to be a part of.

"Maybe you can return in a few days," she said, lifting a section of the floor.

"Why do you not send an army in to take back what is yours?" Johnathan asked.

"We would love to, but we can't." Mari lowered herself through the hole. "You'll see why in a moment."

The others followed, one at a time. The room they were now in was small, and there was only just enough room for them all. Several pipes branched off into three of the walls, none of which were large enough to allow access. There was no fourth wall; instead, what took Shaan, Rebecca, and Jonathan by surprise was the blue and white sparking of the shield wall. They knew instinctively to stay away from it and pushed back against the other walls.

"What do we do now?" Johnathan looked around the room. The air smelled stale and damp.

"We wait," Mari said, sitting down on her heels.

"Wait. For what?" Shaan was eager to continue with his quest.

"For the shield wall to open."

"The shield wall opens. Then why have you not brought your people in this way?"

"This room is an exhaust port for the air ducts. Fresh air is drawn in through one port, and stale air is pumped out through another; this is the stale air vent. The pressure builds up in here, and when it reaches a certain level, the shield wall is opened to allow it to escape. The only problem is that the port opens randomly every four or five hours and only for a few seconds at a time. This is why we cannot get an army into the city; it would not be possible to get enough people inside to make an attack successful," Mari explained.

"That's why you need a key..." Jonathan said, making more of a statement than a question.

"Exactly"

The air in the room was becoming thick and hard to breathe, and Mari turned to Rebecca.

"You may as well sit down and conserve your breath; we have a long wait ahead."

Moroc sat unmoving on his horse, his shoulders back, and his head held high. Neither looking left nor right but straight ahead at the tower. He let his horse pick its way over the rocky terrain towards his goal. The men behind him were not so confident, and many sat uneasily, darting glances this way and that, fearing that at any moment the attack would come, but it did not. They were halfway to the tower, and there had been no sign of the Jarenn, which made them even more wary. What were they up to? Had they all retreated to the tower? The uncertainty was like a slow torture, and it made them imagine sounds and images that did not exist.

The Jarenn looked on from their hiding places. They were under orders not to attack any scouting parties for fear of losing their advantage when the full-scale attack came. The traps were set, and all that they now required was that the battle begin so that they could wreak havoc amongst the invaders before they reached Taal, hopefully diminishing the enemy's strength enough so that the defenders of the tower could hold them at bay.

Daal looked out from one of the lookout posts set high in the tower and watched as Moroc approached. Behind Daal, Nasim pulled an arrow from the quiver at his side and took aim. If he could take Moroc now, it might force the Bastion army to retreat, but before he could set the arrow to flight, Daal had put his hand up in front of Nasim's' face.

"No. Not yet, my friend. We must let them think that they are invincible; that way they will be more confident and less concerned about our tactics," Daal said calmly.

Nasim lowered his weapon. "I hope you are right."

Moroc had reached the gateway of the tower; he took his standard and rammed it into the earth. The flag waved in the wind, rippling, causing the dragon design to come alive. Moroc looked up and met Daal's downward gaze, a large smile crossing his face.

"Are you ready to die yet, old man?" He shouted, and he laughed a great, echoing laugh, then turned his horse and trotted it away, followed closely by his band of men. As they made their way back to the camp, Moroc wondered at the ease of their journey. He had at least expected a little resistance. What were the Jarenn up to?

Rebecca coughed, spluttering, gasping for air. Her ears were ringing, and her heart pounded as if it would burst. The pressure in the room was becoming unbearable, and she felt that at any moment she would pass out. Just when she could take no more, she heard Mari call out.

"Now."

As she looked up, she saw the shield-wall buckle and move away from the entrance, then it made a strange sizzling noise, and all of a sudden, the air rushed from the room and her arm was jerked forward, pulling her up from her sitting position and out of the now open end of the room. In an instant, she was lying in a heap on the dusty floor with the others sprawled around her. Looking around, she could see that the shield wall was now restored to its usual shape, sparking, and crackling with renewed vigor.

Mari was first to her feet. Dusting herself down, she smiled at Jonathan, who was sitting with his hands on his knees and looking up at her.

"You sure move fast for a big guy."

"It has its advantages," Jonathan smiled as Mari held out her hand and helped him to his feet.

Her hand felt warm and soft, and he was reluctant to release it. She too held on for a longer time than seemed necessary, then, looking slightly embarrassed, she pulled slowly away.

"Come, I will show you where you can rest, and if you insist on going back in, I will get you some more appropriate clothing."

At first, the gentle slope of the ground eased their aching limbs after the time spent crouching, but now the dusty path had turned to rock as they climbed higher into the mountains, and even Mari was beginning to breathe hard.

"Just a little further," she panted, "beyond that ridge,"

Mari pointed up to where a ledge of rock jutted out from the red mountain. After a short time, they reached the ridge, and sure enough, the path levelled out, and to the left, between two huge stone pillars, lay a vast plateau. Here were the homes of the Myrina. Not the grand domed structure that they had been forced to leave behind, but tent-like structures made from cloth covered wooden frames. They had been constructed well and built to last, but they were not permanent. From each tent flew a banner, and Shaan wondered what they signified. On questioning Mari, he discovered that each tent housed a particular clan, and it was the symbol of each that waved in the gentle breeze that blew across the plateau. Here and there, women could be seen going about their business, some carrying supplies, others emerging from one tent only to disappear into another. All were dressed in brightly coloured clothes and not, as Shaan had expected, in the same black as Mari wore. As they reached the stone pillars, Shaan watched Mari pull a square object from the folds of her clothing, which she jabbed at with her fingers, then, without saying a word, she returned it to the darkness.

Mari led the others through the encampment past endless tents until she reached a particularly large one. Atop this flew a white flag with three blue wavy lines embroidered on it. The entrance to the tent was open, and Mari stepped inside.

"Please wait," she said to the others, then disappeared within, returning a few minutes later and ushered them inside.

The tent was subdivided into many small rooms, and it was into one of these that Mari took them. Inside, sitting cross-legged on the floor, was an old woman, her face wrinkled and scored by the sands of time.

"Please, come sit a while." The old woman's voice was calm but with a subtle undertone of caution.

Shaan looked at Mari, who gave a small nod. He lowered himself down, sitting cross-legged in a similar manner to the woman. Johnathan and Rebecca did the same. Mari sat next to the woman. There was a silence, and it occurred to Shaan that maybe they were waiting for him to speak.

"I am Shaan Moonblade," he said, introducing himself. "And this is the Countess Rebecca and my good friend Jonathan."

Johnathan nodded at the woman, but she remained motionless, her blue eyes seemingly fixed on Rebecca. Still, she said nothing.

What do I do now? Am I missing some form of etiquette, some act I should carry out? Shaan wondered.

"We would be pleased if you would share our food," the old woman said directly to Rebecca. "You may bring your companions should you wish to."

Shaan tried to speak, but Rebecca tapped him on the leg, causing him to stop. "We thank you," she replied.

"Mari, make the arrangements," the woman ordered, and without a word, Mari left the room to carry out her task.

"Mari tells me that you need our help," the elder paused, "and also that it is because of you that she failed in her mission."

"It was unfortunate that our paths crossed when they did," Rebecca replied, "but if they had not, then I would surely be dead. Mari saved my life, and for that I am forever in her debt. I believe, though, that it was fate that brought us together, for without our meeting, we would be unable to warn you of the evil that is about to be unleashed on your world."

"Oh, you are too late for that; Lucian came many years ago."

"It is not Lucian that I speak of. They are nothing compared to the evil of Krishia."

"Krishia? I have never heard of such a being," the woman frowned.

"Then please allow Shaan to explain," Rebecca said.

"That is an unusual request. A man speaking in council is not generally permitted, but as you are clearly from a different culture to ours, I am sure it seems quite normal to you," the woman said, shaking her head from side to side. "In this case, I will allow you to tell me why I should help you."

The old woman listened to Shaan's story, from how he had met Bron, through the battles he had fought, and to how Mari had come to their rescue in the Lucian city. His story had lasted for an age, and when he eventually reached the end of his tale, he felt sure that he would get the help that he needed.

Shaan's heart sank as he heard the woman say, "In all of your adventures, the only indication that Bron is telling the truth was your encounter with a few men in a forest in the middle of nowhere. Men who could have been ordinary robbers. You have not seen this Krishia or her vast army, or indeed witnessed any of the evil of which you speak. I am sorry, Shaan, but I cannot risk the lives of my people on pure speculation," she said, pausing to take a deep breath. "Do you really believe that this danger exists, or are you just looking for an adventure, Shaan?"

"Shaan speaks the truth," Jonathan gave the old woman a harsh glance.

"I am certain that he does not deliberately try to mislead us, but have you seen any of this evil?" she shot back "And what of you, Rebecca?"

They both had to admit that they had not.

"I do not lie to you," Shaan said quietly. "If I do not succeed with my quests, then all is lost. My people, Rebecca's, and yours will all become slaves to darkness, a darkness from which they will not escape." With this, Shaan rose and left the room.

"You must listen to him," Rebecca begged.

"Must listen?" The woman scowled. "I must do nothing," and

with that, she too rose and left the room.

"Things are not going too well," Jonathan said quietly to Rebecca.

"I can't argue with that," she replied.

At that moment, Mari returned; she looked puzzled.

"Where are the others?"

"They left," Jonathan answered.

"What do you mean, they left?"

"I do not think that your friend is willing to aid us. You saw for yourself that she did not want Shaan to speak in the beginning," Rebecca tried not to show the anger she was feeling.

"It is nothing personal. It's just that we do not allow our men into council meetings. You must understand that it was hard for her to accept that Shaan or Jonathan are equal to you."

"We do not even know her name, why the secrecy?"

"There is no secret, she probably thought it was of no consequence. Her name is Pythea, and she is the leader of our clan and head of the council."

"Why do you not allow men to your meetings?" Rebecca asked.

"When the Lucian came and drove us from our home, they slaughtered our men, and very few escaped. The ones that did are kept away from danger and protected from any harm because without them, our people will die out. Also, a lot of us blame them for what happened, for failing to protect us, and we do not trust them to make decisions about our welfare."

"Well, I do trust mine," Rebecca stated. "And, I will do anything to help him in his quest. In a few years, you will realise this, when the Lucians have spread out from the city and taken even more of your land and killed more, if not all, of your people."

Mari thought about this for a moment. Maybe Rebecca was right. Maybe the men were not to blame, and the Lucian would have succeeded anyway. Perhaps it was not yet time to reinstate men to their old positions, but that time would surely come.

"I will talk to Pythea, but I can promise nothing," and with that, Mari once more left the room.

Rebecca looked at Jonathan. "I hope she can convince Pythea."

"I also do, but somehow I do not think she will."

A girl of about eight or nine entered the room. "A meal has been prepared for you. Please follow me," she said.

They were led into another of the tent's many compartments and were surprised to see Shaan already seated. He looked thoughtful as they approached but said nothing.

"Looks like we are on our own," Jonathan said.

"It looks like it," Shaan echoed. "Do these people really believe that they are safe?"

"I do not think that they have even considered what may be happening outside of their small part of this world, let alone what is happening in another realm, or even if they believe such things exist." Jonathan replied honestly. "We will manage Shaan. We've come this far; I'm not about to give up now."

"Nor I," added Rebecca as she looked deeply into Shaan's eyes.

Halfway through the meal, Mari appeared. She did not look directly at Shaan but spoke quietly.

"I am sorry; there is nothing we can do for you." Then she turned slowly and left the room.

"Mari. Mari," Johnathan called and followed through the folds of the apartment's doorway. He caught up to her a little way down the corridor.

"Mari, we need your help." He reached out and caught her by the arm. She looked round, her eyes dull and filled with pain.

"I cannot help you, Jonathan."

"Mari, please. Without your help, we cannot find our way to

the spear. Without your help, our world and yours are doomed. Millions will die; these will be the lucky ones. Please, Mari, if not for me, do it for yourself and for your people."

Looking up into Johnathan 's eyes, Mari felt drawn and entranced, as if she had known this man all her life. What was it about him? Why did she feel this way? She knew at that moment that she wanted to be with him, to feel a love that she had never felt before.

Mari reached towards Johnathan and was caught up in his arms. She spun around as if in a dance, his lips meeting hers in a long, passionate kiss. Round and round they whirled, their lips never parting until they could stand no more, and they crashed to the floor in a fit of laughter and tears. When the laughter stopped, Mari looked at Johnathan ; the smile was gone.

"If I help you, will you take me with you?"

Jonathan was taken aback. It had been a long time since he had felt this way about a woman; maybe he never had. "I am not sure that I can."

"What do you mean?" Mari queried.

"The way we came into your realm does not allow passage to everyone."

"Now you talk in riddles. If you do not want me to come with you, I will not," Mari said, pulling away from Jonathan's embrace.

"Of course I want you to come, if it is at all possible for you to do so," he reassured her.

Mari thought about this for a while, then said. "Tell Shaan to meet me at dusk near the shield gate."

"The shield gate, where is that?"

"You have a lot to learn about my world, Jonathan. The shield-gate is between the two pillars of stone marking the entrance to the citadel. Oh, and don't allow Shaan to attempt to pass through until I have turned the power off."

"Now it is you that speaks in riddles," Jonathan shook his head.

"The shield-gate works in the same way as the shield-wall around the city," Mari said in way of explanation.

"But I saw no sparks when we approached."

"That is because the size of the gate is much smaller than that of the wall, and therefore it needs less power."

"I still do not understand what you are saying," Jonathan replied, frustration evident in his voice.

"Never mind that now, just meet me by the gate and do not try and step through until I get there," then she put her arms around Jonathan's neck, kissed him gently, rose to her feet, and disappeared down the corridor.

The army of Bastion had grown in the last few days as more soldiers had made their way to the rendezvous, and now, as one, they moved out of the camp. A thousand spears pointed skyward, and like some giant porcupine, it crept forwards towards its prey. Sections of the army moved off to the left and right of the main body, giving it the appearance of a large bird spreading its wings.

One section, led by General Crael, circled the battlefield before suddenly changing direction and charging at full speed towards the tower. It did not get far. The ground below them seemed to give way as the horses raced over it, sending them and their riders plunging onto the sharpened stakes below. Only a few of the riders had managed to pull up before they had reached the pit's edge, having seen what had happened to their comrades, one of whom looked down into the pit and saw the face of General Crael staring back, racked with pain, a stake having pierced his armor below his waist line only to emerge through his shoulder.

On the other side of the battlefield, another section of the army had tried the same maneuver and was making good progress.

In the grass ahead of them, a snake weaved its way through the dense undergrowth, weaving its way around the small bushes and through the thick clumps of grass and weeds until it reached an object it could not pass. The fine netting had been laid in such a way and at such an angle that the snake could not raise its body to climb over it. The snake turned and wriggled its way parallel to the netting, slipping over and under its companions as it looked for an opening. There was none. Without warning, the snake was attacked, with the hoof of a horse crashing down close to its head. Then another and another. The snake did what came naturally and struck out, its fangs sinking deep into the horse's leg and its venom taking immediate effect. The horse reared, throwing its rider to the floor, and the snake struck again. All around, the snake's brothers and sisters were also striking their attackers.

Moroc could not see the flanks of his army, but he knew something was wrong. He should have been able to see the first attacking forces making their way towards the tower by now. "Damn them," he thought, but he had no time to worry about them now. He raised his hand into the air, signaling to General Kai to start his attack. Another brigade of horsemen charged towards the tower, and this time there seemed to be no resistance, not until they were half-way there, when the tie ropes to the saplings were cut, causing them to spring upwards, the wire between decapitating more of Moroc's men, and again the arrows flew as General Kai and his soldiers were cut down.

Moroc looked on in disbelief. What was happening? Why were his men being tricked so easily? Fools, all of them fools. He signaled to the man on his left, who put a horn to his lips and blew. All around the Bastion army halted, turned towards Moroc, and waited. A signal was given to regroup, and the army rapidly formed a more conventional attack pattern. Spreading out in lines and ranks across the battlefield, they would begin their slow march to the tower. Picking their way steadily over the trap-infested ground.

The signalman pointed and at the same time said to Moroc. "My lord. Look."

As one, the Jarenn army rose. Their green armor was polished and glistening. With weapons ready, they waited for Moroc to make his move. There were less than two hundred of them, and Moroc knew that the majority of the army was made up of militia and mercenaries. Only a small percent was true, Jarenn.

"Lambs to the slaughter," he said under his breath. A thousand Bastion warriors advanced, and the battle proper had begun.

Khamel had at last reached Stroika, a city in ruins, its walls smashed and crumbling, its buildings now just piles of rock and ashes, and its people beaten. Those that had survived now took shelter where they could, scavenged for food scraps, or just waited for death to end this nightmare. Krishia had wanted something, something rumored to be in Stroika, but in order to search among the ruins, Khamel would have to look like one of the citizens, not raise suspicion, and certainly not appear to have anything that a scavenger would desire. Her clothes were filthy rags, but had it not been for Krishia, she would still have looked out of place with her fair skin, perfectly manicured nails, and styled hair.

Khamel winced at the memory, the flame, the heat, and the immense pain as the flames had licked at her skin. Her left side was burned and gnarled, her face no longer beautiful but scarred and blistered so that she was no longer recognizable even as a woman. She had lost one eye, and a mangled piece of skin was all that was left of her ear. Yes, she would look just like the other survivors here. Her orders were simple: find what Krishia wanted by any means necessary.

Khamel shuffled along the streets, looking here and there, rummaging in the ruins. This was an impossible task: to find a small object in a huge city. As night drew in, the air became colder, and she pulled her rags tighter around her body. A short way off, she could see a few people gathered around a fire, trying to keep the cold away, and she made her way to them, seeking the same. No one looked up at her or seemed to care that she had joined them; she was one of the survivors, and they must all pull together. Most were discussing the war, the destruction of their homes, and the extermination of their people. This had been no war of conquest; it had been a war of extinction because of the resistance that Stroika had put up against the demands of a tyrant would-be ruler. Two women sat talking in quiet voices so as not to draw attention to themselves, but Khamel was close enough to hear. They talked about before the war, their lives, and how they had so much but now had nothing, but something made Khamel listen more intently; they were talking about the last time they had been together, in the marketplace, watching the performers and listening to the banter between traders and customers.

"The last thing I remember is listening to that actioner try to flog off his cheap jewelry box; I was almost going to bid myself before the attack came".

"Did you say jewelry box?" Khamel inquired, trying not to seem overly interested but merely curious.

The two turned to look at Khamel, then back to each other and continued talking, ignoring her question.

"Excuse me, but..."

One of the women spoke in a chastising tone, "You care about trinkets in a time like this, be gone with you," shooting Khamel a look that meant there was no more conversation to be had.

Khamel scurried away, both in shock at the woman's words

and knowing she now had a clue to the whereabouts of her lost object. Khamel had visited Stroika several times with her parents as a young girl and was aware of the marketplace and its attractions; in fact, it was one of her favorite places to visit while here, and she had begged and pleaded with her father to take her there on each occasion. She remembered the joy, the vibrancy, and the happiness that it brought to the citizens.

After three hours of sifting through debris, smashed market stalls, broken pots, and other goods, she had given up. Sitting with her head in her hands, not caring that it was painful to touch her skin, she knew her task was hopeless, that Krishia would carry out her promise to destroy her whole family, right down to her most distant relative, and have her husband skinned alive just to show others what she did to people who were of no use to her.

The night had drawn in; the darkness now descended upon the city; shadows fell around her; and she stared up into the night sky, praying to a god she knew did not exist for a miracle that would never happen.

Khamel heard a noise, looked towards it, and here and there scurried small creatures, seeking out morsels of food, leaping and hopping from place to place, making high-pitched squeaking noises as they went about their business. She watched one as it made its way under and over various pieces of debris, stopping occasionally to sniff at the air before continuing on its way, and there it was, a faint glow: at first she thought she had imagined it, but no, it was there. Scrambling over to the source of the light, she pulled away rubble and broken timber until she could reach in and grab the object with her hand. The carved wooden box glowed green at the edges, and Khamel's heart started to beat faster.

The moon was creeping out from behind a thin vale of clouds when Mari appeared.

"I was beginning to think that you had forgotten us," Jonathan whispered.

"How could I possibly forget you?" she said, smiling up at him. Then she handed Shaan a bundle of clothing. "Here, put these on."

He did as he was instructed and was now dressed from head to toe in black.

"Now, I will take you into the city, but you must do exactly as I say. Do not ask questions; keep moving unless I stop. When I do, crouch down and don't move no matter what happens. Understood?"

He nodded. "Right, let's go."

"What about us?" asked Johnathan .

"You wait here, it will be quicker and safer if there are only two of us. Besides, I can't keep my eye on all of you," Mari answered.

"She is right, there's nothing you can do this time, Jonathan," Shaan assured him. Then they left, leaving Rebecca and Jonathan alone in the moonlight. Rebecca looked worried.

"They will be fine," Jonathan said, trying to convince himself as much as Rebecca.

Mari pressed what looked like a small black box against the pillar of the shield gate. She yanked Shaan through the opening, and almost immediately there was a popping sound and a brief glimmer between the pillars. Mari explained to Shaan that the device she had used could open the gate for a few moments and no more.

'If only I had the key that turns off the whole shield wall permanently, I could take all of my fighters with me." Mari said "Usually it is just a handful of us at a time; it would take weeks to get a large enough force through".

When they reached the citadel, luck was with them. They had only to wait a few minutes before the shield wall at the air vent opened, and they dashed inside. Mari again led the way through the twisting corridors and ducts until they eventually came to a halt.

"This is it. The altar is directly below us," Mari whispered, and then, putting her ear to the floor, she listened. "I cannot hear any movement. If you're going to do it, it has to be now."

Shaan nodded, and Mari lifted the panel from the floor and peered through the hole. "All clear."

Mari took off her backpack and removed two lengths of black rope. To the end of each was tied a hook, which was also painted black. She gave one to Shaan and retained the other herself. Together, they each lowered their hooks towards the spear. When he had let out enough rope, Shaan gave it a shake and twisted it this way and that until, at the appropriate moment, he pulled, causing the rope to become taut as it hooked onto the spear. Mari did the same, and after a few attempts, her hook too had caught on the spear.

"Well, that was the easy bit," Shaan said. "Gently now,"

They each pulled a little on their ropes, and the spear lifted gracefully from its place of rest. Bit by bit, they eased the spear upward until it was nearly within reach. Across the room, Mari heard the tapping of approaching footsteps. Her concentration momentarily lost; she allowed her shoulder to drop. This had the effect of lowering her end of the spear, and with a screech, it began to slip from the hook on her side, inching further and further to the point of no return.

"Oh no," Mari gasped.

Luck was with her, as if some god were aiding them, the shoulder of the spear's blade reached Shaan's hook and arrested its movement. Quickly, Mari pulled on her rope, again levelling the spear. She looked at Shaan and mouthed the word "sorry." Not daring to move again, they watched the lone figure cross the room until it disappeared through a door at the far end. Droplets of sweat beaded on Shaan's forehead. He looked at Mari and nodded, together they returned their attention to the ropes. Bit by bit, the spear rose until, at last, Shaan reached down and grasped it firmly in his hand. A broad smile crossed his face as he pulled the silver shaft towards the opening. Turning it point down to enable the spear to pass through, he lifted it hand over hand until, with a clang, it hit the ceiling above Shaan's head. The spear's blade was still on the wrong side of the opening, and no matter how he tried, no matter what angle was used, Shaan could not get enough leeway to allow the spear to pass completely through. Mari watched anxiously as Shaan struggled.

"What are we going to do now?" Shaan hissed.

"I don't know. You're the brains here," Mari said, as frustrated as Shaan.

"It's no good; I'll have to go down."

"You can't," Mari warned. "You won't even make it across the room."

"It's not far, if I am quick, I can make it to the main door before anyone realizes," Shaan said hopefully.

"Then what? Even if you get outside, you will not make it through the shield wall," Mari touched Shaan's hand. "I'll go."

"Go where? You have just said that it is impossible to get through the shield wall."

"Do you think you can find your way back from here?" Mari asked.

"Yes.Why?"

"I can make it to the exhaust port through the corridors of the city. I'll meet you there. Whatever happens, do not come looking for me; now give me your jacket."

Shaan disrobed, handed the jacket to Mari, and with that, she dropped through the hole and landed, catlike, some twenty feet below. If Shaan had not seen it for himself, he would not have believed it. Mari signaled for Shaan to drop the spear, which he did. She caught it nimbly and immediately started off across the room. Shaan watched her reach the far end, and then she was gone. He replaced the panel, wound the ropes into a coil, tucked them away in the backpack Mari had left behind, and began to retrace his footsteps back to the exhaust port. It took longer than he had thought. Twice he had to backtrack as he realised, he was going the wrong way, but at last, here he was. Mari was not here yet, but he had expected that it would take her longer as she would have to move slowly and stealthily through the city's labyrinth of corridors, avoiding contact with the Lucian. An hour passed and still she had not appeared. Shaan had begun to worry a long time before this, and several times he had almost left the safety of the exhaust port to go in search of her. He sat, listening. Then, from beyond the wall, he heard the steady patter of footsteps. Closer and closer they came. Had they found him? Had they captured Mari and made her talk? The panel that hid the entrance to the exhaust port was pulled away, and Shaan readied himself to strike.

On leaving the main hall, Mari had stopped briefly to rip Shaan's jacket into strips that she bound around the spear to disguise it, and on more than one occasion she thought she would be caught, each time crouching against a wall with the spear laid flat against the wall and floor. Her heart had beaten fast as she tried to steady her breathing, each time evading the Lucians as they walked past or came out of a room to go into another. She was beginning to think she was getting too deep with these strangers.

The sun was creeping over the horizon, casting long shadows over the ground on which Rebecca and Jonathan sat. Neither had slept, and now with bleary eyes they stared into the distance, looking for any sign that the others had been successful in their mission.

"They should have been back by now," Jonathan said with concern in his voice. "I should go looking for them."

"I would offer to come with you." Rebecca replied, nodding towards the gate, indicating that neither of them could pass.

Out of the corner of her eye, she had seen something or someone.

"Look," she said, pointing down the pathway.

Around the corner came a shadowy figure, followed a few seconds later by another, taller figure.

"They made it." Rebecca breathed a sigh of relief.

Shaan and Mari stepped through the shield gate. It closed behind them as before.

Rebecca ran to Shaan, calling, "You did it. You got the spear."

"Hope for your people maybe, but not for mine," Mari said quietly.

"I wish there was something we could do," Rebecca put her arm around Mari's shoulder. It was then that she noticed what Mari was holding.

"What is that?" She asked, looking down at the strange square object.

Mari turned the box over in her hands and held it up so that Rebecca could see better.

"It is a key to the shield gate. My people managed to make this one, but it only lasts for a few seconds at a time. It was a key similar to this that I sought in the city."

Rebecca reached into the folds of her clothing.

"Like this?" She asked, holding out the cube she had collected while in Lucian's office. Mari's eyes widened. Could it be true?

"Where did you get that?"

"I found it in the room where you saved my life, just before you rescued me from Risanne. I had no idea what it was," Rebecca said in surprise.

"It is the answer to our dreams," Mari smiled. "The greatest gift you could ever give us."

"Then it is yours," Rebecca said, handing the cube to Mari.

Pythea had risen and bathed, dressed in the colours of her office, and was on her way to her chambers when she saw Kira.

"Good day to you, Kira. Have you seen Mari anywhere?"

"Not yet, but you know what she is like. Off on one of her training runs no doubt," Kira replied.

"Yes, no doubt," Pythea said as if trying to convince herself.

Inside her chamber, she sat at her desk and pushed some papers into a pile. Something bothered her. It was unlike Mari to leave without saying where she was going. Then, on her desk, Pythea noticed the parcel. A box wrapped in plain paper with a note attached. She picked up the note and read it quietly to herself.

"My friends have given us the gift of life. The chance to reclaim our homes and become again the people we once were. Now it is my turn to give. I go now to aid them in their fight, as I believe it is the fight for us all. I will return when they no longer need me and will again become your daughter. My love is with you always. Mari."

CHAPTER FOURTEEN

Shaan splashed through the shallow water that washed up and into the entrance of the cave. He knew that this way would bring him back to Cannchester. Rebecca, Jonathan, and their new companion, Mari, had taken the route to Aidenvalle to rest and prepare for the final battle against Krishia and her forces. This journey was one that Shaan had to complete alone.

Had his orders been carried out? Had the sword, Caliburn, been returned to Arielle? If not, where would it be? He had to find Sir Philippe, if indeed he had survived, for although the battle had been won, there would still have been some of Theodore's men who would seek revenge for the humiliating defeat that had been caused them. Outnumbered by ten to one, Shaan's army had still crushed them. A smile came to Shaan's lips as he remembered this, but it was short-lived, for although he was born a warrior, he hated the senseless killing brought about by one man's or woman's jealousy and greed.

As Shaan approached the cave's opening, the shrill of a gull soaring high above made him stare upwards into the bright blue sky. The smell of the sea entered his nostrils, and the smile returned. He splashed in the water like a child on his first visit to the coast, his arms outstretched, spinning round and round. After three complete turns, he stopped, the image in his head clearing. He stood perfectly still and rubbed his eyes.

In front of him, the rocks rose sharply out of the water. The tops of these rocks were covered in grassy outcrops, and on top of these sat a castle, but not just any castle. This was the castle of his father, the castle of his mother, and before that, the castle of the Duke of Dumnonia. "Trevena."

Shaan cupped his hand over his mouth as if to stop himself from saying the name aloud lest anyone should hear.

Even though the signs of war lay heavily on her walls and battlements, she still looked grand. Still one of the finest castles in the land. No one lived here now. Not since Prethus had conquered her and then had been killed himself, had anyone dared to inhabit her.

The local legends had said that the castle was cursed and that anyone who came here was doomed. Ghosts were supposed to roam the corridors, and phantoms and banshees wailed at the moon from her high towers. Even Shaan's mother and her three other children had left the castle after the death of Prethus, never to return. Only Shaan and one other knew the truth. Gaius had brought him here as a child, although Shaan had not known the significance of it at the time, to tell him stories of the great warrior Prethus and how his lost son would one day turn the divided lands into a kingdom.

When asked who the son of Prethus was, Gaius would only reply,

"Who knows? Maybe it is you, Shaan,"

then he would laugh in a hearty manner and slap Shaan on the back, most times sending him stumbling several paces forward, and then he would point at a gull or some other bird and explain the principles of flight, which somehow Shaan could never quite grasp.

The tide was out, and the rocky causeway enticed him towards the castle, but he hesitated. He would have loved to have explored the grounds and walked through the magnificent halls and rooms once again, but time was running out, and so he changed direction, heading inland along a valley and up the sloping pathway that led to the village. The path grew steeper as he neared the first of the dwellings. Looking to his right, he could see the wooden spire of the church. Thoughts of the past returned only to be shattered by the voice of a small boy.

"It's the King, it's the King!" He joyfully shouted, the sound of his voice now accompanied by the patter of his feet as he ran towards Shaan. "It is you, ain't it, sir?" The boy stopped and stared up at Shaan with bright blue eyes as big as saucers.

"What makes you think that I am the king?" Shaan asked, kneeling on one knee so as not to intimidate the lad.

"Everyone knows what the king looks like. "There's no one who could pretend to be you, sir." The boy seemed pleased with his answer.

"Have you not heard that the king is dead?"

"I do not believe that it is true. Anyway, it can't be true because you are here."

A woman walked briskly down the road and came up to the boy, taking him by the hand.

"Come now, Tom. Haven't I told you not to talk to strangers?" she asked, looking at Shaan. "I hope my boy did not offend you, sir, but he hasn't stopped talking about the King since we heard that he had been killed," she said, raising her eyes to the sky, "God bless him."

"And you believe him dead?" Shaan asked.

"But, ma, that's him," the boy said, pulling at his mother's dress.

"Hush now, sorry about the boy sir," she said, and pulling the boy by the hand, she led him, protesting, down the road.

Shaan smiled, waited a few moments, then made off in the opposite direction. In order to get to Cannchester, he would need some form of transportation. He walked through the village. The few locals that he met wished him a good day, but none recognised him as the boy had. Was this to be his fate? Forgotten so soon. Gaius had once said that it was the curse of man that he forgets, and it seemed that he had been right. Then it occurred to him that he had not travelled this way for many years, so how could he expect to be recognized?

At the far end of the village was a farm, and it was here that Shaan hoped to acquire a horse. He walked purposefully down the dirt track that led to the farmhouse and up to the wooden door. He knocked three times and waited, but there was no reply. He tried again with the same result. From the rear of the house came a snarling and grunting sound, and then a man shouting.

"Curse you, you creature from hell," the voice bellowed. "I'll send you back there too."

It could only be the Chrysak. Had Dresslon fallen already? Shaan ran towards the sickening sounds, preparing to do battle once again. Down the side passage of the house, sweeping past bushes and trampling flowers as he went. Rounding the corner, he came face to face with the beast from hell. It was not a Chrysak warrior, as he had suspected, but a large silver-grey-haired dog. A huge staghound, the largest that Shaan had ever seen. It took no notice of Shaan but instead continued to snarl at the farmer, who was halfway up a tree, a large patch missing from the seat of his trousers. He shook a stick at the dog.

"Back demon before I knock your brains out," and with that, he took a swing at the dog, missing so badly that he nearly lost his balance.

Now he hung from a branch like a pig trussed up for roasting. The dog saw this as a once-in-a-lifetime opportunity, and he jumped up, tearing another strip of cloth from the farmer's trousers. The farmer yelled, obviously; the dog had ripped more than material with that strike.

Shaan had to act fast. He gave a loud whistle, and the dog turned and stared at him. Shaan stared back, and it suddenly dawned on him that he had no weapon. The dog looked at Shaan, then at the farmer, and then back at Shaan again. Without a sound, it leapt at Shaan, catching him high on the chest and knocking him to the floor. The dog's paws were on each of Shaan's shoulders, and its weight prevented him from rising. Its mouth came nearer and nearer to Shaan's face, its huge white teeth glistening in the bright daylight. Then, without warning, it struck out with its long tongue, licking the full length of Shaan's face, its thick tail lashing vigorously from side to side.

"Back, hellhound." It was the farmer, who had now climbed down from the tree and was waving a large stick.

The dog moved its attention back to the farmer, growling. It removed its paws from Shaan and crept slowly towards its tormentor.

"No. Don't!" Shaan shouted as he rose to his feet. "It's alright, here, girl, come on," he said gently. " The hound turned to look at Shaan, unsure what to do.

"Drop the stick," Shaan commanded.

The farmer hesitated; he was not certain that it was the best plan of action.

"Do as I say. Drop it," Shaan said again.

This time, the farmer did as he was told. On seeing this, a sparkle came to the dog's eyes, and he glared at the farmer and gave a loud, ferocious bark. The farmer turned and ran. He did not stop until he reached the door of the house. Opening it quickly, he rushed inside and slammed the door behind him.

Shaan could not help but laugh, and he did so even louder when he watched the dog sit down and wag its tail, obviously pleased with its work. Shaan stroked the dog on the neck, pushing its long fur backwards and forwards, causing its tail to wag faster. After a few seconds, it rose to its feet, yapped once in pleasure, and then trotted off out of sight.

The farmer looked nervously out from the safety of his kitchen.

"It's alright, she's gone," Shaan called out.

"What do you want?" came the reply, but the door stayed shut.

"I need a horse," this was not the way that Shaan had imagined the conversation taking place.

"I don't have one," the farmer replied, "and even if I did, I wouldn't let you have him."

"I am willing to pay any price you name," Shaan pleaded. "The kingdom is threatened, and I have to get to Cannchester quickly."

"Who do you think you are, the king or something? I told you, I don't have one."

A dog barked a short distance away, and Shaan broke off his discussion with the farmer to investigate. Walking down a short path, he came upon the staghound standing by the gate to a grassy meadow. In the meadow, tethered to the fence, was a large mare. Her coat was as black as the night sky, and as Shaan approached, her ears pricked up.

"Easy girl," Shaan whispered. "Easy," he reached out and patted her, then took hold of the reins. By Shaan's own law, horse thieves were hanged, but this was an emergency, and besides, he was not stealing the horse; he was only borrowing it. Opening the gate, he led the horse out of the field, leapt up onto its back, and with a nudge of his feet, sent it straight into a canter, the sound of the farmers cursing ringing in his ears and continued down the road that led away from the village. It was going to be a long ride to Cannchester, and without a saddle, it would seem even longer.

The broken bodies of hundreds of warriors lay strewn across the battlefield of Taal, and the Jarenn were in retreat. They had run out of tricks, although not before sending many Bastion soldiers to their deaths. Jason, now covered in wounds from the cuts of a dozen swords, had taken his men high up on a nearby ridge, where they now had a large unit of the enemy caught in a crossfire. Arrow after arrow rained down from above, and there was nowhere for them to shelter. Jason felt sorry for the pitiful creatures that were dropping by the dozen, but after all, it was they who attacked his homeland, and all they had to do was surrender, and the bloodshed would stop.

He looked around at the carnage that continued all around. They had killed a great many of the enemy's forces, but still they kept coming, and it was clear that the Jarenn would not be able to hold out for much longer. It was then that he noticed that something very strange was happening. The Bastion was no longer engaging in any new battles. As one finished, either with victory or defeat, they waited for their comrades, who slowly joined them. This was most unexpected. In a short time, the two armies stood face-to-face with the blood-covered battlefield between them. The ranks of the Bastion army parted, and a figure emerged from within. She was dressed from head to toe in red samite, the cloth drawn tightly over her head and clinging just as tightly to her perfectly proportioned body. Her feet and legs were covered with long black boots that, from the knee up, curled around her thighs in the shape of a dragon's wing. Hanging about her shoulders was a long black cloak that fanned outwards and draped down onto the floor and around her neck hung an amulet that glowed from within.

Krishia had never felt better or looked more beautiful. She walked gracefully through the corridor formed by her soldiers and stood before the amazed Jarenn army. She lofted her jewel-encrusted staff skywards and spoke in a voice that, although soft, carried to the far reaches of the battlefield so that all could hear.

"Surrender now and all your lives will be spared; continue and you will all die. It is a simple choice, as I am sure you realise that you cannot win this battle. My forces are too powerful and yours are too small to give you even a hope of victory. Save yourselves while you still can."

"Do you think we are fools?" A voice came from the Jarenn ranks. "We know that if we surrender, you will kill us all."

"Not so. Are we not all warriors, and we fight by the same code of honor as you?" Krishia replied calmly.

"You liar," the voice shouted back angrily, and a swishing sound followed it as an arrow shot out towards Krishia.

It was a perfect shot; surely she would not be able to get out of the way in time. She did not even try; the arrow flew straight to her, and just as it should have struck its target, it changed, ceased to be an arrow, and was now a shower of white petals like those of the cherry blossom tree.

"Why thank you?" Krishia flashed a smile at her attacker. "You see, there is nothing that you can do to harm me. Now what do you say? Will you join me or die?"

This time, a throwing knife flew from a different part of the Jarenn ranks. The knife promptly turned into a shower of tiny sparks that glistened like stars in the night sky and then faded away.

"I'll take that as a no then, shall I?" Krishia said with the smile still on her lips, and with that, the soldier who had thrown the knife cried out in pain as his face seemed to melt and the limp body toppled over and crashed to the ground.

"Kill them. Kill them all," she raged.

There was a great roar of battle cries as Krishia's army swept by and the battle resumed.

"I tried to be nice. No one can say I didn't try," Krishia said to the driver as she climbed back into her carriage.

General Tulak's armies had travelled for days, knowing that they could not take Varsile, having been severely depleted, they had headed south. A messenger had been sent to order them to Taal, where they were to meet up with Krishia's main forces for reasons he did not know. It seemed that he was to be given just enough information and no more, as if he were no longer trusted by the high-ranking chain of command. He felt betrayed, let down by his masters; no reinforcements were sent, no aid was available as it had been at Stroika; why had he been abandoned? Had he not swept all before him? He also wondered why the messenger had not brought him the usual messages from his wife, the ones to say she missed him, was worried about him, and asked for news of the war. He had, though, sent his message to her, written in the code only they knew, so that she could know the truth about the situation and know he was soon to be coming home to her.

Night was drawing in when Shaan reined in his horse. His body ached from the effort of riding bareback, and he was hungry and thirsty. A nearby stream quenched his thirst, but now he needed to find some food. He had no weapons apart from the small knife that Bron had given him, and he knew that whatever he was going to eat, he would have to catch with his bare hands. Out of the corner of his eye, he spotted it, small, furry, and with long ears. Rabbit. "Perfect," Shaan thought. With slow, deliberate movements, he turned to face his quarry. The rabbit pricked up his ears, standing up on his hind legs, sniffing the air. Shaan flexed his knees, being careful not to alert his dinner, and then with a flash he dived with outstretched arms. "Yes," Shaan said aloud. Pulling his arms towards his chest, he looked down. nothing. Shaan looked up just in time to see a white bobtail disappear down a hole a short distance away. "Damn."

Shaan shot a glance to his left, alerted by a loud bark. A few paces away sat a huge animal covered in long grey fur, a ball of brown and green feathers in her mouth.

"Well, what have we got here?" Shaan stood and walked over to where the dog sat, wagging its tail vigorously. "Hello dog. I thought I had seen the last of you at the farmhouse," the dog barked as if in answer, dropping the pheasant at Shaan's feet. "Why thank you, my lady," Shaan laughed. "This will taste better than rabbit, I'll wager."

Finding some kindling and flints nearby, it was not long before Shaan had a fire roaring, and within the hour, both he and the dog were enjoying roast fowl. An hour later, the dog was lying on its stomach, watching Shaan closely. When she was sure that he was asleep, she inched closer and closer until her head rested in Shaan's lap, and she too drifted off into whatever world it is that dogs go to when they are asleep.

In the grounds of Castle Cannchester, a bird sang, its melody drifting softly to where Bedilore sat. He stopped what he was doing and looked up. The bird was nowhere in sight, yet its chirping was loud and clear. Bedilore looked left and right, up and down, but the singer was not to be seen. Again, the sweet song sang out. It was such a beautiful tune that Bedilore had to find out where it came from. He rose to his feet and cocked his head to one side, listening. There it was again; from around the corner of the stables it came. Following the harmony, like a lodestone inexplicably drawn north, he rounded the corner. Bedilore's eyes widened, and his mouth opened, for there, sitting on a low wall, whistling and chirping like a bird, was a man. But not just any man

"Shaan. Is it you?" Tears came to Bedilore's eyes. "Is it really you?"

A huge smile crossed the man's face. "Hello, old friend," he said.

Bedilore dropped to his knees. "Praise be to God!"

Shaan stretched out an arm and helped his friend to his feet.

"God and Gaius," he proclaimed. "Come, my friend, we have much to talk about."

Putting his arm around Bedilore's shoulder, Shaan steered him towards the castle's entrance. "Tis good to be home."

The silver-grey hound followed behind, its tail lashing from one side to the other.

"Come quick. Galwraith, Berel," Bedilore shouted. "Marrakech, Lyonell," then spinning around in a kind of joyful dance. "Ah, we are one again, Meneduke; Thomas, come and see."

From all directions, the Knights came, running to the sound of Bedilore's voice. Whatever could have happened, had he gone mad? they wondered. As one, they came into the great hall, and almost as one, they came to a halt, eyes staring in disbelief. Then slowly, a whisper started.

"Shaan. It's Shaan," they murmured.

Shaan looked at them. Now it was his turn to shed a tear. "Are you all that is left of my knights?" he said quietly. "My God. What have I done?"

With that, his head dropped, unable to look his fellow warriors in the eye. "I am so sorry. I have betrayed you all."

Thomas was the first to speak. "No. You did what you had to do. What any of us would have done in your position," he walked over to Shaan and knelt down on one knee. "You saved us. Saved the whole kingdom from darkness," then, one after the other, all the knights kneeled before their king.

From the back of the hall came a voice. "What's happening? What's all the..." the voice stopped abruptly.

"Welcome, Sir Philippe," Shaan said. "Please join us."

CHAPTER FIFTEEN

After they had eaten, during which time Shaan had recounted his adventures to date, he and Sir Philippe had mounted their horses and rode to the shore of a large lake, a lake that Shaan knew well, for it was here that he had been given the great sword Caliburn by the lady Aenea after he had broken its twin, Moonblade, during a fight with Davide. The water was calm, as if no wave dared ripple across its surface.

After a few minutes, they came to a spot where a rowing boat was tethered to a wooden post. Shaan dismounted and, looking up at Philippe, said, "Wait here." Philippe was about to protest but thought better of it.

Shaan pushed the boat into the water and jumped aboard. Grabbing the oars, he set about rowing towards an island set in the middle of the lake. The island was surrounded by trees, but Shaan knew that at its center was a chapel, and the inhabitant of that chapel was the only one who could help him now.

Having reached the land, he pulled the boat a short way up the loose shingle that formed the shore so that it would not drift away. He pushed past some bushes and threaded his way between the trees until he reached the tiny sandstone chapel. Gently turning the handle, he opened the door.

The interior of the chapel was plain and without decoration, save for a wooden cross at the far end and a stone table that served as an altar. Although there were no windows, the inside of the chapel was as bright as daylight, lit by the glow of hundreds of candles.

Shaan entered the chapel and knelt, head bowed, for a few seconds, then rose again to his feet. As he did so, a woman emerged from a door adjacent to where Shaan now stood. She glided to the alter as if walking on air, seeming not to notice Shaan. She stopped and put down the chalice that she was carrying. It was only then that she turned to look at Shaan.

Her face and hands were as white as marble, as if she were a statue, but it was her eyes that showed that she was alive, deep blue, they stared at Shaan for a few seconds before she spoke.

"Welcome, Shaan," she said emotionlessly, her voice seemed to have a slight echo to it "I heard that you had been killed."

"I do not believe so," Shaan replied with a smile, "although these days I am not sure what I believe. Maybe I am dead, and this is some dream world that I now reside in."

"You do not dream, Shaan, all that you see is real."

"If you tell me that it is so, then I will believe you."

Shaan looked into the deep blue eyes. "How do you fare, lady Aenea?" He had noticed that she appeared preoccupied.

"It is always a little hard when one of my kind leaves," Aenea replied.

"You grieve for Gaius, my lady?"

"I do"

"Then he is dead."

"He no longer lives on this plane," was all she replied, refusing to be drawn further on the subject. "You came here not to talk of Gaius, but for a different reason," Aenea beckoned to Shaan. "Come."

Shaan was led through a door to the side of the altar and down a spiral staircase of wrought iron fashioned into an intricate design. The floor of this new room was barren rock, and the sound of running water could be heard echoing through the room. It was much darker on this level, as only a handful of candles burned, casting eerie shadows on the surrounding walls. Shaan followed Aenea to the end of the room and discovered where the sound of water was coming from; here the water cascaded down the walls into a shimmering pool. In the middle of this pool, a rocky platform rose out of the water, and hovering horizontally above this was an object that Shaan knew well. Strange forces held the sword in place, forces that Shaan did not understand.

"Caliburn," Shaan said, almost in disbelief.

"Yes. She always comes home when she is no longer needed," and for the first time Aeneas voice seemed to lighten, although her expression had not changed. "A word of warning, Shaan. "Krishia is no ordinary mortal; if she gains possession of Caliburn, it will spell the end of light in this world forever. If you take the sword from this place now, you will be committing yourself to being the protector of mankind until Krishia is destroyed. If you fail to banish her, then you will be cursed by humanity for all time."

"I have no choice, Lady Aenea. If I do not have the sword, then all is lost anyway."

"Are you sure there is no other way, Shaan?"

"I do not think that I can destroy Krishia without it."

"Then you must take Caliburn," Aenea said, but added softly, "and may God be with you."

Shaan waded into the water, first up to his boot tops, and then, having filled them with water, it began to rise further up his legs, and by the time he had reached the platform, it was swirling about his waist. He pulled himself up onto the rock and stood with his feet apart in front of the mighty battle blade. He was reminded of the past, when, as a young man of seventeen, he had been given the sword's twin, Moonblade, by Prethus before he had died, a sword he had broken in anger, and that sword in turn had been replaced by Aenea. Reaching out, he took hold of Caliburn with both hands and then held it aloft. "For God and Humanity."

Krishia had summoned Moroc to her chambers. "How goes the battle?" she demanded to know. "Can I expect the tower to fall today?"

"The battle goes well, my queen. The Jarenn have been forced back into the tower and have barricaded themselves in. It will only be a matter of time before victory is ours."

"Time!" Krishia shouted. "I do not have time. I want them destroyed now."

"We have lost many men, your majesty, but they are few now, and they cannot resist us long," Moroc answered.

"You had better be right," then with a smile, "or I shall be needing a new commander."

"If we had the Dragon, then it would be over very quickly," Moroc said with a smug look on his face. Dare he push her this hard?

"Summoning a dragon is not a party trick, Moroc. I have only just recovered from the last time I had to help you out. It will be a while before I have the strength to do that again," Krishia turned away from Moroc. "By then you will have taken the tower," she stressed.

Krishia fingered her amulet, knowing that it had fully restored her powers but not wishing for Moroc to know this. She had allowed Khamel to live for now; her mission was complete, and the object of her search had been found and delivered to its rightful owner.

Moroc knew that the audience was over, so with the words "Yes, your highness," he left the room, cursing. Had he not been loyal? Had he not swept all before him in the name of Krishia? Even now he had forced the great, and some said invincible, Jarenn scurrying like scolded dogs back to their fortress. Well, maybe they weren't scurrying, and perhaps he had lost over two-thirds of his army to a much smaller force, but they had been full of tricks and had not conducted themselves properly in the art of war, which of course, he admired. Krishia had no right to be angry with him, and he swore to himself that one day he would get even.

Philippe looked out over the lake and watched the rowboat make its way slowly towards him. As it neared the bank, he called out to Shaan,

"Did you find it?"

"I did, my friend," Shaan called back, "and now we must ride once again, against the forces of darkness."

Philippe ran into the water and helped Shaan pull the boat ashore, and then together they mounted their steeds and rode back to Cannchester.

"I hope that the rest of the knights will join me," Shaan said hopefully.

"How can they not when you are their king?" Philippe asked.

"Was their king," Shaan replied. "My time in this place is over, Philippe. I have served my purpose, and now someone else must take the throne and lead the people to greater heights than I ever could," he added thoughtfully, almost to himself. "I think that I was a good king for a while, but it cost me my chance to be a man. I lived only for the land, but now I must live for myself."

"I think I understand what you mean, my lord," Philippe replied, though he seemed unsure. "One thing is certain, and that is that I will follow you to the ends of the earth if you ask me to," he continued proudly.

"And beyond?" Shaan asked.

Soon the hooves of the two horses were clattering over the cobblestones of the courtyard of Castle Cannchester as Shaan and Philippe returned. Thomas met them in the courtyard and greeted them with a smile. "Good afternoon, gentlemen."

"And a good afternoon to you too, Sir Thomas," Shaan returned the greeting. "What do you do on this fine day?"

"I am just exercising my sword arm," said Thomas, holding out his right arm to reveal the sword he had been practicing with.

"Fighting shadows?" Shaan laughed. "How would you like to do battle with a real army?"

"Why, are we under attack?" Thomas said he was spinning round, with his sword pointing forward, to catch sight of any advancing foe.

"No, at least not yet," Shaan said seriously, "but fetch the others and I will explain."

Without hesitation, all the knights had agreed to aid Shaan and had packed weapons and provisions and followed Shaan out of Cannchester.

They looked a splendid sight as they rode once more, flanked by two standard bearers, their armor shining brightly in the glorious sunshine that now filled the sky. It seemed that someone was smiling down on them as they made their way west to Trevena and beyond.

Two days later, they rode through the town, stopping briefly to throw a bag of coins containing enough money to buy ten horses to the farmer whose horse Shaan had 'borrowed' a few days before. As they filed past the houses and wheeled around a corner to begin their descent to the sea, Shaan heard a small boy's voice behind them.

"See, ma, see. I told you it was the King."

Shaan waved, "Hello, Tom! I hope one day you will ride by my side too, or at least write of my adventures.

"I will, sir, I will" came the reply, "I promise."

They were accompanied on their descent by the sound of running water splashing and whirling as the stream to their left made its way to the sea. Ahead of them ran the staghound, head held high and tail thrashing about as if she knew where they were going.

A figure stared out from a window set high in the castle's wall as the knights led their horses into the sea and from there into the cave opposite.

"That's right, take the fight to her, my boy," the figure whispered, "but beware the dragon."

"Beware the dragon.... Beware the dragon," a voice echoed in Shaan's head. He turned in his saddle and looked at Sir Thomas, who rode behind him. "What's that you say?"

"I did not say anything, my lord," Thomas replied.

Shaan shook his head, puzzled. He was sure that the voice had come from behind him.

"Are you alright, Shaan?" Thomas asked.

"Yes, yes, I am fine," he replied, turning again towards the cave.

Although Shaan had described the cave to them, there was not one knight who was not amazed as they each led their horse out of the passage and into the cavern, which held the round table.

"How did it get here?", "Why is it here?" and other such questions were muttered.

"First we will go to Aidenvalle, where we will meet my companions, and then we will pray together for the last time before we do battle," Shaan announced. He looked at the markings on the table to see which indicated the passage they must take.

Johnathan 's sword swept downward, and it took all of Rebecca's strength to parry the lethal blow. Now she attacked, stabbing out with her own sword and forcing her opponent back. Again, she thrust out, but this time Jonathan stepped to one side, causing Rebecca to come forward, and now she was standing next to him. Johnathan made a move to take a small blade from his belt with which to attack at close range, but before he could do so, Rebecca kicked out with her leg and caught him behind the right knee, sending him sprawling to the floor, her sword arcing over to be placed on Johnathan's throat.

Mari laughed. "She learns quick," and she jumped up from where she had been sitting cross-legged. "Come, my love," she said, reaching out a hand to help Johnathan rise, "that is not a dignified position for a man of your reputation to be in."

"It is a situation I would gladly have reversed," he answered. "Well done, Rebecca, if I had not taught you myself, I would not have believed it possible."

"My husband was a good teacher, but you are a great teacher, Jonathan. In less than a week, I feel that I could take on anyone."

"Be careful not to get overconfident," Jonathan warned. "It is one thing to fight the same man day after day; you get to know his moves and the way he thinks. But remember, everyone is different, and all fighters will have their own special moves and favorite tactics."

"I will be careful," Rebecca said, feeling a little less assured, but she knew that she was now more prepared than she had ever been in her entire life.

"Someone is coming," Mari announced. She looked over at Jonathan, who was listening intently.

"Ten horses, I should say," he replied.

"Eleven," Mari argued.

"What is it?" asked Rebecca, who had heard nothing.

"We have company," Mari answered as she and Johnathan began running towards the wall of the keep. Clambering up the stone staircase, they peered out from behind a rampart.

"Told you," Mari shot a smile at Johnathan .

Toward them came eleven horsemen. Nine in shining armor

and two in plain chain mail, bearing standards that fluttered in the gentle afternoon breeze.

"What is that?" Mari pointed to the furious beast that ran just in front of the lead horse.

"It's a dog," Jonathan replied. "Do you not have them in your world?"

"I do not think so," Mari answered, "but then, I have never been far away from my home before, and nobody has ever told me of such a creature."

"Who do you think it is?" Johnathan asked.

"It's Shaan!" replied Rebecca joyously.

"How can you tell?"

"I just know," and with that, Rebecca was bounding down the staircase and towards the entrance to the courtyard.

Shaan saw someone emerge from the building's gateway and knew immediately who it was. He kicked his horse to a gallop and raced towards the waving figure. Within moments, he had leapt from his horse, half running, and swept her into his arms. He kissed her face and neck as she clung on to him tightly.

"I missed you," he said softly.

It had only been a few days since they had last been together, but to Shaan, it had seemed like a year. "Rebecca, what have you done to me? I feel like a boy again," he laughed.

"You make me feel young again too," she replied, kissing him back.

"Well, well. Who is this beautiful maiden?"

Shaan looked around. The others had caught up, and Philippe stared down at them from his magnificent palomino horse.

"Gentlemen, may I introduce the Countess Rebecca?"

Shaan stood back a little so that they could see her.

"Rebecca, these are the best friends that any man could have."

He then went on to introduce each knight by name, and as they were called out, they gave a small nod in Rebecca's direction. By the time he had finished Johnathan and Mari had joined them.

"Knights, these are also two very special friends without whom I would not be here today. Mari of Myrina and Jonathan of..."

"We have already met, have we not, pilgrim?" Sir Philippe glared at Jonathan.

"I believe that we have." Johnathan smiled.

"You know this man?" Shaan enquired.

"Yes, Philippe replied. "Do not trust him, Shaan."

"Why not?"

"He has already lied to us. He came looking for you, Shaan, disguised as a humble pilgrim. We trusted him, fed him, and gave him refuge, and he has betrayed that trust."

"I know all of that, Philippe. It is true that in the beginning Jonathan was not all that he appeared to be, but he is our ally now," Shaan said.

"If you say that it is so, then I will not argue with you, my lord," Philippe replied. Then, looking down at Jonathan, he said: "Even so, I will be alert to anything that threatens our safety."

With that, Philippe turned his horse and trotted over to where Sir Bedilore sat watching the unfolding scene. They immediately struck up a conversation, casting an occasional glance over towards Jonathan.

"They will come round," Shaan insisted.

"I suppose I only have myself to blame," Jonathan answered. "Do not worry, Shaan; I mean you no harm."

"I know that, my friend," Shaan replied reassuringly.

CHAPTER SIXTEEN

Ling Chuan sat at the great table, its eerie green glow shining up at his face and making him look almost alien. Around him were gathered the members of the council and their advisers.

"We have no choice," one of the councilors was stating loudly. "We must recruit another army to aid us."

"We cannot allow the gateways of the tower to become public knowledge," another argued back.

"There is no other way," said the first. "If the tower is taken, then untold damage will be done."

"It is a chance that we must take," Ling Chuan spoke for the first time. "If it becomes common knowledge that the tower gives access to other realms, then it could lead to a war on a scale that none of us could comprehend. Every creature in every land in every realm with even a small army would seek to control the tower, and it could mean a war that would last for all eternity. Even Krishia's rule would be better than that."

The others fell silent and stopped their arguing. They realised that Ling Chuan was right.

"Then what are we to do?" asked Jason.

"We must destroy the tower," Ling Chuan said solemnly.

"Surely there must be another way?" Daal protested.

"I am sorry," Ling Chuan insisted. "After the explosives have been positioned, each man will be allowed to enter the realm of his choice before the detonation."

"No," a voice boomed from the back of the hall. The doors had opened to reveal a small man with a wizened face, from which protruded a strange object that appeared to be on fire, sending a spiral of white smoke drifting towards the ceiling. "He will be here soon."

Members of the council fought for a view, mumbling to each other. "Who is it?" "How did he get in?" and "What's that in his mouth?"

One who obviously recognised the man said, "It's that crazy woodsman, Grom, or whatever he's called."

"My name is Bron,"

The man corrected himself. "Bron."

"And just who is it that will be here soon?" Ling Chuan asked.

"Shaan Moonblade," Bron stated. "And his knights."

"Impossible. Moonblade is dead.

"What makes you think that?"

"Travelers who come this way tell us many things," Ling Chuan retorted. "He was killed by Theodore, I believe."

"Then you believe wrong, sir. It was Shaan who was the victor of that fight, and although gravely wounded, he was taken to Aidenvalle and healed by the great Gaius."

"I might have known Gaius would be involved in this," Ling Chuan said scornfully. "Hasn't he learned his lesson yet? He should stop meddling with the affairs of humans."

"His meddling may just save your precious tower," Bron retaliated.

Ling Chuan looked thoughtful. He was not a rash man and took time to make sure that his decisions were right. After a few seconds of silence, he spoke again.

"Where is Moonblade now?" He asked.

"I'm not altogether sure," Bron replied, sucking deeply on his pipe and blowing a great plume of white smoke into the air. "But I feel that he is very close."

"You 'feel' he is close," Ling Chuan said accusingly. "Your

feelings will not help save the tower. We can survive for no more than two days. What happens if your hero does not come forth by then?"

Bron had, by now, walked the length of the room and was standing in front of Ling Chuan, who had turned in his seat to face him.

"May I suggest that you go ahead with the planting of your explosives, and by all means, if Shaan has not arrived in two days, detonate them?"

A man dressed in the robes of a general stood up and shouted. "What about our men? How many more must we allow to be slaughtered? I say that we destroy the tower now."

"Galihar, please be seated," Ling Chuan said softly, his voice barely rising above a whisper, yet all could hear him. "We are sworn to protect the tower above all else. Even above ourselves. We will allow Bron two days to bring us his champion."

"Thank you," Bron said, giving a barely noticeable bow in Ling Chuan's direction. "And now, if I may, I would like to make use of the tower myself."

As the sun set, Shaan sat looking down at the burning fires in the valley below. From here, he could see that the tower of Taal still stood. Around the outside of the tower's walls were camped the armies of Bastion. Shaan had expected to see a battle raging, but there was none.

"I wonder what they are up to. They have not taken the tower yet," he said more to himself than to Johnathan , who was sitting next to Shaan astride his own horse.

"They must be getting ready for the final battle. It is common battle practice in a long siege to rest fully the day before you risk a full assault," Jonathan answered.

"How many men do you estimate are left in Krishia's army?"

Jonathan counted the campfires and tents and made a quick estimation. "Five hundred, maybe more."

"Then I don't see how we are going to win this fight," Shaan rubbed his chin with his hand thoughtfully. "Even against Theodore, I was not this outnumbered."

"I think I have..." Johnathan started but was cut off by the sound of Mari running towards them.

"We've got company," she panted.

Johnathan jumped from his mount to greet her. "Krishia's men?"

"I don't know, but there are about thirty of them."

"Where are the others?" Shaan asked.

"They've taken cover in the trees." Thomas and Philippe have gone to take a closer look.

"We had better leave the horses here and take a look ourselves," Shaan said as he dismounted. "Lead the way, Mari."

Mari turned towards the trees, but before she had taken a step, two figures emerged from the darkness, their hands tied, being urged on by the sharpened lances aimed at their backs. These were closely followed by several horsemen. Shaan instinctively drew Caliburn from its scabbard. Jonathan also brought his sword to hand, and they waited for the enemy to approach. Mari did not have a sword but instead carried a long-bladed knife, but this too would be very effective at close range. As the riders and prisoners approached, their faces began to materialize. First Thomas, then Philippe. They did not look as though they were carrying any injuries, which indicated to Shaan that they had been caught completely by surprise and had been unable to put up a struggle. He looked up at the riders; there was something very familiar about their style of dress. The lead rider was now fully visible to Shaan, and he immediately recognised him. A smile crossed Shaan's lips. The smile turned into a chuckle, and the chuckle into a laugh. Johnathan looked at Shaan and frowned.

"What's so funny?"

Shaan coughed, trying to stop himself from laughing, but he couldn't.

"I'm sorry. I suppose it's not very funny really," and with this he broke into laughter again.

"Shaan," Johnathan hissed.

Suddenly, a look of recognition crossed the leader's face, and he leapt from his horse and ran up to where Shaan stood.

"Is it you?" He inquired, "Is it really you?"

Shaan embraced the other man, saying, "Hello Jobe, it's good to see you again. What are you doing here?"

"I heard that you needed some assistance; besides, it was getting too quiet without you around," Jobe said. "It seems we turned up just in time. We caught these two sneaking around in the bushes," he added, looking around at Thomas and Philippe. "What do you want me to do with them?"

Shaan smiled. "Now let me see, I think... you should let them go."

"Let them go?" Jobe looked puzzled.

"Yes, let them go," Shaan walked behind the two prisoners and slit their bindings. "Jobe, I'd like you to meet Sir Thomas and Sir Philippe."

"They are friends of yours?" Jobe asked.

"Very good friends," Shaan replied.

"Then I apologise deeply. I hope we were not too rough with you," Jobe held out his hand towards the others.

Shaan sat in the circle of men discussing their options. It seemed that they stood little chance of victory. None were afraid to die, but each would prefer to have a fair chance to survive.

"If only Gaius were here to provide a fog to hide us as he did against Theodore, then we may have been able to surprise them," Bedilore said.

"We could provide such a cover," Jobe offered, "but it would help little." Then he added thoughtfully. "If we knew what they had planned and where they would strike first, then we might also employ some other tricks, but it would be futile to attempt anything using guesswork."

"We are not mind readers, Jobe. If only we were," Thomas said grimly.

"If only I had not been so afraid," Shaan looked down at the earth. "If I had done as I was asked, then we could solve this puzzle."

Johnathan rose and left the circle.

"What do you mean?" Arios asked. "What should you have done?"

"I was told to gather certain objects that I would need," Shaan answered. "I failed to bring one of them with me, and now I may have damned the whole of humanity to slavery."

"What was the object that you left behind, Shaan?" Arios continued.

At that moment, a cloud of dust erupted in the center of the circle. When the dust had settled, the sack that Jonathan had thrown became visible.

"What's this?" Jobe asked, jumping up and walking over to the sack. He pulled out a small knife that had been tucked in his belt and slit the cord. He reached inside and retrieved the object that he sought. It was the steel helmet of Othuset.

"What's so precious about this?"

"Well… Shaan?" Johnathan stared in Shaan's direction.

"I cannot. The Helm of Othuset is evil," Shaan said gravely.

"You must," Jonathan insisted. "It is our only hope."

Shaan looked around at the expectant faces gathered around him.

"Yes, you are right," he conceded,

With slow, deliberate movements, he took the Helm of Othuset from Jobe's outstretched hand. He lifted the helmet to his head and hesitated for a second before lowering it. Voices echoed in his mind.

"What's he doing?", "How can that old Helm help us?" the voices of his comrades inquired.

Shaan tried to concentrate harder. In his mind, he pictured the enemy camp below. Imagining being in one of the tents that he had spied earlier, he could see the vision of a man. Tall and dressed in black leather. Beside him, another man spoke.

"Your plan is insane, Moroc. If we move our armies away, then the Jarenn will have the upper hand."

"Nonsense, I will explain again," Moroc growled. "When we retreat, the Jarenn will think that we are beaten and will come out of their hiding hole to finish us off."

"What if they don't?"

"I would. Anyway, if they do not come out of the tower, then what have we lost? We can simply move our armies back into position again," said Moroc, who seemed agitated by the other man's resistance to his plan.

"If you are wrong about this, Moroc, the Queen will have your head."

"And if I am right," Moroc paused before adding, "maybe I'll have hers."

"That's treasonous talk, Moroc." The other said looking almost shocked. "What would you do if I went to her now and told of your treachery?"

"You will not do that, General Kai," Moroc said, pulling himself up to his full height. "You know as well as I do that Krishia's power is weakening. If we do not gain control of the tower, then she may not even have the strength to return home."

"I know nothing of the sort," Kai said, stroking his chin. "But for now, I'll say nothing."

Johnathan , Jobe, and the rest watched closely. Shaan's eyes were closed, but they could clearly see movement beneath the lids, as if he were looking around at something that they could not see. Sometime later, the blue eyes flickered open, and slowly, Shaan removed the helmet.

Mari, dressed in her usual black, stood, holding Johnathan , but her mind was clearly on the task ahead.

"It should be me who goes," Jonathan was saying. "This is not your fight. You do not have to do this, Mari."

"Oh yes, I do, Jonathan," she whispered. "You know that I am the best suited for this mission. It's something I have done a dozen times, and besides, this is my fight. It is our fight. The fight for all of mankind."

"In my mind, I know that you are right, but my heart says that you should stay here." Jonathan looked at the young woman in his arms.

"I'll be back before you've even missed me," Mari smiled, kissed Jonathan on the lips, turned, and disappeared into the night.

The bushes behind him rustled, and Jonathan called out. "Mari.

"Oh, it's you, Shaan."

"Is she away?" Shaan asked.

"Yes," was the curt reply.

"She'll be alright," Shaan assured him, putting his hand on his friend's shoulder.

"Yes, you're right. I'm sorry I was rude to you," Jonathan said. "Do you know, Shaan, I think that for the first time in my life I'm scared."

"That is nothing to be ashamed of, I have felt the same on many occasions," Shaan admitted. "But I find that it makes me fight even harder."

"Hey, you two, why so miserable?"

It was Rebecca. She had emerged from the cover of the bushes so quietly that neither of the men had heard her approach.

"Mari is more than able to look after herself, and so are both of you," she linked her arm through Shaan's and then Johnathan's.

"Come on, we must rest now, for when the sun rises, we will know no peace until Krishia and her cronies are gone," then she led them back to the camp to prepare for the battle to come.

Mari crept through the blackness of night, towards the Bastion camp.

She had to pass close by in order to reach the Tower of Taal and pass on the plans that Shaan had entrusted her with. If she failed, then all would be lost. Now she was close enough to smell the enemy's cooking and to hear them talking in their tents, telling each other how they would claim many Jarenn lives tomorrow and how brave they were.

"Are you in for a surprise?" she thought.

At that moment, a hand touched her on the shoulder. She jumped, completely taken by surprise. It shouldn't have happened; maybe the last few days had taken more out of her than she would admit. She turned around slowly.

"What the heck are you doing here?" A drunken voice said It

was a Bastion guard. He had obviously been making the most of what could be his last night. Mari's mind whirred. What to do? If she killed him, he would be missed. If she escaped, he would report her to the others. Her hand moved down to the dagger at her side. She raised herself up to her full height.

"You are drunk," Mari said in a voice of authority. "I should report you to the captain."

The guard reeled at this statement. "Whash? Who'd ya thinks you are then?" He slurred.

"Surely you are not so drunk that you do not recognise me,"

Mari knew that she was pushing her luck now, and she began to draw the knife from its sheath. The guard, though, was not so sure. He cursed his partner.

"It'll be alright. Have another to keep out the cold." He had been persuaded. Now he was being confronted by one of Moroc's women, and he could hardly see, let alone talk properly.

"Yes, of course I do," he muttered. "I'm Shorry M 'lady."

"It is just as well that I am not the enemy," she said, softening her voice. "It's alright. I understand that it is the night before victory, and maybe you are celebrating a little early. Go on, be on your way now, and I'll say nothing."

"Thank you, ma'am. I'm really shorry to have bothered you," the guard said as best he could.

Then he staggered past Mari and headed back into the night. "Thank the gods for that," they both thought.

"That was too close," Mari murmured to herself as she continued through the darkness. Away from the camp now, she allowed herself to breathe a little easier. Above her, the towers wall rose, smooth and seemingly impenetrable. She crouched, listening. The only sound came from the crickets and other insects that came out at night to feed. Taking the rope from around her waist, she unfurled a long length; one end was attached to a three-pronged hook, which she swung round in an ever-increasing arc before finally releasing it to sail skywards towards the wall's rim. The hook caught the first time. Mari pulled back on the rope to make sure that it could take her weight, then slowly she began to haul herself up, climbing hand over hand and using her legs to gain extra grip. The wall was high, and it took a long time to scale it, but exhausted and aching, Mari pulled herself up, swung a leg over, and came to a sitting position. She was just about to jump to the brick walkway below when a spear was thrust into her ribs, biting at the skin under her tunic.

"Well, well. What have we here?" the aggressor said.

Mari grabbed at the spear, which only served to get it pushed harder into her side, this time, nearly toppling her from the wall.

"Be careful!" laughed the spearman. "Come on now, off the wall," the spear was retracted slightly, allowing Mari to jump into a much safer position. Standing now, she could see that the man before her was dressed in the green robes of the Jarenn. She pulled off the hood, that had up until now, covered her face.

"By the gods, you're a woman," the startled Jarenn guard said.

"What did you expect, an owl?" Mari answered sarcastically.

How did you make it over the wall? The guard asked.

"Maybe I flew."

"Very funny. You'll not be laughing when you're hanging by your toes," he threatened. "Now go that way," he ordered, jabbing the spear at Mari.

Mari was forced along the walkway and through a door at the far end, where they were met by another Jarenn guard.

"What have you got there, Nasim?" Hulum asked.

"An owl," came the reply.

"What?"

"Never mind, it's a long story. We had better take this one

straight to Daal," Nasim said. "Carimus, you take the watch."

With this, a man brushed past Mari and her captors and disappeared through the door.

"Right, down the stairs," and with that she was bundled, half stumbling, to the lower levels of the tower.

When they emerged into a corridor, Mari was led along it and through a large wooden door. It was worth the prodding because at least now she would meet someone important and be able to deliver her message. Hulum opened a door and roughly pushed Mari inside, slamming it closed behind her. She turned to the door and shouted.

"There was no need for that," she said, then turned back to meet the occupants of the room but saw nothing but barren walls.

"Let me out! You don't know what you're doing," Mari shouted.

But there was no one there to hear.

"Why are we not taking the woman to see Daal?" Nasim asked.

"He is resting at the moment; besides, she's not going anywhere," Hulum replied.

CHAPTER SEVENTEEN

Saris came running up the stairway and out to where Carimus stood watching the commotion below. "What's happening?"

"I'm not quite sure, sir. It looks like they are packing up, ready to move out," Carimus said. "They must have had enough. We certainly showed them, didn't we, sir?"

Saris rubbed his chin. "I'm not convinced. They must know that we cannot survive many more of their assaults. I have a strange feeling about this," he said as he left Carimus and descended back to the tower's lower levels.

"What's the hurry, Saris?" Benn called as the other pushed past, almost running.

"Something's going on," Saris answered. "Come on, we have to see Ling Chuan."

Mari could hear the sound of running feet. She pressed her ear to the door but could not make out what was being said, whatever it was, she was sure it had something to do with the Bastion.

"Let me out! I need to talk to Ling Chuan," she shouted to no avail.

"I've waited long enough for these fools to release me," she said to herself. "Now to find my own way out."

She leant heavily on the door. It refused to move. She looked around; there were no windows, and the ceiling was too high for her to reach, even when standing on the table. Mari sniffed at the air. It smelled damp and stale. The building was obviously incredibly old. Looking closely at the walls, she could see that the mortar was crumbling and in need of repair. If only she had some way of scraping at the mortar. The guards had taken her knife, so she had to come up with another implement.

"Of course," she muttered, undoing her belt and pulling it from around her waist. Using the steel buckle, she set to work.

The doors to the great hall blew open. Ling Chuan and his advisers looked up from their discussion. Saris and Benn rushed forward, giving a slight bow. "We have urgent news, sir."

"The Bastion army is preparing to move away."

"Yes, I know," Ling Chuan spoke softly as if unconcerned.

"You already know?" Benn stared, puzzled.

"Please be seated," Ling Chuan motioned. "What we have to decide now is what to do about it."

Saris and Benn sat behind the crystal table and gazed at the green light shining from within.

"Well gentlemen. What suggestions do you have?"

Benn was the first to speak. "The way I see it, is that if we let them go then they will return with more men and heavier weapons. I think that we should finish them now."

"I'm not so sure," Saris said thoughtfully. "What if they have really given up? Why put more of our men to death for no reason? I think we should let them go."

"And if they return?" Benn asked.

"If they do return, we will have had time to strengthen our defenses, recruited more men and next time we will be better prepared," Saris completed his argument.

"We must not let them go. We cannot allow them to continue their injustices against the world," Benn said angrily.

"Unfortunately, we cannot protect all of the realms. We do not even have the resources to protect this one," Ling Chuan stated. "Neither do we have the right to. Our purpose is to keep the tower neutral and that is all."

Mari had managed to produce a small pile of mortar on the floor in front of her. She wiggled her fingers into the gap she had made around the stone and pushed and pulled as best she could. The stone moved, a little at first, then a bit more and when Mari was sure that it was loose enough, she lay on her back and kicked out with both feet. The stone slid backwards. Mari kicked again, and this time, with a great cloud of dust, the stone fell. Turning over, she crouched on her hands and knees and peered through the hole. Beyond was a room similar to the one she was in now. It was a tight squeeze, but with a good deal of pulling and wriggling, she managed to work her way through. Standing up, Mari retied the belt around her waist, and then softly, she crept up to the door. Twisting the handle, she pulled firmly. The door opened, and Mari moved swiftly into the corridor.

"Now to finish what I came for," she thought.

Mari had only gone a short distance when a guard appeared from around a corner.

"Where do you think you're going?" he snarled.

Mari did not answer, instead, she moved her right hand in an arc past the guard's face and upwards towards the ceiling. This momentarily distracted the guard and his eyes turned to watch the passing hand. At this, Mari's left hand shot out catching the guard under the chin and sending him crashing to the floor. Mari wasted no time and before he could react, she had brought her right hand smashing down on the back of the guard's head. His body went limp, and he lay face down, unmoving, on the cold stone.

"Sorry, no time to chat," Mari said as she sprang to her feet, braking into a run.

"We have all voted, and accept the majority decision." Ling

Chuan was saying. "We will send a force out to end this threat here and now."

Benn sat down, a relieved look on his face, that was until Mari burst in. "Don't order the attack," she panted.

Johnathan watched as the Bastion army began to move away. "I hope she made it," he said.

"For the sake of us all," Arios added.

Shaan and Jobe had now joined them, and it was Shaan who spoke. "We had better get ready."

"Are the traps in place?" Johnathan asked.

"As many as we could lay in the short time we had," Jobe answered. "Don't worry, they are in for a few surprises."

Most of Shaan's small army had already broken camp to take up their positions and only a handful remained waiting outside Shaan's tent. The flap was pulled slowly back, and Shaan emerged. He stood tall and strong; his body covered in the armor that had once belonged to Rani, although it had been adjusted for its new owner before they had left Aidenvalle. On his hip hung the sword Caliburn. On his left arm, he bore Lady Bellas Shield and in his right hand he carried the spear of Loris. Sitting atop his head was the Helm of Othus, the helm of knowing. The very sight of him was enough to send a shiver of fear through his own men let alone those of his enemy. Rebecca stood beside him now, resplendent in her burgundy leathers that had been highly polished so that the sun shone off them, reflecting bright light into the faces of those who looked on. A sword also hanging by her side. From among the crowd came a third. It was Jonathan, armed to the teeth and ready for battle.

"Is it time, Shaan?" Jonathan asked quietly.

"It is time, my friend," came the soft reply, and then louder, to all assembled. "Today we fight not just for ourselves or this country, but for all mankind," and raising the spear skywards. "Victory!" He shouted.

"Victory!" Came the echoing battle cry from all around. "Victory!"

In the courtyard of the tower, men mounted their horses, they were all dressed in the purest green silks. Some carried flags of green and black that were so long that the ends touched the cobbled paving. Among them, astride a palomino horse sat Mari, her black clothing making her stand out from the rest. Beside her stood Daal, his fine hair and beard fluttering in the gentle breeze.

"You don't have to do this. You can stay in the tower in safety until it is over," he said.

"Yes, I do Daal. I believe that my destiny lies beyond these walls," Mari replied looking straight ahead.

"Don't worry, she'll be fine," Saris said with a smile. "Who would dare to harm such a lovely young woman?" He looked over and winked at Mari. "Besides, I'll take care of you."

"I can take care of myself," she replied, nudging her horse forward through the Jarenn ranks.

"She's got a lot of spirit," Saris called to his father.

"Maybe too much," came his whispered reply.

"It would appear that the Bastion forces have all moved away from the tower, sir." Reported Ben.

"How fares Moonblade and his knights?" Ling Chuan asked.

"Very well, sir, considering they are vastly outnumbered," Ben replied, then he continued with a slight smile on his face. "They also appear to know as many battle tricks as we do, sir. The Bastion army doesn't know which way to turn. Fires here, explosions there. It's almost like watching ourselves. Something else that's strange, no matter what tactics the Bastion army tries, Shaan's army seems to be one step ahead. It's as if they know every move that their opponent is going to make." Then his face became serious again. "Even so, their numbers are dwindling. I'm not sure that they can last much longer."

"Then it is time for us to make our move," Ling Chuan said, rising to his feet. "General Galihar, give the orders to attack."

"Yes sir," answered the General with a salute.

This was the moment he had been waiting for. No more tricks, no more hiding. Hand to hand combat, a real man's war.

On a hillside, just a short distance from the battlefield, General Tulak sat astride his horse, surveying the scene below. He watched the armies of both sides, the ebb and flow of battle, the deaths of men on either side and yet he did not enter the fray. Two days earlier he had been resting in his tent when the flap had opened and in walked a hooded figure, he could not make out who it was, but he could tell by the way it stood that it was a woman. Leaning up on one arm, he gazed from where he lay as she stood in the tent's entrance before coming inside and allowing the flap to close behind her. His hand grasped the dagger hidden by his furs, waiting to see how it would play out.

"Hello, my love," he knew the voice in an instant, clambering to his feet and rushing forward to take his wife in his arms. Khamel pulled back, avoiding his outstretched arms.

"No, please," she begged, "I just wanted to see you," and she turned to leave, but Tulak caught her arm, pulling her back to him.

"What is wrong? Come to me, wife," Tulak spoke in a warm loving voice. "How I have missed you, and the comfort you bring."

Khamel pushed into his body, embracing him tightly, her head resting on his shoulder. Tulak tried to pull back a little, but she hung on even more tightly.

"Let me see you, that beautiful face; Let me kiss your lips, and feel like we are one again."

Gripping her biceps, it took all of his force to push her away,

"Why are you resisting me?"

"Please, no," He could hear the sadness in her voice, "you cannot look at me, I am not as you remember."

Tulak slid his hands gently upwards over her arms, then shoulders, until they reached the material of her hooded cloak, softly sliding his hands inside, he slid the hood back and down. This time she did not resist, all her energy was spent, and she was unable to stop her husband from doing as he wished. She knew that he would eventually find out anyway, so it was best to get it over with. Her fear, that he would no longer want her, she was not the beautiful young lady he had loved so much and married with such pride. She was a beast, ugly, scarred, worthless, something to be discarded and thrown away.

Tulak was shocked, he had seen war, the terror of it, the loss of life, the scars of battle, but on his wife? How could this be? Leaning close, he kissed her face and lips, gently so as not to cause pain.

"My wife, what happened? Why did I enter this war when I should have been protecting you?"

"There is nothing you can do my husband, what is done is done,"

"Signal an attack to the right flank," Shaan ordered. He had seen, with the help of the Helm of Othuset, that the enemy was about to break off on that side to start a surprise attack. So far, his forces had had the upper hand with this new insight, and the Bastion army had suffered heavy losses, but so had his. Suddenly and without warning, his mind's eye was filled with a terrifying vision. The most ferocious dragon that Shaan had ever encountered. Its eyes stared directly at Shaan, and its huge jaw opened, issuing forth flames of blue, green, and yellow, that struck out and engulfed him. Pain filled Shaan's head as the fire seemed to consume him. All energy and consciousness fled his body, and he slumped forward.

From across the battlefield, Johnathan saw what had happened and he broke off his fight with a Bastion general and spurred his horse in Shaan's direction, much to the disgust of his opponent. He arrived at his friend's side just as he slipped from his saddle and fell to the floor. Leaping from his horse, he knelt beside him.

"Shaan, what's wrong? Are you wounded?"

Shaan did not reply but lay clutching his head, his face contorted with pain. Johnathan could see no sign of a wound.

"The Helm," a woman's voice shouted. "Remove the Helm."

Jonathan reached out and pulled the offending article from Shaan's head. As quickly as it had come, the pain vanished and Shaan lay with beads of sweat running down his face.

"Thank you, Rebecca," Johnathan said, and he looked around to see where the voice had come from, but Rebecca was not there, in fact, he could make out her burgundy clothed figure some distance away, fighting alongside Jobe and Arios. If it wasn't Rebecca who had called out, then who had it been? Shaan was now in a sitting position and had pulled his shield towards him.

"Johnathan , I'd like to introduce you to someone. This is Lady Bellas Shield."

The face on the shield came to life. "Good to meet you, Johnathan ,"

Johnathan said nothing, just stared open-mouthed.

"We are just about to have company," she continued.

Shaan and Johnathan both looked up at the same time to see a band of Bastion cavalry bearing down on them.

They rose to their feet just as the first of the attackers reached them. Shaan swung Caliburn in a huge arc, sweeping the legs from the leader's horse sending it and the rider crashing before moving in quickly to finish the job. Johnathan had drawn an arrow with lightning speed and had taken the next rider through the neck with a white-tipped dart.

A spear struck the ground near Shaan's feet, its thrower cursing his bad aim and spinning his horse round he drew, his sword and came in for another try. Shaan pulled the spear free while at the same time ducking under the swinging blade of his luckless foe. He turned and threw the spear at the retreating horseman, catching him between the shoulder blades with his own weapon. Johnathan had dispatched the fourth rider, and, seeing this, the fifth had decided that there was easier game to be found elsewhere on the battlefield and had ridden off at speed.

Johnathan had time now to think about what he had seen. "You kept that secret well," he said pointing at the shield.

"It's rude to point," Lady Bellas Shield chastised.

"I don't tell you everything." Shaan answered. "Besides, you might tell Rebecca and she would get jealous," he added with a wink.

General Galihar was not sure that he had ever had so much fun. It had been years since he had been in a real battle. He sliced this way and that, cutting down the enemy on all sides. Jason was not having such a good day. Four fierce warriors surrounded him. Stabbing out, he sliced into the arm of one who immediately took a step backwards, this was Jason's chance to escape, he swung his sword around his head, screamed a loud war cry and rushed forward. The first blade caught him in the side and stopped him in his tracks, the second, in his throat. Jason's limp body slumped to the ground.

From the hills to the north of the battlefield, a figure sat watching the events below. She watched first one side attack and then the other. Moves and countermoves. The Bastion army, although a fraction of its original size, was on the edge of victory. Now only a handful of the Jarenn and their allies remained. Krishia smiled, maybe she would let Moroc live after all, besides, she could always get another army. Now that the tower of Taal was hers, she would rule the planes of the multiverse with an iron fist, no one and nothing could stop her. But wait, what was happening below?

"What's that fool doing now?" She cursed, rising to her feet.

Mari kicked high, smashing the jaw of her adversary, and as her feet landed on the ground, she spun around, slashing out with her long knife, ending his life. She had taken many lives today, which she was not proud of, but if it meant the freedom of mankind, then it was something that she had to do. Just for a moment, she could take a well-earned breather. A little way off she spotted Johnathan taking on three more of the enemy. He looked in no danger though, a gleam in his eyes as he cut and stabbed at the foe. First one, then another toppled, until all were dead. He glanced over at Mari and smiled. Mari was about to smile back when she noticed the bowman, behind Jonathan, stringing an arrow. Without hesitation, she ran towards Johnathan , crying out, but he could not hear her over the sounds of battle. Leaping over the bodies of dead warriors, both Bastion and Jarenn alike. Reaching Johnathan , she flung her arms around his neck and spun him around, pressing her body tightly against his.

"All this celebration for the victory over three men?"

Johnathan teased. "You should have been around when I took on eight a while back."

Mari looked up at Johnathan , a smile twisted with pain on her lips. Pools of tears welled in her eyes. "I'm sorry," she whispered.

"Sorry for what?"

"I wanted to stay with you forever." The words were forced

from her as she fought to draw breath.

"Mari, what's wrong?" Johnathan cried as her body became heavy, and he dropped his sword and supported her under her arms and in doing so, he felt the wooden shaft protruding from her back. As she sank slowly to the ground, Johnathan sank with her. He never saw the second arrow's flight, but Shaan did, and it ricocheted off his shield away from its target. Shaan stood shielding Jonathan from any more danger.

Blood now dripped from the corner of Mari's mouth. "I have loved you since the first day we met," then she coughed and gripped Johnathan 's hand tightly. "I'm scared Johnathan , so scared."

"Me too," he replied, looking down at Mari.

"I'm so cold"

"Don't leave me Mari," He whispered, almost afraid that if he raised his voice the angels would hear and swoop down to take Mari from him.

It was no good, her hand went limp in his grasp and her eyes slowly closed. "No!" He roared as he sprang to his feet snatching, up his sword, he brushed Shaan aside and ran headlong towards the man who had taken his love. "No!" The cry rang out as an arrow whistled by his head. Before the bowman could string another, Johnathan had buried his sword up to the hilt. With a roar, he lifted the murderous enemy off the ground, skewered like a piece of roasting meat. Johnathan watched the life drain from the man before discarding the carcass in a heap on the muddy, bloodstained battlefield. By the time he had returned to where Mari lay, she had been covered with a cloak. All that remained of Shaan's army and the few surviving Jarenn had also gathered there.

Shaan stood, Caliburn in one hand, the Shield of Lady Bella in the other, and the spear of Loris slung across his back. Next to him stood Rebecca, her burgundy leathers darker now with the blood of the enemy streaked over them. Jobe and Arios stood back-to-back awaiting the next attack, both covered in hundreds of tiny cuts and wounds. Benn, unable to stand due to a wound to the leg, sat on a rock while Saris wrapped a strip of cloth around the leg to try to stem the flow of blood. General Galihar had mustered the few remaining soldiers under his command into a defensive position. Philippe, Thomas, and Bedilore were the only knights left standing.

Moroc positively glowed with pleasure, even if he had lost almost an entire army, victory was his. Before him were the remnants of the opposing army, bloodied and beaten. An army that, in a few moments, would be wiped from existence. The fifty strong Bastion force waited for the order to attack: weapons ready.

"What are you waiting for?" Marcus asked. "Send them in, finish it."

"Patience Marcus. Now, I'll show you why I am in command."

Moroc raised an arm. "Bowmen."

Thomas watched the Bastion bowmen assemble. "What are they up to?"

"Very interesting, they are going to finish us off with arrows," Johnathan replied. "They don't want to risk hand to hand combat."

"Cowards," a young Jarenn survivor shouted out. "Come on. Do you have no honor?"

But the Bastion took no notice as they took arrows from quivers and took aim.

"So, it ends here," Shaan said more to himself than anyone else.

From somewhere came a low humming sound. Shaan looked around.

"Rebecca, do you hear that?"

"Yes, where is it coming from?" she answered. The humming grew louder, turning into a chant. "It's the shield," she exclaimed.

Shaan looked at the Shield, her eyes were shut, and she looked expressionless, only her lips moved, the sound growing louder and louder. Now the shield vibrated, gently at first, then more violently, until it took all of Shaan's strength to hold on. He wanted to let go, to run from whatever was about to happen, but something inside told him he must not. With a loud crackle, a band of blue lightning crept up the shield from bottom to top. Some of Morocs warriors turned and ran, these were the lucky ones. Marcus' horse reared and bolted, not entirely without the riders help. Suddenly the lightning burst outwards from the shield in a great arc of blue and green, striking at the closest Bastion soldiers, burning through the fleshy bodies like a scythe cutting them in two with a searing white-hot heat. The victims cried out in agony but were dead before the screams had ended. The ring of lightning raced on through rank after rank until most lay dead, their bodies nothing more than smoldering corpses, the unlucky ones were still alive, but cut in half and still in the throes of death, their screams filling the air.

How Moroc had survived he did not know. Maybe it was because he had been a distance away from the others. He did not wish to even consider why, at the moment, content to lie hidden in the trench into which he had been thrown when his horse had bolted along with Marcus's, the blast had passed over him. The Jarenn had won this time, but there would be others, and next time he would be better prepared.

Cheers rang out from both Shaan's remaining men and the Jarenn in the tower.

"Shaan, you did it," Rebecca yelled with joy. "You did it."

"She did it," he said, lifting Lady Bellas Shield into the air. "I don't know what she did, but she did it,"

Shaan placed the shield on the ground and looked at it. The face was unmoving and once again resembled a picture.

"I can't believe that we are alive," Bedilore shouted triumphantly. "I thought we were dead for sure."

"So did I," a woman's voice said softly, "but believe me, you will be very soon."

Everyone turned at the same time to see Krishia standing directly behind them.

"You're becoming a real pain,"

Saris growled as he unsheathed his sword and ran full speed at Krishia, thrusting out as he reached his target. So great was the force of his strike that the blade broke as it struck Krishia in the midriff. Saris looked at Krishia, expecting to see blood pouring from an open wound. The red samite of Krishia's costume had been ripped away by the force of the blow, and now her skin could be seen beneath, but it was not the skin of a normal woman, this skin was green and covered in scales, and the sword had made no impact, not even a small nick.

Krishia stood, hands on hips, and gave a loud, bellowing laugh.

"You think you can hurt me, you insignificant little mortal?" and she laughed again.

The laughter turned into a snarl.

"Alright, no more fooling around,"

The red samite of her skin-tight clothing tore apart as her body began to grow, and the necklace tightened and snapped, sending her pendent down into the mud. Shaan watched Krishia begin to change, first slowly and then more rapidly. When she had almost tripled in size, she fell forward onto her hands and knees. From her fingers sprouted razor-sharp claws, and from her back, grew leathery wings. Krishia's metamorphosis was complete, and in her place, seven meters high, stood a fearsome dragon.

Saris backed off to rejoin his comrades. He had seen this dragon before and knew what destruction it was capable of, and now he understood how it had been undetected until it attacked. This was the creature that had not only destroyed the town of Talmarc but had also killed all of the people that had lived there, and only by using their Jarenn-taught skills had he and his father survived.

With weapons drawn, Shaan and the others circled the beast. A young soldier, one of Jobe's men, was the first to attack. Running at the dragon from the rear, he threw his spear with a mighty yell. The spear clattered against the rock-hard scales and fell harmlessly to the floor. The soldier made to retreat, but before he could, the dragon gave a flick of its tail, sending the man high into the air. He was dead long before his body crashed to the ground. Now they all attacked at the same time, slashing, and stabbing with their many different weapons, but to no avail. The dragon raised its head, and with a mighty roar, smoke drifting from its nostrils, it breathed out with all its might. The men nearest to the head ran, stumbling away from the expected flames, but none came. Again, the dragon roared and exhaled, again there was no fire. It seemed that Krishia had not fully recovered from her last transformation, and the loss of her pendant while she transformed had halted that restoration.

"Not as powerful as you thought, Krishia?" Saris mocked. "Is that the best you can do?"

As if in answer the, Dragon lashed out with a wing, catching Saris on the top of the head and knocking him down. Before he could recover, the dragon stepped forward and placed a talon laden foot on Saris' chest. The dragon looked down at Saris as if in fascination. Slowly it put more pressure on its captive's body, squeezing the life from him. Saris screamed out in agony. At this,

Shaan charged, swinging Caliburn around his head, and with a crash like thunder, he smashed the ancient blade against the dragon's head. A flash of blinding golden and orange light burst forth, and a great shower of sparks rained down all around. Shaan was sure that the blow had been so powerful that it must have severed the Dragon's head clean off. When his eyes cleared, Shaan saw that the Dragon was still in one piece. The head stayed on, but a long gash had been sliced into the Dragons skin. It had been stunned though, and it eased the weight from Saris so that Thomas and Philippe had been able to pull him clear. The Dragon shook its head as if to clear its thoughts then stared, through huge amber eyes, directly at Shaan.

Johnathan was the first to notice, and then Jobe. Looking beyond the dragon they could see men on horseback bearing down on them. Men dressed in Krishias colours, swords drawn, their loud battle cries carrying across the battlefield. With their fate already sealed, death staring them in the eyes they rushed past the dragon and took up a defiant stand in the face of the oncoming storm, hoping to buy enough time for Shann to defeat his foe.

Shaan lifted Caliburn ready to strike again, but before he could move the blade further, a claw sent it spinning from his hand. The claw now closed tightly around Shaan's body and lifted him high into the air. The pain was excruciating, but he refused to cry out. Blood poured from the cuts made by the sharp talons, and Shaan could feel the consciousness leaving his body, and he fought hard against it. He felt himself being drawn towards the Dragon's mouth, and in a low growling voice, it spoke to him.

"You have caused me much trouble, Shaan Moonblade, and now," it paused, taking a deep breath, "you will die."

The huge mouth opened, revealing yellow rotting teeth, the stench was almost unbearable, and Shaan tried to hold his breath. A forked tongue slithered out and covered him in a sticky slime. The gaping mouth drew nearer, and a long-pointed fang brushed against Shaan's leg. At the last possible moment, he snatched the spear from his back, spinning the shaft in his hands so that the blade pointed downwards, he drove it down towards the Dragons neck. The tip of the spear glanced off the scales, slid past the dragon's head, and Shaan, weakened from the grip of the claws, could no longer keep his hold on it, and it fell to the ground. Shaan was spent, his bloodied body racked in pain, the light faded from his eyes, and he went limp. He hung from the dragons claw like a rag doll as blackness overtook him.

The six riders brushed past Johnathan and Jobe without so much as a glance and instead bore down on the dragon, circling it and stabbing and thrusting their swords at it from all angles. One rider who had broken off from the others leaned far over in his saddle and reached out, and scooping up the spear of Loris, he turned his stead towards the dragon. leaning forward in his seat, he kicked his horse to a gallop. The dragon, on seeing this, turned its head, stretched forwards, mouth agape, fangs ready to destroy this fool. At the last moment, the rider steered his horse slightly to one side, passing the open jaw and griping the spear as tightly as he could continued his charge. The spear stabbed into the dragon's eye, its momentum driving it deep into its target.

The Dragon gave out a deafening howl, reared up on its hind legs, wings beating furiously, taking the rider high into the air as he clung on with all his might, then spun around shaking its head, trying to dislodge the cause of its agony. Tulaks' weight as he clung on only served to drive the spear deeper, and with a sickening noise of snapping bone and gristle, the long shaft was driven into the dragon's brain. It stiffened, stood perfectly still and stared at Tulak with its one good eye, "For Khamel" were the last words it heard, then it buckled and fell, sending a cloud of dust and debris billowing into the air.

Through the dusty haze, Johnathan could barely make out the

outline of the fallen beast. He rushed forward with Rebecca in hot pursuit, to where Shaan lay, trapped in the Dragons claws. Together, with Jobe, they prised the talons apart and dragged Shaan's battered body free.

Tulak and his remaining men were leaving the battlefield; They saluted their hitherto enemy, but there was no celebration, no feeling of victory, however, there was a sense of freedom. Tulak would return to Khamel and be the husband she deserved.

CHAPTER EIGHTEEN

Rebecca stared down at the freshly dug grave, her eyes glistening from the tears she had shed. The ceremony had been conducted with full state honors, those reserved for heads of government and royalty.

"We came so far; I can't believe it would end this way."

"Nor I," Johnathan agreed. "All the things we did, the dangers we came through. I thought that nothing could stop us, that we were invincible."

Rebecca looked up at Johnathan . "Time to go, our work is finished here. The tower is safe, and for now, at least, so is humanity."

"Where do you go from here, Rebecca? Will you be returning to your homeland?" Johnathan asked.

"I don't know," she replied. "What do you think?" she said, looking to her left.

"I think that we could all do with a rest, and I can think of nowhere more beautiful," Shaan said. "Will you join us, Johnathan ?"

"Thank you, but I need to be on my own for a while," Johnathan glanced down at Mari's grave. "I need to find myself again."

"I understand. Take care, Johnathan ," Shaan embraced his friend.

"Farewell, Shaan," Johnathan turned to Rebecca and kissed her cheek.

"Farewell, Rebecca." And with that, he climbed into his saddle, kicked his horse on, and rode away. To where, only he knew.

Shaan stood in the cave once more, he took a long look at Lady Bellas Shield. She had not spoken since the final battle, her face still and unmoving as if it were just a painting.

"She will recover in time, Shaan," Bron spoke softly.

"I hope so, we have lost so many," Shaan thought of his Knights who had given their lives. Only Philippe, Bedilore, and Thomas had survived. They had earlier returned to Cannchester.

Jobe, Arios, and their surviving men had also used the tower to get back to their homes. Shaan handed the Shield to Bron along with the Helm of Othus and the Spear of Loris.

"What will you do with them?" he asked.

"They must be separated again, lest they fall into the wrong hands," Bron warned. "I will scatter them through the realms once more."

"Take care, Bron," Shaan said as Bron walked into the darkness.

"We will meet again, Shaan Moonblade." The other's voice echoed. Then the little man was gone, and Shaan and Rebecca stood alone.

Rebecca took Shaan's hand and led him down one of the passages. "Let's go home."

In a room in a castle high on a hill in Trevena sat a figure in black, its long black hair held back by a silver band. The figure stared deeply into the crystal, seeing things past, things present, and things to come.

"There's a storm brewing. One even more powerful than Krishia," Gaius thought to himself.

THE END

www.ingramcontent.com/pod-product-compliance
Lightning Source LLC
Chambersburg PA
CBHW060924120626
46557CB00003B/868